TWO LOVE SONGS

"My horse?" Blayde whispered. "Is my horse out there somewhere?"

"Your horse is safe," Tasmin replied. "I will get him for you if you promise not to run away. You are too weak to walk."

"I need you, don't I?" he asked.

Tasmin returned his emerald gaze. She froze to the spot, unable to move or look away. Her lips burned for his kiss. A kiss of fire . . . that had been the Gypsy's prediction. "Two love songs you will hear . . ." But he was a *gajo* . . . she must not let desire overwhelm her. In spite of herself, she moved closer to him.

Before she could react, he had pulled her down into his lap and captured her lips in a devouring kiss. Tremors of excitement raced through her body. Her entire being became a fiery mass of anticipation as her lips molded to his and the heat of his body burned into her . . .

Veronica Blake
Texas Princess

ZEBRA BOOKS
KENSINGTON PUBLISHING CORP.

ZEBRA BOOKS

are published by

Kensington Publishing Corp.
475 Park Avenue South
New York, NY 10016

First printing: February, 1992

Printed in the United States of America

THIS BOOK IS DEDICATED
TO TWO VERY SPECIAL PEOPLE...

To my beautiful and handsome grandson,
Derek,
whose arrival has produced more joy
than mere words could portray.

And to my dear friend Kathy Pierce.
She is living the fairy tale,
which most of us believed
dwelled only in the pages of a romance novel.

Prologue

Gentle waves lapped over the ivory sand like timid tongues, growing ever closer to the overhanging cliffs that loomed above the beach like stone sentries. A heavy sphere hung low in the velvety night sky, casting an eerie glow across the crests of water and lending a shimmering effect to the flawless white sand that bordered the base of the jagged cliffs. Untouched and unmarred by time, this beach had been a silent host to a million tides, a playground for billions of wayward waves. Now it lent its soft alabaster shore to a man and a woman, lovers who were as wild and free as the moon that shone overhead and the rolling sea that licked at its coastline.

Unencumbered by clothes, their tanned bodies lay upon the ivory pebbles; legs entwined and torsos meddled together as if they were one. Moonbeams danced across their dark, sweat-drenched skin. A contented smile curved the woman's lips as she looked up toward the ebony sky . . . a Gypsy sky, mysterious and endless, like the road her people had forever traveled.

The man beside her sighed softly in his peaceful slumber. His obvious contentment filled her with a sense of awe; was it possible to be this happy, or was this just a dream from which they would soon waken to discover that fate had only been playing a cruel game? She reminded herself that to dwell on these thoughts would be a waste of this mystical night, a night when no ghosts were invited to walk across their fragile and mending hearts.

She drew in a ragged breath, burying the memories of the past in the deepest recesses of her mind. Tonight, and for the rest of her life, she wanted only to devote all her thoughts toward the man who lay at her side. She glanced at his handsome face again, wondering if he knew how much she loved him. Perhaps she should waken him to reaffirm her undying love so that he would never be able to forget. They rarely made love in the house at the top of the cliff. Although she had begun to adjust to living in a house, there were times when her Gypsy soul could not withstand the suffocating confinement of the dwelling. Her husband understood her need to be free, for he cherished her wild spirit, and never did he want her to feel imprisoned by their love.

A billowing wave of her raven hair cascaded over his muscled shoulder when she rested her head against him. Nestled in the down hair which carpeted his broad chest, her cheek was the receptor for each beat of his heart. Her fingers raked through the mass of auburn curls, which started at the base of his collarbone and grew in a beckoning trail to his waistline. Once her hand had slid downward, her inquisitive fingers continued to travel lower, as if they had a will of their own. But then, they knew this path by heart, knew every inch of this man, just as his fingers knew every inch of her.

A throaty groan signaled that the man no longer slept, and within seconds he had wrapped his strong arms around her and drawn her against him in an enslaving embrace. His lips sought her mouth with a hunger that only she could satisfy, while their tongues entwined, anxious to taste the sweet nectar within. The entire lengths of their bodies touched in an intimate manner, every core of their essence united with a fiery passion that could outshine even the glow of the moon.

Without disturbing the manner in which they molded together, the man rolled the woman over, pinning her slender form beneath his, his gentle actions so proficient that not even their lips separated in the transition. Their kisses only intensified, while their bodies grew damp with perspiration and the excitement of the ritual which they both knew would soon occur. Exploring hands traced each curve, every hollow and crevice, never tiring of this ardent quest, until at last there was no holding back.

She never knew what to expect from this man, and perhaps, that was one of the countless reasons she loved him so passionately. At times he would spend hours teasing her body, her senses, with tantalizing kisses and caresses until she begged for release from this sweet torture. At other times—like now—he would take her with a savage urgency that seemed to defy all reasoning, almost as if he feared time would run out.

The man paused for a moment in his relentless assault upon her lips to raise his head up so that he could gaze at her in the moonlight. The sight of her made his senses exalt as he asked himself once again: did she truly exist? Or was she the product of Gypsy witchery, whose image would disappear if he should ever stop believing in magic? His emerald eyes devoured her beautiful, mysterious face. Her beauty was beyond any that he had ever encountered; dark skin glistened like bronzed silk over a countenance that was sensuous and regal, with eyes as sparkling and black as the star-studded night sky. Her long hair spewed across the silvery sand like a profusion of thick raven clouds. He watched as her tongue traced a beckoning outline along her parted lips, an enticing gesture that left them wet and sparkling, and left him trembling with such a deep yearning that whatever fears had possessed his thoughts now floated away with the warm night breezes.

The sounds of lapping water mingled with moans of ecstasy as the man eased his hips between the woman's satiny thighs. He immersed himself in the warm, moist crevice hidden in this secret area—his domain. Never would he grow tired of discovering the wonder of her over and over again. Each time he made love to her, he felt as though it was a new beginning; each time he held her in his arms, the pain of the past grew dimmer. He made love to her now as feverishly as if there would be no tomorrow. Then, with a shuddering sigh, he took a final, victorious plunge, spilling into her the seeds of his eternal love. "I will cherish you forever," he said in a raspy voice. His hand raised up and entangled itself in the wild abundance of her hair as he drew her head back for another ravishing kiss.

When they parted, she gasped for air, then made the demand he knew she would make. "Say it?" she whispered.

"Gypsy Witch," he muttered, then buried his face in the mass of raven tresses. His nostrils drank in her ambrosial aroma, a sweet, natural scent that reminded him of wildflowers and deep grasses.

"Say it?" she asked again.

He sighed and raised up to meet her flashing dark gaze. "I once told you, only a witch could make me say those words again." Even as his voice faded, a gentle smile curved his mouth as he added in a tone that had grown as tender as a caress, "I love you." His green eyes misted with the emotion that this declaration always aroused. He rolled from her unmoving form and lay back against the sand; then, almost frantically, his arms encircled her waist, drawing her as close to his body as humanly possible.

She made no attempt to converse with him, knowing that he would not answer. She understood the silence that followed their lovemaking, understood even more how difficult it was for him to love her so completely. Her head tilted back so that she could look up toward the heavens while she said a silent prayer of thanks to the Gypsy God for bringing them together in spite of all the adversities in their lives. For there had been a time not so long ago when the pain from the past threatened to hold him forever in its deadly grip . . . a time when the flames of destiny had burned so low that it seemed they would be doused forever . . .

Chapter One

Passion forgotten seeps through the soul
Like raindrops from shrouded skies
And stokes the flames of Gypsy Fires . . .

Among the glow of the campfire and spiraling trails of smoke, the dancing Gypsy appeared almost ethereal. Hip-length hair of ebony swirled like Medusa's serpents about her lithe form, concealing her upper body with its thick tresses, then tumbling away briefly in the darkness of the night to reveal glimpses of the girl's angelic face and flashing eyes. From the fringed green scarf encircling her waist hung a tambourine, which she grabbed after making several turns around the circumference of the large fire. Raising her arms over her head in a graceful poised position, and keeping rhythm with the dulcimer and violin played by accompanying Gypsy comrades, she tapped the tambourine with her open palm. In a twirling frenzy she continued to move through the smoky haze, her body pulsating with the intensity of the music. As she bent and swayed in exuberant abandonment, her bare feet touched down in light and quick movements, barely disturbing the thick layer of dust which carpeted the ground.

She wore a dress of chili-pepper red; the full skirt resembled torrid flames as it encircled her legs, exposing long, slender limbs that glistened in hues of golden brown. From every pore she radiated fiery passion which was enveloped by her exotic movements like columns of smoke from a blazing wildfire. To those who watched it was as if she had become akin to the spirits of the night.

The music continued for a few minutes longer, but the barbaric beat began to ebb into a gentler strain. Soft whisperings of the violin filled the air as it clung to the fading chords of a haunting melody. The oak-infested draw which housed the Gypsy camp on this sultry evening was alive with a sense of the intangible, a mystical something that lingered even after the girl ceased to dance and the last of the music floated over the treetops with the gentle night breezes. A combination of exquisite beauty, along with the provocative innocence the girl portrayed, always left her audiences with a feeling of enchantment after witnessing one of her breath-taking performances. But to the *gajo* who was a guest in the Gypsy camp, the effect was much more profound.

Blayde Chandler did not want to meet her eyes when she stopped before him on bended knees, but he had no power to avoid her gaze. When the girl

14

first started to dance, he felt as though he had been transported into a land of fairy tales and goddesses. He became enraptured by the swirling of her red dress and the graceful beauty of her movements. But as her performance continued, an unwelcome sensation began to overcome him, a feeling he thought he was no longer capable of experiencing. Although he had never believed them, he now recalled the ancient stories his grandmother had told him about Gypsies and their strange incantations and forms of sorcery. A shiver ravaged him as he wondered if the young girl kneeling before him was a temptress who had cast a spell upon him and resurrected the forgotten emotions which he had buried long ago.

The breath caught in Blayde's throat as he watched the girl raise her head. Like unveiling a rare masterpiece, her long, tapered fingers raked through the heavy tresses which curtained her face as she pushed the raven mass over her shoulders. A voice in his head told him to turn away—to get away—but he could not respond when his eyes were drawn to her face and held prisoner by her magnetic presence. He guessed her age to be anywhere from twelve to twenty, but she was the most beautiful woman-child he had ever looked upon. Her mouth curved into a smile laced with innocence and a hint of sensuality, a smile that seemed to reflect the gentle glow of the moon and the savage heat of the fire. Blayde expected to see an evil glint in her dark gaze, a coldness in her face, something—anything—that would confirm the presence of sorcery; because

15

when their eyes met, he knew he had fallen victim to a power over which he had no control.

"It is rare that we share our campfire with a *gajo*. But in honor of this special occasion, Tasmin has dedicated her dance to you." Romalio smiled proudly with this announcement, then added, "She is soon to be my wife. Am I not a lucky man?"

Blayde nodded, though words of congratulation eluded him. As the dark beauty rose to her feet, his eyes followed every movement. She lingered for an instant longer, her catlike gaze locked with the eyes of the stranger. Then, with a shy smile, she glanced at the Gypsy king who was her intended before rushing off to join the other women and children who were retiring to the *vardos* for the night. Blayde stared after her until she had disappeared into the back of one of the canvas-topped wagons, yet, it was still several seconds until his mind could function in a normal manner.

"Do you have a wife, *Gajo?*" The smile remained intact upon the Gypsy's face, but his dark eyes flashed with bolts of silver as his gaze wandered toward the wagons. Though he tried to ingore the sharp pang which shot through his breast, his nagging jealousy remained. Tasmin was a rare prize of beauty and talent, and at times Romalio's fear of losing her overpowered his reason.

Chirping crickets from nearby Chico Creek deafened the night as a cluster of ominous-looking clouds stole away the moonlight. Blayde Chandler glanced up at the eerie sight of the shrouded moon, then averted his eyes back towards the smoldering fire before he answered Romalio's question.

"I did once, but not anymore."

Within the stranger's slow drawl was a piercing tone of sadness that made Romalio fill with a sense of remorse. He almost expected to see tears in the stranger's eyes when he glanced at him again. But instead the Gypsy was startled by the blatant expression of hatred that had overtaken the man's face. Absently the king tugged at the gold earring that hung in his left ear as he felt himself growing uneasy. He wanted to ask his guest what had happened to his wife, but the dangerous aura the man emitted rendered him speechless.

With an unexpected jolt, Blayde's tense body jumped as if an icy wind had invaded him, even though the evening air still clung to the humid heat of the dwindling day. When he glanced back at the surprised face of his Gypsy host, a mild look of embarrassment replaced his previous hostility. It was rare for Blayde to allow his inner thoughts to surface when he was in the presence of others, but the odd way the dancer had affected him left him vulnerable to the simmering cauldron of emotions which he usually kept well-hidden. Uncurling his six-foot frame from its cross-legged sitting position, Blayde rode to his feet and drew in a heavy sigh that was burdened with the painful memories the Gypsy's question had summoned.

"I reckon it's time I retired to my own camp," he said in his deep voice, which was heavily accented with remnants of his Texan upbringing.

Romalio nodded in agreement as he pushed

himself up from the ground. He tried to hide the immense relief he felt to be rid of their guest while he waited for the man's departure. Gajos seldom associated with Roms—as the Gypsies called themselves—and it was even more uncommon for the king to invite a *gajo* into their camp. Normally, he was suspicious of all non-Gypsies, and the responsibility he felt towards his kinsmen made him even more cautious. When the lone man wandered into their campsite earlier this evening, however, Romalio had extended his people's hospitality. He told himself—and the others—it was time they learned to be more trusting of the Americans among whom they now lived. But the Gypsy leader no longer felt so confident as he noticed the wariness of the *gajo's* movements. Why hadn't he paid more attention to this man's unruly appearance before now? A week's growth of reddish-brown stubble covered his lower face, and strands of unkempt hair of the same color hung past his shoulders in a length unfashionable among most *gajos*. His trailworn clothes were creased with dust as if he had been riding long and hard, and his holstered six-shooter appeared to be a permanent fixture against his muscled thigh. Tonight I was careless, Romalio told himself.

Aware that he was under close observation, Blayde tossed the cold remains of his coffee on the ground, then shoved the empty tin cup into one of the side compartments of his saddlebags. With ease he tossed the heavy leather bags over his shoulder before glancing back at the man who still watched him with guarded eyes. For a reason he could not

18

fathom, Blayde had been drawn into the Gypsy camp tonight with a deep hungering for human companionship, even if it was from one who seemed so foreign and odd to his eyes and customs.

His gaze traveled over the unusual garb worn by the Gypsy king and the handful of men who stood around the campfire watching him. Each loose-fitting tunic was tied with bands of brightly-hued scarves, and the raven curls that hugged the curve of each man's necks were bound by more colored scarves, then topped with a flat, wide-brimmed hat. With their beaklike noses, high cheekbones, and smooth, dark complexions, the men who made up the adult male population of the Gypsy tribe all appeared to have descended from the same set of genes. Even with these similar characteristics, however, Romalio's nobility was evident: he was the only man who wore a large gold hoop in his ear-lobe, which marked him as a true-blooded Gypsy chief. He had an air of aristocracy and confidence. Yet where the lovely Tasmin was concerned, his self-assurance weakened.

"Thanks for the coffee and interestin' conversation," Blayde said in earnest as he repositioned his hat low on his forehead. With the exception of his grandmother's tales, this was his first encounter with actual Gypsies. He was surprised by their generosity, and fascinated with the stories they related to him about their nomadic way of life and how they stopped occasionally in populated areas to earn money or to trade their exotic wares for other necessities.

This particular band of Gypsies had been part of a large immigration from Eastern Europe and had been in America since 1883—less than two years. Already their travels had led them from one end of the continent to the other. In this northern section of California they had been picking grapes in exchange for various commodities. Since he had met them on this sparsely traveled backroad, Blayde wondered if the extent of their activities in this area was questionable. Gypsies were notorious for their thievery, and when Blayde recalled the large herd of well-groomed horseflesh hobbled at the edge of the campsite, he couldn't help but wonder how many grape farmers were missing a horse or two after the Gypsy caravan passed through their lands.

A nervous feeling began to work its way through Blayde's bones as he thought of his own horse tied to the branch of a spreading oak a few hundred yards from the Gypsies' herd. His worry increased when he looked back toward the group of Gypsies and met with the piercing stare of one of the men who had placed himself at their leader's side. Where had this man appeared from? Blayde wondered. He had not noticed him in the camp earlier, and he would have taken note of a man who wore such an unmistakable look of contempt upon his dark, brooding face.

Must be lettin' my imagination get the best of me, Blayde told himself as he directed his attention away from the hateful glare of the Gypsy. Avoiding further conversation, he turned and headed toward the edge of the camp with a growing concern which he hoped would not show. With each step he took,

20

however, his wild imaginings increased. His head filled with visions of discovering his prized horse gone from the oak tree where he had left him, then became consumed by the uninvited memory of the beautiful dancer.

Upon seeing that his horse had not been disturbed, Blayde halted his hasty steps and closed his eyes in an effort to wipe out the image of the Gypsy girl. *Tasmin:* even her name provoked his slumbering desires. Never had he glimpsed eyes that sparkled so brightly or skin so silken that it begged to be caressed. He wondered what it would be like for a man to capture a spirit as wild as hers. Would his kisses bring that incandescent shine into her dark eyes, or cause her bronzed skin to glow softly with the heated blush of passion? Damn it! What spell had that witch cast upon him? It had been years since he had thought of a woman in that manner, and it was a bitter blow to Emma's memory that he should be aroused by a vixen who had undoubtedly used black magic to obtain his attention. *I never should have come here,* Blayde repeated to himself as he opened his eyes, then felt his heart lurch frantically in his chest.

"For a piece o' silver, I'll tell your fortune, *Gajo.*"

In a wordless stupor, Blayde stared at the girl who stood before him. She seemed to have appeared out of nowhere as she had not been present when he had first reached the cluster of oaks. She was holding a candle, which combined with the pale moonlight flickering through the treetops, granted him with a clear view of her face. For an instant he hoped she

21

was the same one who had danced around the campfire, and he grew infuriated at himself when he realized how disappointed he felt to discover that she was someone else. However, he could not help but notice that although she was not as stunning as the dancer, this girl also possessed the regal beauty which seemed to be a trait among the women of her dark-skinned race.

Finding his lost voice, he finally managed to stammer, "I-I haven't got any money with me." He thought of the gold piece in his shirt pocket, but he had no intention of giving it to this girl in exchange for listening to her gibberish.

Undaunted by his refusal to pay for her services, the girl reached out and clasped his hand without warning. Blayde drew in a sharp gasp of surprise at her sudden gesture. Instinctively he started to pull away, but her next words caused him to grow numb and limp within her embrace.

"After tonight, *Gajo,* the pain of the past will become a hollow echo in the inferno of your heart." The Gypsy's hold tightened as she pulled Blayde out from the shadows of the oak branches. The dark clouds no longer hid the moon when she turned his palm upward, then held her burning candle above his hand. Her eyes narrowed as she brought her face close to his open hand and studied the predominant lines running through his weathered palm. When he offered no further resistance, the fortune-teller continued to hold his hand while she tossed her head back and stared into his eyes with a boldness that left Blayde completely unnerved.

22

Whether her gaze held him for a moment or an hour, he was not sure. The time did not matter; he was mesmerized by her penetrating stare. It was as if she could see inside him, and Blayde found himself trying to wipe his mind clean of all memories and thoughts, so that she could not pry them out of his head. He wished a gale of wind would blow the flame from her candle and the clouds would once again cover the moon, because maybe, if it was pitch black, she could not look into his soul. When she spoke again, it was in hushed tones which made her words seem even more foreboding.

"All your life you'll remember what this poor Gypsy girl will tell you on this night."

Blayde wanted to remind her that he was not planning to give her any money for this nonsense. But again it seemed as though he had no voice or mind of his own. Where her hand encased his, it felt as though a fire had been built, and the heat engulfed his entire body in sweat as he waited to hear the Gypsy speak the words he sensed he never would forget.

The girl's eyes did not waver from Blayde's face as she continued to watch him with intense concentration. By reading his palm, she already knew several things about this stranger. She had noted how the life line ran through his palm in a long narrow gauge, indicating a man strong of character. His heart line revealed him to be a noble lover who was devoted to his mate, yet the many branches rising and falling from the heart line suggested he was capable of feeling hatred as passionately as love. Yet, it was the

23

unspeakable pain lurking in the depths of his emerald-colored gaze which drew her complete attention. Persia could usually read a person's inner thoughts just by watching his eyes and expressions for a few moments. Unhappiness was easy for her to detect, but she found herself baffled by the conflicting emotions which kept flashing across this *gajo's* haunted face. What tragedy in his past would cause him so much agony that it would spew from him like lava from an erupting volcano?

With each passing second, she grew more anxious to know what it was about him that she could not expel from his shattered heart or coax from his tormented gaze. But her rare ability to achieve this knowledge failed her on this humid night. Persia felt rivulets of perspiration trickle down the sides of her face as she realized this man's past was far too complex for her to unravel in such a short time. To predict his future, however, was a much simpler task. Glancing away from his troubled face, she took a deep breath to help sort her thoughts, then once again focused on the listless hand she still held in her grasp.

"Pain is your constant companion, *Gajo.*" Persia reached up and placed his palm against his thudding breast, then pressed her own hand over the same spot. "But love will once again smooth the jagged edges of this fractured heart." She saw his head move negatively from side to side, and noticed the anger flare up in his eyes. "You do not believe this poor Gypsy girl now. And you will try to show that I am wrong by resisting this new love with every strength you can summon forth, but—" she held her hand against his chest using more pressure when she added, "Nothing from the past, or no one, will be able to halt a love that is destined to be."

Unexpectedly, she dropped his hand and stepped back into the shadows of the trees as though she needed to put distance between the two of them before she called out her final warning. "Be careful, *Gajo*, for the joy of this love can not be felt without added pain to a heart that is already too burdened." As she spun around, her pantherlike strides took her out of sight as suddenly as she had appeared.

Blayde stared at the spot where she had been until his eyes misted with the strain of peering into the obscure oak forest. With a grunt of fury at his own stupidity, he hurried to his tethered mount. As he untied the horse from the oak tree, and began to make his way back to the area where he had planned to bed down for the night, he tried to block out the Gypsy's words—meaningless words! Still, they echoed through his mind long after he had ridden past his intended campsite.

It was approaching midnight before Blayde felt safe enough to make camp. He was certain he had not been followed by any of the Gypsies, but his apprehension remained. When he stretched out on his bedroll, he realized it was useless to think he would be able to rest tonight. He kept remembering every sordid event of the past three years, and it was these memories he had been hoping to elude for an hour or two by visiting the Gypsy camp. But there was no escape. Blayde reached up to his breast pocket seeking the faded photograph he always kept within reach. For a moment his weary mind did not comprehend what had happened, but then he recalled the gold piece that had also been in his pocket with the photo.

"Thievin' little witch!" he said between clenched teeth as he thought of the way the fortune-teller had placed her hand over his heart. He had been so distraught at the time she could have easily slipped the money—as well as the picture—from his pocket.

"Poor Gypsy girl—ha! Well, she won't get away with it!" Come first light of dawn, he was headed back to the Gypsy camp to reclaim his stolen property.

Chapter Two

From a distance they almost appeared to be twins. Both were petite in stature, with raven hair that hung past their waists in thick, shiny cascades. The garments they wore were similar, too, the usual Gypsy fashion of colorful skirts, ruffled blouses, and silky scarves. From their wrists, ears, and necks, gold jewelry reflected the glow of the morning sun and shimmered brilliantly against their bronzed skin. Both were beautiful, with flashing eyes of ebony and striking features that conjured up regal images of bejeweled saris and mysterious Asian fables. Their appearance suggested that they would be more at home in domed castles of white marble on the banks of the Danube, rather than here on the thorny banks of Chico Creek.

Upon closer observation, it was apparent the two young women were not twins, for one of them possessed a beauty that far outshone that of most women of any race, and though she was considered to be royalty by her people, even in their native homeland, Princess Tasmin Lovell's life would not be any different than it was now. The ways of the Gypsies had not changed in hundreds of years; only the locations differed as they wandered from one continent to another. The idea of settling in one place was suffocating to their wild hearts, and death would be preferable over loss of their precious freedom. Staying in an area for too long a time could also prove dangerous, since the lifestyle of the Roms was not accepted by society in any country.

As the two girls emerged from the oak woodland and approached the waters of the narrow creek, Persia gave a terrified squeal and jumped back from the bank.

"What is it?" Tasmin asked in alarm as she stopped her trek toward the icy water and turned to her friend with concern.

"A spider!" Persia's frightened expression turned to one of annoyance when the other girl's lyrical laugh filtered through the cool morning air. "What would Romalio think if he knew of how you joke at the customs?"

Tasmin's black gaze clouded for an instant, hinting that an unwelcome thought had passed through her mind. But she quickly regained her composure and shrugged as her mouth curved with a mischievous grin. "In Romalio's eyes I can do no wrong." Her flirtatious laugh echoed once more across the rippling sound of the water as she hiked her skirt up around her shapely thighs and took a timid step into the cold creek. A layer of mist encircled her ankles when she immersed her feet in the freezing water. "My toes are growing numb," she said as she jumped back to the edge of the muddy bank. When she glanced at her friend again, she was not surprised to see the pout on Persia's pretty face. "I'm sorry," she said, trying to sound sincere. "I know it is bad luck to see a spider so early in the morning, but some of those old beliefs seem silly now that we are in this country."

"*Sarla, tugno,*" Persia said with a definite toss of her dark head. "Morning sadness!" she repeated with a shudder and a worried glance at the spot where she had glimpsed the spider. As a tribal fortune teller, she was an ardent believer in ancient superstitions, and her friend's frivolous attitude only strengthened her convictions. Now, though, her thoughts were not entirely on the spider. She had caught the strange glint that had shadowed Tasmin's dark gaze, and though she was not sure how to approach the subject, she knew she had to speak to her friend about the knowledge her insight had unveiled about the *gajo* who had visited their camp.

"Last night something happened that I must talk to you about. The *gajo* . . . I read his palm." Persia noticed a red flush move through Tasmin's cheeks when she mentioned the man, and once again, she saw the strange glint invade her friend's eyes. "His future, and yours, are connected."

Though Persia's revelation made a shiver run down her spine, Tasmin gave her head a defiant toss, sending her long hair flying over her shoulder in wild disarray as she pretended not to hear the other girl's words. She bent down to straighten the colored tiers of her skirt, then let out a jubilant chuckle. "Ha! Look here—it is a Daddy longleg. He is a sign of good luck." When she twirled around to face her friend, her gaze twinkled like diamonds in a black sea as she laughed again, an infectious sound which seemed to flutter through the air like the gentle wings of a butterfly.

Although she was annoyed at Tasmin for refusing to discuss the *gajo,* it was impossible for Persia to remain upset. Maybe now was not the time to tell Tasmin how she had foreseen the overwhelming changes in which she was about to partake, Persia told herself as she watched her friend laughing and frolicking on the creek bank. Tasmin's enthusiasm overflowed to anyone who was in her presence for any length of time. Even when she was a small child her passion for life had filled her tribesmen with joy. It was no wonder that their king, Romalio, had patiently waited for her to grow into womanhood before deciding to choose a bride. A deep sadness filled Persia as she thought of how many people would be affected by the events that her unusual powers had allowed her to glimpse when she had read the *gajo's* palm and looked into his sorrowful gaze. She almost wished she did not possess her rare insight, because at times it made her aware of things she did not want to know. But she had always known that destiny was more powerful than any mortal man or woman, and Tasmin's destiny had rested in the palm of the *gajo.*

A concession of distant rumblings drew their

attention away from the thoughts that engrossed each of them. "Was that gunshot?" Persia asked, cocking her head in the direction of their campsite. The two friends had walked a long distance from the *vardos* to obtain privacy for their morning grooming. The dense forest of oaks concealed the convoy of wagons from sight and muffled sound.

"Soobli must be hunting," Tasmin said with a nonchalant shrug when several more shots echoed in the distance. Her brother, Soobli, served as the *masengo*—the ritual slayer—for their tribe because he was the best with a gun, and rarely did he allow them to go without meat for their meals. The *masengo* was permitted to hunt only when food was needed. Soobli, however, fulfilled his obligation to kill with a vengeance that sometimes worried his tribesmen. A frown creased Tasmin's smooth complexion as she thought of the cruel personality her brother had acquired over the past few years. "Sounds like we'll have meat for many days." Her attempt to hide her disapproval of her brother did not go unnoticed by the perceptive Persia, but she did not offer her own thoughts about Soobli since her thoughts and Tasmin's were much the same.

Tasmin turned from her friend, hoping Persia would not pursue the conversation about her brother, and especially about the *gajo*. She was not ready to discuss the feelings she had experienced when she had knelt before him last night. Nor was she prepared to talk about the impure thoughts that had possessed her dreams during the brief periods when sleep had overtaken her weary being. Persia's suggestion that the man would be a part of her future, however, was ridiculous—only Romalio would be in Tasmin's life. For once, she thought, Persia's foresight had gone astray.

Tasmin pretended to place her full concentration on the plaid scarf she used to corral her thick, hip-length hair. Quickly folding the scarf into a triangle, then tossing it over her head, she tied a loose knot at the base of her throat. Several rebellious strands escaped, and the large, gold hoops that dangled from her earlobes peeked out from the untamed mane of hair which framed her lovely face in dark tendrils. Casually she tied her *jodaka* apron around her waist, then with her hands resting on the curve of her hips, she paused when another round of gunshots rang out in the distance. When she met her friend's worried gaze, they both sensed that Soobli was not hunting for food.

Neither woman took time to voice her fears as she began to run toward the cluster of oaks. Tasmin and Persia had been in America long enough to know that there were few areas here where they were welcome and would not be harassed. Not only were they strangers in a foreign land, but their people had gained a notorious reputation as thieves and cheats. Due to their practice of ancient customs, which were odd to *gaje,* and because of the uncanny talent of some of their womenfolk to predict the future, many *gaje* believed Gypsies dabbled in witchcraft.

They had been run out of Romania for similar reasons, and America had offered no refuge. As Tasmin and Persia raced toward camp, they recalled

32

the brutal attacks their people had already suffered in this land during the past two years. Both had lost loved ones to angry lynch parties who had accused the Gypsies of horse stealing or black magic, and now they feared more of their people were being slaughtered because misfortune had befallen someone whose path they had crossed recently.

Besides numerous accusations of thievery, the Gypsies found themselves at fault for disasters beyond a mortal man's control. In Kansas last year, they had been accused of using black magic to cause a tornado, and only several months ago, when they had been traveling to California, a plague had broken out in a small town in Nevada a few days after the Gypsies had passed through. Though no Gypsies were infected with the virus, the townsmen chased the Rumanians down, then tarred-and-feathered several of the men. Before they had finished their carnage one Gypsy was dead and their entire food and water supply had been destroyed.

The tribe began to avoid civilization, sticking to backroads and sparsely-populated areas, and never staying too long in one place. Romalio's friendliness towards the *gajo* last night had surprised his people, and if the stranger had led an attack against the Gypsies, Tasmin and Persia both knew everyone would blame Romalio for inviting the stranger into their camp. Normally, they would have not permitted the *gajo* to leave until the Gypsy caravan had also been on its way, then they could have made certain he did not follow them. Romalio had not taken any of these usual precautions last night, and now they wondered if they would all regret their king's rash decision.

With these thoughts raging through her mind, Tasmin was also filled with a sense of regret. Like Romalio, she too had trusted the *gajo,* although her feeings toward the green-eyed man had gone far beyond trust. Last night, however, she had quickly escaped to her *vardo* in an effort to dismiss the strange sensations the *gajo* had awakened in her innocent heart. Yet by this morning she was still trying to convince herself of how much she loved Romalio. For a Gypsy to desire someone not one of their own was *marime*—impure and sinful—and though she knew Persia could sense how the *gajo* had affected her, Tasmin told herself she would never admit to the indecent thoughts that the stranger had provoked with nothing more than his piercing green gaze.

Now, as she and Persia raced through the shadowed forest towards their campsite, she realized how foolish she had been to think that a *gajo* had looked at her as though he was glimpsing both their destinies when their eyes met. It must have been the magic of her dance, the glow of the moon, something unexplainable that made her imagine the affinity she thought she felt for the stranger. It was only wanton lust, or maybe even hatred, that she had seen flickering in his guarded eyes.

As the two girls neared the campsite, shouts and screams, accompanied heavy clouds of black smoke in the forest of oaks, made it evident that their people were once again under siege. A strangled cry lodged in Tasmin's throat when they ran into the clearing and witnessed the brutal attack upon their kinsmen and friends. Several of the *vardos* had been torched, and already they were nothing more than skeletal shells. Confusion ruled the secluded glade as the murderous *gajo* charged through the small encampment like enraged demons on horseback, shooting their guns wildly and throwing flaming torches at the remaining wagons.

"O Del, please don't let this happen again!" Tasmin sobbed outloud, though she knew it was too late to ask the Gypsy God for help. Across the meadow she glimpsed Romalio and her brother fighting side by side with two *gajo* who had taken the battle to the ground and were engaging the Gypsy king and Soobli in a deadly fistfight. Tasmin cried out to them, but her voice was lost to the roar of the fires and the chaos of the attack. She started to run toward the Gypsy king but was halted by the sight of two children standing in the center of the fiery battleground. Too terrified to move, the tiny youngsters clung to one another, their ebony eyes wide with horror, their mouths open with cries that could not be heard above the sounds of destruction.

Tasmin glanced around frantically for Persia, intending to ask her to grab the children and run for the shelter of the forest. But her dear friend had already left her side. Tasmin reminded herself that Nanna, Persia's seventy-eight-year-old grandmother, would be Persia's first concern. She had no doubt fled to the old woman's *vardo*. Though she desperately wanted to help Romalio, Tasmin did not give another thought to her next move. The children, Cyri and Danso, were her niece and nephew. Danso was barely two when his mother had died giving birth to Cyri. For the past three years Tasmin had been helping Soobli raise his motherless children, and she would give her own life to save them, if necessary.

Without hesitation, Tasmin rushed toward the frightened youngsters. Their faces lit with relief when they spotted her running in their direction. In spite of the battle that raged around them, the small children bravely charged forward to meet their aunt. Tasmin screamed in horror when a horsemen swooped past the children, then she thanked O Del when he ignored them in his haste to chase down a young Gypsy girl who was running toward the forest. She debated as to whether or not she should try to help the girl, whose name was Vilo, but then realized there was little she could do. Besides, her niece and nephew were also helpless. She turned away from the sight of the man as he leapt from his horse and tackled the fleeing girl to the ground. Vilo was her friend, as were all the people in this camp, and Tasmin could not bring herself to witness whatever was about to happen to the girl.

She bent down, scooping Cyri up into her arms. Then, clasping ahold of Danso's tiny hand, she began to run in the same direction she and Persia had followed this morning when they had gone on their fateful walk to the creek. Tasmin's only thought was to get the children to safety, and there was not time to determine whether or not this was

36

the wisest choice. Though Cyri was a small child for her three years, her weight slowed Tasmin's gait. Danso tugged at her hand, urging her to hurry as they ran into the morning shadows of the dense forest. Running beneath the heavy branches of the ancient oaks, Tasmin was overcome with a sense of defeat. Although it appeared that they were not being followed, she still had the feeling that she could not stop, not even long enough to look behind her as they charged through the trees.

As this feeling of utter panic overwhelmed her, Tasmin hastened her steps to the point where she was now dragging Danso behind her, although he was trying his best to match her frantic stride. The sounds of death and mayhem became muffled and distant. Still, an inner voice told Tasmin not to stop until she was certain the children were safe. Sharp pains shot through her tiring limps and her heart threatened to pound through her breast as she pushed herself to continue. Danso grew too weak to keep up with her, so ignoring her own agony, Tasmin picked him up from the ground and carried both of the children in her arms. Her feet stumbled over gnarled roots and rocks that jutted up from the bases of the large trees until at last she emerged from the oak forest.

"Can you walk?" she asked each of the children as they approached the sloping banks of Chico Creek. There was no way she could carry them while trying to wade through the water. Their faces remained masked with fear; still, both Cyri and Danso nodded their small, dark heads in reply to their aunt's question. Placing one child on each side and clasping ahold of each miniature hand, Tasmin started down the creek bank.

"Will my father be killed?" Danso asked in a breathless voice, while his short legs fought for balance on the sandy slope.

A sense of helplessnes invaded Tasmin when she glanced down at her tiny nephew. Was it wrong for them to continue to run? But what difference could she have made if they had stayed in the camp? At least now, there was a chance to save the lives of two innocent children, and it was doubtful that she would have been able to help her brother, or Romalio, if she had remained. As she gazed at each of the children, she tried to tell herself that she had made the right choice. Still, a nagging voice deep inside kept calling her a coward for deserting her family and friends. Would life be worth living if they returned to discover that all of them were dead and she found herself alone with two children to care for in a world that despised them because they were Gypsies? With a heart filled with the heaviness of indecision, Tasmin halted her frantic pace, and stared down at Danso.

"Do you think I should go back to the camp and try to help your father and the others?"

He tilted his head back so that he could look directly into his aunt's face. The morning sun was beginning to rise over the tops of the towering oaks, making his dark gaze squint against the glaring rays. The worried expression on his round face made him look much older than his mere six years as he nodded in reply.

Tasmin glanced down at the little girl who stood motionless at her other side. "Cyri, do you think we should go back?"

Imitating her brother's gesture, the little girl gave her tossled dark head a firm nod.

A trembling sigh rumbled through Tasmin's breast. Her decision to flee with the children had seemed logical in her panicked state of mind. Now she wondered if she had chosen the way of a coward. Perhaps, they had no right to escape when their families and friends were forced to stay and fight, Tasmin told herself as she tightened her grip on the two tiny hands she held, then turned them around so that the three of them were facing the ominous-looking forest once again.

Chapter Three

Although Tasmin knew she had to return to the camp, she had no intention of placing Cyri and Danso in danger again. Frantically she surveyed the area surrounding the creekbed. The only shelter was the heavy thicket of bushes which grew abundant along the shallow banks of Chico Creek. Leaning down so that she was at eye level with the youngsters, she pulled them close to her. The unabashed trust that flashed through their large ebony gazes filled Tasmin with a sense of inadequacy. How she wished she could be worthy of their devotion, but she was as scared as they were at this moment.

"I will go back and try to help your father and the others, but you must stay here." Since Gypsy children were taught to be obedient and never to challenge the authority of an adult, neither of them dared to disagree. Still, Tasmin could see the fear flood through their expressions at the thought of being left alone here on the muddy banks of the creek. "There is nothing to fear," she said in a shaking voice which betrayed her words. "Your father and I will return to get you when it is safe." She attempted to calm her quivering speech, but she could tell by their anguished appearances that in spite of their youth and innocence, both children could see through her brave front.

She rose quickly to a standing position, because if she looked at their sorrowful little faces any longer she knew she would not be able to leave them behind. Yet she could not hide like a coward in the thicket with them, or they might never forgive her for not going back to help their father. Nor would she be able to forgive herself. Without further comment, she began to lead them toward the most dense area of the thicket. They followed in silence, while their young thoughts were consumed with the terror of never seeing their aunt or father again.

The brush was not an ideal hiding spot since it housed a bevy of insects and was laden with branches which spouted pointed thorns. Tasmin had to carefully push them aside so that she could clear a low path through which she and the children could crawl. Still, the sharp spines poked at their tender skin and shredded their clothes as they made their way on hands and knees in a slow procession. Several feet into the thicket they came to a small opening where the brush had left a spot barren of branches. Here Tasmin stopped and began to push back the loose twigs that covered the ground. When she had cleared the area as much as possible she scooted the children into the center of the tiny hiding

41

place. A jagged pain shot through her breast when she noticed the bloody scratches on their soft cheeks and arms. Their expressions of horror as they stared at their aunt, made Tasmin aware that her own face and arms were equally as mangled. Not even the children though, mentioned the burning pain that accompanied the wounds.

"If you get thirsty, you can go to the creek to get a drink. But make sure it is safe. If I don't come ba—" She cut off her words sharply. Indecision tore at her as she wondered if it would be wise to give the children instructions on what they should do if no one ever came back to get them, or if it would be better not to add to their terror by letting them know her worst fears. Her heart felt as though it was going to shatter with the agony that seared through her breast as she looked at their terrified young faces once again. She could not love her own children any more than she loved these two, and the idea of them being left alone to fend for themselves in this cruel land was unbearable.

"We will be back soon," she said in the most definite tone she could manage. She reached out and pulled them close to her breast, giving each a kiss on the forehead before she forced herself to turn loose of them. "I love you," she whispered. Holding back her tears was not possible, so before they noticed that she was crying, and before she lost her waning courage, she turned away and began to crawl back through the heavy brush. The sounds of their soft whimperings raked through her soul as harshly as the spiny branches tore at her skin as she crawled out

42

from the thicket, but she did not allow herself stop.

When she was clear of the thick branches, she stepped back and scrutinized the brush. The dense bushes hid the children completely from view, and after she took a branch and swept across the opening where they had entered the thicket, there was nothing that would give a clue to the precious contents hidden within the thorny branches. Over the treetops a glorious array of sunshine greeted Tasmin when she turned away from the brush and began to retrace her steps back to the campsite.

Morning dew sparkled like tiny diamonds on the edges of the pointed branches and across the thatches of green grass that grew wild along the creek bank. How could O Del allow the sun to shine so gloriously on such a black day? Tasmin wondered as she drew closer to the towering grove of oaks. The sound of gunfire had stopped. All was silent now, and the permeating quiet had settled over the trees like a cloak of doom. While Tasmin walked through the forest on her way back to the fated glade she noticed how the smell of gunshot lingered in the air, a fiendish reminder of the death and destruction which had been bestowed upon her people on this terrible day.

At the edge of the clearing she halted her steps and surveyed the remains of what had once been their peaceful campsite. The battle no longer waged, and for a moment Tasmin did not realize that the perpetrators were already gone. She had drawn her knife from the hidden pocket in her *jodaka* apron, prepared to do battle beside the rest of her comrades against the ambushers. But she had arrived too late. Despair washed over the young woman when she glimpsed the smoking carcasses of the burnt *vardos*. Eight of the eleven wagons had been spared, but the loss of the wagons did not matter when compared to the horror they were constantly forced to endure merely because they were Gypsies.

"Praise O Del! Tasmin, you are safe!"

Tasmin snapped from her trance, then turned to the man who had called out her name and was now rushing toward her. As Romalio's strong arms encircled her numb body, Tasmin felt the last of her strength drain from her quaking limbs. Normally, it would be considered *marime* for him to hold her in this manner, but now neither of them cared that they were committing a sin. She slumped against the broad chest of the king and allowed him to cradle her as though she was a helpless child. His shirt was drenched with sweat and the odor of smoke, but never had those offensive smells been so welcome to her nostrils.

"I was so scared, Princess," he said softly as his cheek rested atop her head. "I could not find you anywhere. Until I saw you walk out of the trees, I was afraid those bengs—those devils—had taken you with them, and I could not bear the thought of such a fate for my beloved."

Tasmin felt the knife she still clasped in her hand slip from her limp fingers as he held her tighter. Her thoughts were consumed with the realization of what a brave man her king was—how could she tell him of her own cowardliness? "I have shamed you,"

44

she cried as she buried her face against his chest in disgrace.

Romalio drew back and stared down at the woman he loved more than life itself. The guilty expression on her battle-torn face filled him with dread and aroused a rash of distorted thoughts to consume his mind. "How could you ever shame me?" he asked in a worried voice as he envisioned her being dragged into the forest, then raped by one or more of the attackers. Even a violation that was beyond her control was considered *marime,* and as the king, Romalio could choose as his *Phuri Dae*—the wife of a king—only a woman who had never been touched by any man, regardless of the circumstances.

"I—I—" Tasmin glanced back over her shoulder toward the forest, thinking of her plight to escape with the children. Her hesitation made Romalio fear the worst. "I ran like a coward," she said, then quickly added, "But my fear was for Cyri and Danso." As she spoke, a new terror occurred to her. What if, at this very moment, the ambushers were headed toward the creek? A horrified cry escaped from her lips as she began to pull away from Romalio's grasp. "I must go back to get them. If the attackers find them, they may be in more danger than they were before. Oh, Romalio, I have been very foolish."

In spite of her display of panic for the children, Romalio heaved a sigh of relief. Because of his position in the tribe, he had learned to be a patient and rational man. But his fear of Tasmin's honor had been desperate enough to destroy all of his reserve. Because he was afraid she would turn and charge back into the forest to retrieve the children without waiting to hear his next words, he pulled her close to him again. "They are safe, Princess." With a toss of his head, he motioned toward the far end of the campsite, adding, "The outlaws did not ride toward the creek, and you were not a coward because you chose to take Cyri and Danso to safety. It was a commendable thing you did, but it was even more brave of you to return to the camp when you might have been placing your own life in danger by doing so."

The knowledge that the ambushers had not headed toward the area where she had hidden the children helped to ease a bit of her panic. Beneath Romalio's drooping mustache, a weak smile touched the corner's of his mouth when he noticed she had relaxed slightly. His next words, however, sent her back into a state of turmoil.

"Now, go gather up the *chavvies*—the children—and bring them back to the camp. When you return, I will be gone. But know this, every moment I am away, my heart will still be here with you my beloved princess."

"Wh—where are you going?" Since it was not Romalio's nature to leave his people at a time when they needed him the most, a deep sense of foreboding washed over Tasmin as she waited for his reply.

Romalio drew in a deep breath and glanced down at the ground, wishing that he did not have to tell

46

Tasmin where he was going, or why. At last, he raised his dark eyes to her face and allowed their raven gazes to lock in silence for a moment before he began to speak. "I must ride after the outlaws who attacked us."

A disbelieving gasp flew from Tasmin's lips, and before she could stop herself from questioning her king, she blurted out, "Why? What good will it do to hunt them down? You could be killed!" Usually, when their tribe had been attacked, they would immediately flee as far away from the old campsite as possible, in the hopes that their trail could not be traced. Romalio's words sounded like a death sentence for the entire tribe.

"I must go," he said with sadness edging into his voice. He glanced away from her face again as if he could not bear to look at her while he spoke. "They have taken several of our women as captives. That is why I feared so greatly for your fate."

When the meaning of what Romalio was saying began to sink into Tasmin's reluctant mind, she felt as though she had just been struck down by one of the massive branches of the ancient oaks. The thought of being hostage to a group of murderous madmen was worse than death, and there was not a Gypsy woman alive who would not prefer to die rather than to be forced to submit to a *gajo beng*. Since every woman in this tribe was Tasmin's friend, she found that she could not bring herself to ask who had been kidnapped.

"Persia was one of them," Romalio said in a quiet tone, knowing the question that was rushing

47

through her mind, and wishing he did not have to confirm it. "And also Savana and Vilo."

The image of Vilo being tackled to the ground by one of the murderous devils returned to her with vivid recollection and made Tasmin cringe in horror at the memory of the last time she had seen the young girl. Vilo, who was barely more than a child, had turned fourteen years old just weeks ago. But already she was becoming a budding beauty as her youthful body ripened with impending womanhood. Again Tasmin was overcome with guilt as she wondered if she could have somehow helped Vilo, and possibly changed the horrible fate the young girl was enduring at this moment.

Of those who had been abducted, only one, Savana, was a married woman. Her husband, Teril, was a jealous man, prone to violence if one of the other men looked at his *bori*—bride—in a way that he did not find appropriate. Should Savana survive and be returned to the tribe, Teril would undoubtably consider her *marime* and reject her as his wife. Tasmin loved all three of the young women as friends, but it was for Persia that she suffered the most. The two of them had been best of friends since they were barely two years old, when Tasmin's widowed mother had joined this tribe sixteen years earlier.

"You must find them," she said, her voice breaking with emotion as she tried to hold back threatening tears. "You must," she repeated before bowing her head as a defiant teardrop rolled down her cheek.

In a tender gesture, Romalio reached out to wipe the tear away with the tips of his fingers. "My brave princess," he said quietly, then added, "I will do my best." He bent down and gave her a brief kiss which was barely more than a brush of their lips, and lasted no more than an instant. Then, without another word, he forced himself to turn loose of her and walk away. Every inch of him ached to hold her close again, to kiss her with every ounce of passion that was contained in his enflamed body. At this moment, he felt a desperate urge to pick her up in his arms, carry her into the forest, and make love to her beneath the Gypsy sky until both of them had forgotten all the bad things that had happened today. This was impossible, of course. Thoughts of this sort were *marime*, so he quickly asked O Del to forgive him for allowing his mind to ponder on these impurities when he had so many grave tasks to confront.

Tasmin watched him as he walked through the shattered remains of their camp. The shock of their first kiss still burned bittersweet upon her lips. Under normal circumstances, she knew he never would have been so bold as to kiss her before they were married, but today was not an ordinary day. Nor was Romalio an ordinary man, she reminded herself. He was a great man, whose goodness overflowed to all those who knew him. That he had chosen her to be his wife made her a very lucky woman, and because her own father had also been a king, it was even more fitting for her to become the *Phuri Dae*. So why had she dreamt all night of the

49

sad-eyed *gajo?* And why was it that when Romalio had kissed her, she had wished she could recapture just a bit of the desire that the quiet stranger had aroused in her last night when she had knelt before him? Rage began to burn in Tasmin's veins like wildfire as she wondered how she could allow these wicked thoughts to enter her head at a time when there was so much sorrow all around her.

Reluctantly, she began to move through the disheveled camp. From the edge of the forest it had appeared nearly everything was destroyed and that the death toll had been numerous. Tasmin was overcome with relief to hear that there had only been a few deaths. A couple of the elderly people had been killed, and one younger man had taken a bullet through the heart. Miraculously no one else had been murdered, although there were several more who had suffered injuries. Persia's grandmother had survived the attack, and fortunately, so had her *vardo.* Tasmin could not help but to worry about how the old woman was handling Persia's abduction, so she took a few minutes to tend to her before she left to retrieve Cyri and Danso. Nanna was as dear to Tasmin as if she had been her own grandmother, but such was the way among the *familia*—the extended Gypsy families who traveled together every day of their lives.

When Tasmin's mother had died five years earlier, Nanna had unselfishly moved the orphaned girl into the *vardo* where she and Persia lived. Even though she was almost too old to care for even one teenaged girl, Nanna had managed to provide for both girls with her uncanny skills for predicting the future. Many Gypsy fortune-tellers had a difficult time convincing *gaje* that their visions were accurate. Nanna, however, needed only to level her unwavering Black gaze at the face of the person whose future she was glimpsing, and they seemed to know that she was not merely entertaining them for a silver or gold piece. It was from Nanna that Persia had inherited her skills as a fortune-teller, though even Persia had to admit that no one would ever be as wise as her grandmother.

"Will she come back to us?" Tasmin asked the old fortune teller as she handed her a steaming cup of tea.

Nanna's gnarled hands shook when she reached out to clasp ahold of the cup. Today's ambush had taken a toll on her elderly body and mind. Her thoughts kept drifting back to *Puro tem*, the old country. Though the Gypsies had been run out of Romania, she longed to return to the land of her birth, and it saddened her to know that she was going to die in this country where her people were hated with such vengeance.

She pushed the image of her childhood lands from her thoughts, forcing herself to concentrate on Tasmin's question. The heavy folds of her aging skin sagged in tired lines over her cheekbones as she sighed heavily and met the young woman's worried gaze. "Some things I see with clarity, others are not so plain for me to see. I never foresee an attack, and now," she paused and glanced down at the teacup she held in her trembling hands, then shook her head with uncertainty, "the tea leaves are confused." Her gray head tilted downward so that she could peer closer into the cup with her knowing eyes. "Today they say we will have *bok* and *kushti bok.*"

Tasmin clasped the old woman's arm in relief. "*Bok* and *kushti bok,*" she repeated in an excited tone. "Bad luck and good luck. We have already had the bad. The good luck has to mean that our menfolk will return safely with Persia and the others."

"Perhaps," Nanna sighed. A rattling sound echoed through the *vardo* when the old woman's shaking hands turned loose of the black china cup she had just set down on the tiny table which stood next to her bed. Tasmin glanced at the teacup, thinking it ironic how Gypsies believed that black china would bring them good luck. A burdened sigh emitted from Nanna, drawing Tasmin's attention back to the old woman. The eyes that usually appeared so knowing and alert, were now void of anything but sorrow as they settled on the face of the younger woman. "Go fetch the *chavvies,* now," she said in a weary voice. "They grow anxious for your return."

With Nanna's command, Tasmin started towards the narrow doorway at the end of the *vardo.* Abruptly, as though she had forgotten something, she paused and turned back toward the old woman. Leaning down, she planted a kiss on top of the woman's gray head, then without further hesitation, she left the *vardo.* Though Nanna did not pretend to acknowledge Tasmin's tender gesture, a thin smile curved her lips after the girl had disappeared through the door. She closed her tired eyes, hoping that her dreams would transport her across the vast waters of the ocean, back to *Puro tem* once again.

Outside Nanna's *vardo,* the men were preparing to go in pursuit of the outlaws who had kidnapped the three young women. Among the small posse Tasmin glimpsed Romalio's proud form sitting on top of his horse. His wide-brimmed hat was pulled low over the scarf that covered his thick, black curls. Beneath the hat his handsome face was host to a worried frown. It pained Tasmin to think of the responsibility he must shoulder for the entire tribe. Yet rarely did he lose his patience, and never had she heard him complain. Once again, she became filled with guilt because she had allowed the *gajo* to replace Romalio in her thoughts, even if just for a brief time.

As the men began to ride toward the edge of the glade, Romalio stopped and turned around to glance back toward the smoldering campsite once more. The anguished expression on his face softened into one of love when he spotted Tasmin standing beside Nanna's *vardo.* His hand rose into the air for a final wave, lingering there for a long minute, before he finally forced himself to turn away and follow the rest of the men.

Tasmin watched until he had disappeared from view. Still, his image continued to haunt her long after he was gone. His love for her was obvious, but as he had turned away, it seemed that his face had become shadowed with remorse. Maybe she had only imaged his strange look, she told herself, just as she thought she had glimpsed her own destiny in the eyes of the *gajo*. Tasmin felt her knees grow weak, and a deep trembling began to work its way through her being. Could Romalio sense the *marime* thoughts about the *gajo* that had invaded her body and mind? A vicious shiver ravaged her in spite of the humid heat that was already beginning to control the morning air. Somehow, she vowed to herself, she must shake these unnerving thoughts about the *gajo*, she must wipe the memory of his haunting green gaze from her mind once and for all! Then, when Romalio returned, she would put every ounce of her energy toward preparing herself to be a wife who was worthy of such a great man . . . that is, if Romalio returned.

Chapter Four

Blayde Chandler crouched down in the thick underbrush and waited with the patience of a coiled rattler. Had he heard a noise? Or were his nerves playing tricks on him again? He held his breath, listening. Nothing. A cold sweat drenched his taut body, despite the heat which radiated from the morning sun. He thought about untying the red handkerchief from around his neck to wipe the sweat away from his eyes, but it was just a thought. Until he was certain he had only imagined a noise in the brush he would not make another move. Even as the perspiration dripped from the spiked tips of his long, dark lashes and settled in the corners of his eyes like fiery coals, Blayde remained as still as a dead man. Each of his senses were keenly alive, though, as his ears sorted out the earthy sounds of the insects and rustling brush of the deep thicket that bordered the creekbed. He felt the weight of his six-shooter against his thigh. For three years now the gun had been his constant companion, yet there were times when it still felt strange . . . heavy and burdensome. The weight of the weapon, though, could never compare with the heaviness he had carried in his aching heart in all that time.

With a determined attempt to ignore the veil of sweat that played havoc with his vision, the bounty hunter focused on the barely indistinguishable trail his well-trained eyes had noticed beneath the low hanging branches. He waited, still nothing. Must be hearin' things, he told himself again. When he had stopped to water his horse at the creek a few minutes ago, he thought he had heard something in the thicket behind him. The dangerous profession he had pursued since leaving Texas had taught him to be cautious at all times. The second he had been alerted, he had dived beneath the nearest clump of brush and listened for another sound. Here he had remained, unmoving, his hand resting on his holster, though he was confident the gun could be drawn and fired in less than the blink of an eye if he needed to protect himself.

When the seconds began to expand into minutes, Blayde decided that he was letting his nerves get the better of him. The noise he had heard was probably something as insignificant as a bird or snake. Lately it seemed that he was on edge more than usual, and if he was going to accomplish what he had set out to do, he knew it was imperative for him to remain in control of his frayed emotions. A fidgety man could easily get himself killed by being overcautious. A man with nerves like iron or one who did not care whether he lived or died, was the type of man who was needed to complete the job Blayde Chandler had assumed. For the past several years he had been the epitome of a man who did not care about his own life. However, he was not ready to die . . . not until his mission was completed.

Just as Blayde had convinced himself that he was being foolish, he heard another noise. This time, he knew it was not his imagination. Something—or someone—was in the brush only a few yards from the spot where he was hiding. Quietly, but with lightning speed, he drew his six-shooter from its holster. Another sound from the thick underbrush caused him to cock the hammer without a second thought. He had distinctly heard whispered voices, and he reasoned that if someone was lurking in those thorny bushes, it was not to his benefit. But whoever was in there had the advantage. They probably knew exactly where he was, but unless he just started shooting into the thick brush, he had no way of knowing their location.

Since he had nothing to lose by disclosing his own position, Blayde decided to make an attempt to determine the site of his unknown stalkers. "My gun is aimed right between your eyes," he hollered, hoping his trick would work. "Come out, or I'll start shooting!"

He knew his ploy would either bring about movement in the brush or, most likely, a round of gunfire in response. In preparation for the latter, he lowered his head and waited for the attack he was certain would come. Instead, he was shocked to hear a tiny voice cry out, "Please, *Gajo,* don't shoot us."

Blayde raised his head, and in confusion, cocked his ear toward the voice. Was that a kid he had heard in there? He scooted forward until his face was level with the low-hanging branches and peered into the profusion of thorns and leaves. From this viewpoint he could glimpse snatches of bright-colored clothing, but the identity of the person in the thicket was still concealed.

"Who's in there?" he demanded. "Come out and show yourself!" He saw movement in the brush and heard high-pitched whisperings again, which left him with little doubt that his would-be assailants were no more than a couple of children. Still, he could not fathom why they were hiding in this thorny thicket, since it was definitely not the type of place children would pick as a playground. He rolled over and gave the area a quick surveillance, but just as it had been when he had ridden up, he saw no one else. Movement under the branches diverted his attention back to the brush, where he was stunned to see two tiny Gypsy children scooting out from their hiding place. As they crawled toward him he cautiously watched the area from where they had emerged, although it appeared that they were the only two who were hiding in the brush. But still he wondered why they were there.

Blayde pushed himself up from the brush and rose to his feet, though he did not holster his gun just yet. Maybe this was a trick of some sort; Gypsies were famous for their sneaky pranks. Perhaps these children were meant to divert his attention so the true culprit could hit him over the head and rob him of the rest of his belongings. That thievin' fortune-teller might have told her cohorts what an easy target he was after she had stolen from him last night with such little effort. He looked around again but stil saw nothing else that would arouse his suspicion. When he glanced back, the children were standing before him with the most frightened expressions he had ever witnessed.

A sick feeling crashed down around him as he stared at their tiny faces and realized how scared they were of him. He released the hammer of his six-shooter and shoved the gun back in its holster as if it was on fire. "What are you two doin' here?" he demanded in a harsher tone than he had intended. At once, he was overcome with more self-reproach when they cringed at the booming sound of his voice. He couldn't help but to notice the ragged condition of their clothes, and the drying blood that caked their dirty faces and also their arms and legs.

The boy, who was trying his hardest to be brave, pulled his sister close to his side in a protective manner. His dark eyes stared up at Blayde in wide-eyed terror, but he made no attempt to reply, even when Blayde repeated his question. Without an answer, the gunslinger was left to his own assumptions. He had heard that Gypsies stole children and raised them as their own, but it seemed that these two had been deserted. "Are you lost?" he asked, seeking another answer that might explain why they were here. Neither of them made any attempt to give him a clue, however.

In aggravation, Blayde clamped his hands down on his hips and exhaled an annoyed sigh. "Well, I'm takin' you back to the Gypsy camp with me. Maybe havin' the two of you with me will give me some bargaining power," he reasoned, although he was

59

speaking mostly to himself, since the children had no idea what he was talking about. He hoped to be shown some gratitude when he returned these two ragamuffins, and perhaps the grateful Gypsies would make that stealin' wench return the picture and money she had stolen from him. The money didn't matter, he reminded himself, but Emma's picture could never be replaced.

"Come on, now, let's get going. I'm sure your parents are wondering where you are." Blayde motioned for them to follow him to his silver roan horse, who stood quietly—and patiently—at the edge of the creek where his master had left him. Blayde halted his hasty pace and waited, impatiently, while the children followed him with dragging footsteps. As he watched them, he was overcome with the feeling that something was drastically wrong. These kids were too small to be so far from their campsite. Also, they were much too frightened about something, and he was certain his threats had not been enough to produce such terror. They had fled into that thorny thicket to hide from something, or someone, and Blayde was growing more anxious by the second to discover what it was that they had been running from. If those thievin' Gypsies had gone off and left their own children here to perish, he was going to make them pay for a lot more than stealing his belongings.

With a child in each arm, he swung them onto the back of his horse, then hoisted himself up behind them. A rush of memories flooded his mind, and for a short time he was so smitten with grief that he found it hard to rein in his emotions. He told himself that the stinging sensation in his eyes was caused by the reflection of the morning sun shimmering on the water in the creek. Had it only been three years since he had taken Timmy for rides on Eclipse, and the boy would sit in front of him, just as this little Gypsy boy was doing now? As his only defense against the overwhelming pain, he had worked so hard at avoiding these memories that it seemed a hundred years had passed since he had held Timmy in his arms. But it had been in another lifetime, and Blayde Chandler was a different man then.

As he had forcefully trained himself to do during the past several years, he wiped clean the recollections of that other life, and blinked away the fiery moisture in his eyes, then focused his attention on his passengers, whose tiny bodies were encircled by his tense arms. There was nothing about these dark Gypsy children that should remind him of his fair-haired Timmy, so why was he recalling all those unbearable memories now?

"Hold on tight so you don't fall and break your necks," he said in a gruff voice. He would not let these little beggars affect him, he vowed. But then he was reminded of how the Gypsy dancer had affected him, and of the unyielding way her image had refused to leave his tortured dreams all through the long night. Damn these people! There had to be some truth to the belief that they used black magic and witchcraft to cast spells over unsuspecting souls. Why else would his mind insist on reminiscing about Timmy and Emma . . . and desires that he had put to rest a long time ago?

Chapter Five

While Tasmin retraced her steps back through the oak forest, a growing sense of panic washed over her. Although Romalio had assured her that the outlaws had not come in this direction, she worried that too much time had passed since she had left the children in the thicket. No doubt their fear increased with each passing second they were left alone—although she still could not begrudge herself the time she had taken to tend to Nanna. The tribe referred to the old woman as *rawnie*, which meant "great lady," and this was truly an appropriate title for Nanna. Tasmin was thirteen when her mother died of a deadly fever. They were living in Romania then, and Tasmin was afraid that she would be sent back to her father's tribe to live with her paternal grandparents. But because Nanna had taken her in, she did not have to leave Persia, nor any of the other people she had come to love in this tribe.

Tasmin's mother had belonged to Nanna's tribe when she was growing up, but marriage to the king of another band of wandering Roms had led her to live with her husband's people. Since he was of a noble bloodline, Tasmin and Soobli were bestowed with the titles of "Princess" and "Prince" among their tribesmen. But when Tasmin's father was killed in a battle with Romanian villagers, Tasmin's mother took the girl and her brother back to her own tribe. Soobli, five years older than his sister, had planned to return to their father's tribe when he was grown, where he hoped to regain his prestigious position. However, since all bands of Gypsies never stop their endless wandering, Soobli could not locate them and was forced to return to his mother's people. Milza, a young woman in the tribe, caught his eye shortly after he had rejoined the familia. Danso and Cyri were the results of their union. When his wife had died en route to America while they had been emigrating from Europe, Soobli's discontent with his mother's tribe increased. Many times he spoke about returning to Romania to continue his search for their father's people. Tasmin worried that he sometimes resented his obligation to his children, and if not for them, he would have already returned to their homeland.

When it was announced that his sister would marry Romalio and become the *Phuri dae,* Soobli made no secret of his joy over this prospect, especially since her position would also increase his power among the tribe. His quest for domination caused Tasmin concern, but she kept telling herself Soobli would not use his impending authority to bring harm to their people. Still, she could not help but worry about how her marriage to Romalio would affect her brother's attitude when he was considered a royal figure once again.

Now, however, her concern was for his children. When she stepped from the thick glade of trees and met with the *gajo,* who apparently held her niece and nephew prisoner, all her common sense disappeared. They stared at one another for only a second, although the surprise of their sudden encounter was evident on both their shocked faces. Tasmin's mind could envision only that he was kidnapping them for some demonic purpose, such as white slavery or torture. She knew first-hand of how much her people were hated by the *gajo,* and today's ambush added proof to this knowledge. That this man also might have been the one who had led the attack, served as a basis for her rage and fueled her courage.

A rash of Romanian profanities flew from her mouth as she charged forward like a crazed lioness. Her force against the side of Blayde's horse threw him off guard, and before he could function coherently, he and the two children tumbled to the ground like a trio of rag dolls. He had not regained his full composure when the woman jumped on top of him, but he found his floundering senses once he saw the blade of her knife flash through the air before his eyes. Instinct caused him to try to protect himself by grabbing for the knife, but he was not swift enough. The sharp blade sliced through the palm of his hand before coming to a thudding halt in the muscles of his shoulder. His last thought before unconsciousness slipped over his stunned mind was that this damned Gypsy witch had cut his gun hand!

Tasmin recoiled in horror when she felt his struggling body go limp. The expression on his face was one of disbelief and pain as his eyes closed in silent agony. Although she was only trying to protect the children, an ill feeling gripped Tasmin when she realized that she was capable of killing someone.

"He was taking us back to the camp," Danso said in a panicked voice. "I was going to ask him to help you and father." His wide-eyed stare looked down at the gaping wound in the man's shoulder, while it appeared that the boy went into a trance as he watched a circle of dark red blood soak the man's tan shirt. Cyri held her tiny hands over her tightly-closed eyes, afraid to see the gory vision of blood and torn skin.

"O Del! What have I done?" Tasmin gasped. "I thought he was kidnapping you." Although she was certain she had killed the man with her irrational attack, she fell to her knees at his side and leaned close to his chest to listen for a heartbeat. She had barely touched her ear to his bloody chest when she was surprised by his sudden burst back to consciousness. Before she was aware of what was taking place, the man had reversed their positions and now had her pinned beneath his hard body. Tasmin did not even have time to cry out, and until she felt the burden of his weight, along with the sticky warmth of his blood soaking through her thin blouse, she was too shocked to realize what had happened.

In a frenzy of fear for their aunt, Danso and Cyri jumped on top of Blayde's back and began to pound, kick, and bite at the man who was once again foe rather than friend. Blayde, weakened by his wounds, was almost knocked unconscious again with the force of the children's attack. His mind waged a desperate battle with his body in a vain effort to keep from passing out again, while he also tried to shake the children from his back. His main concern, though, was the wildcat he had pinned beneath him, especially since he already knew that she was capable of killing him without a moment's hesitation. In the pandemonium that followed, however, Blayde surprised himself with his ability to retain his tight hold on the woman, in spite of the shooting pain which bolted from his hand to his shoulder like a million fireballs burning through his veins. The combined aggravation of the two children tormenting his backside was nearly his undoing, however. But when he realized that the woman was hollering at the two children to leave him alone, he was even more shocked.

When they finally became aware of what their aunt was saying to them, Danso and Cyri rolled from the man's back, then huddled together several feet from where he still held Tasmin captive. Since they were sure the *gajo* was going to hurt their aunt, they could not understand why she had demanded that they stop trying to help her.

"They are scared for me," Tasmin said in a gasping whisper as she fought to catch her breath. The force of the man knocking her to the ground had stolen the wind from her lungs, and the extra weight of the children had caused her even more distress. Now, though, she focused her attention on the man whose face hovered only inches above her. Their noses were almost touching, and each of them could feel the hot, labored breaths of the other against his face. The ebony gaze of the Gypsy princess flashed with bolts of silver as she stared into the emerald green eyes of the *gajo,* and although she had admitted to him that the children were afraid of him, she would never permit him to see how frightened she was of his intentions.

Unable to look away, Blayde was overpowered by the same feelings of helplessness and desire that she had awoke in him last night when their eyes had met for the first time. It was as though this Gypsy witch had the power to ignite a fire in his soul with no more than her hypnotic black gaze. If he had not been so weak from the wounds she had inflicted upon him, he would have continued to stare at her, continued to feel these forgotten emotions that only she seemed to have to power to summon forth, but his arms were shaking so violently that it was affecting his vision and making it difficult for him to focus on her face.

His deteriorating state was evident to Tasmin, but she was uncertain as to what she should do next. In his present condition, she could probably overtake him again, but she could not make herself move. Even in the wake of all this insanity, she found herself only wanting to immerse herself in his green gaze for a while longer, in the hopes that she would once again glimpse her own fate . . . a fate that was somehow entangled with his. A moment ago she had tried to kill him, but now the strange sense of affinity she felt toward him was the only thought her spinning mind was able to comprehend. Persia's words came back to taunt her, but Tasmin had been too stubborn to permit Persia to tell what she had seen in the *gajo's* palm. If she had, perhaps she would not be so cloaked in confusion now. Thinking of her dear friend reminded Tasmin of the ambush and made her fill with guilt for allowing her lascivious thoughts to rule her mind once again.

"Were you riding with the devils who attacked our camp this morning?" Tasmin asked, her voice still raspy and low from lack of air. The damp area where his blood had soaked her blouse felt sticky and caused her to worry about the amount of blood he was losing.

Her question surprised Blayde. He eased the weight of his body up from her slightly, then winced with the pain that even this small movement caused in his shoulder and hand. "Your camp was attacked?"

Tasmin started to accuse him of leading the rest of the *gaje* to their campsite, but somehow she knew that he had not been involved. Though she did not possess the great mind-reading powers with which Nanna and Persia had been gifted, Tasmin felt that she could usually tell whether a person was lying to her or not by the reaction in their eyes. A liar could never hold his eyes steady for too long a time when confronted with an unwavering stare. But this *gajo* had a way of locking his gaze with hers, and wiping out all her common sense. "I—I ran from the camp when we were ambushed and hid the *chavvies* in the thicket." She tore her eyes from his face and glanced towards the children, adding, "Then I returned to help my people. I thought you were stealing them when I saw them on your horse."

68

A strange glint lit Blayde's green eyes when he thought of the irony of her accusation. Gypsies stole children, and he found it almost humorous that she would think he was capable of such a terrible deed. Even though she was dead wrong, he ignored her insinuation that he was as low as her people and refrained from making a snide retort in his own defense. Still, as much as he mistrusted Gypsies, Blayde did not want to see any harm come to them, either. "How bad was the attack?" he asked as he pushed himself up from the unmoving form of the woman with his uninjured arm. He sat back on his heels, afraid that if he attempted to stand, he would lose consciousness again. The gash in his hand was not as serious as he had first thought, but the witch had done a thorough job of slashing open his shoulder. The tan shirt he wore hung limply from the wound in ragged shreds, and the blood from both of his wounds covered most all of his front side in a deep shade of crimson.

Tasmin gasped when she noticed how much blood was still oozing from the gash in his shoulder. "Let me help you," she said as she eased herself up from the ground. As she rose to her feet her eyes were drawn down to her own garments, which were as gruesome a sight as the man's clothes. "You must let me tend to your shoulder." Her sincerity was not false, but Blayde gave his head a negative shake.

"You've done enough already," he answered in a sarcastic tone, cradling his injured arm and hand in his other arm as if they were an infant. He attempted to rise, but when he stood, his knees were almost too weak to support his weight. His head felt light and his vision grew distorted as he fought to overcome the dizziness and to remain standing.

Without hesitation, Tasmin rushed to his side and wrapped her arms around his middle. She felt him stiffen when he became aware that she was supporting him, but he was growing too unsteady to push her away. "You will die if I don't help you."

"Wasn't that what you had in mind?" His voice was as shaky as his limp, but the contempt he felt toward her was still evident in his tone.

Tasmin opened her mouth to retort with her own debasing remark, but decided that exchanging barbs with him would not help any of them. He needed help, while Danso and Cyri needed reassurance. She motioned toward the horse. "Danso, Cyri, help me to get him on his horse. Then we will go back to the camp and wait for your father to return." The fear disappeared from the childrens' faces at once when she mentioned their father and the camp.

"Our father is safe?" Danso asked as he and his sister approached the *gajo*.

"Yes," Tasmin said in a voice that was beginning to sound labored from the burden of the man. "But he had to go away for a little while. He will probably be back by the time we return." She wished her confident-sounding words could be true, but it was doubtful that the demons who had stolen her friends would be so quickly overtaken. She cringed at the thought of what might have already happened to Persia and the others by the time Romalio and his men caught up to the outlaws. Even worse was that the men would probably have to fight another battle to recapture the women, which could also mean

70

more deaths among the dwindling Gypsy population.

"Let's hurry," she said as she tried to turn her morbid thoughts away from the fate of her loved ones. With every bit of energy she could summon she began to drag the man toward his horse. He was nearly unconscious again and leaned heavily on Tasmin as she and the children struggled to hoist him onto his silver roan. The strain of mounting the horse left Blayde in a state of pained submission. He could feel the woman's hands against his hips as she tried to support him in his saddle. The children were leading his horse through the trees, and although he did not want to return to the camp with them, he was in too much agony to resist.

To keep himself from giving in to the blackness which threatened to engulf him, Blayde concentrated on the enraged fury this Gypsy witch had aroused with her foolish actions, which was almost as great as the desire her presence summoned forth in his reluctant being. He kept telling himself that if he died at the hands of this evil woman, the past three years would all have been in vain. He thought of the creed he had lived by during this embittered time . . . *an eye for an eye.* How could he join Emma and Timmy without first avenging their deaths? As these insane thoughts consumed his pain-ridden mind, he vowed that he would haunt this raven-eyed witch for all eternity if she prevented him from fulfilling his last desperate mission.

Chapter Six

Once Blayde realized he was in one of the Gypsy wagons, his eyes purposely closed again. He tried to focus his groggy senses on what the two women were whispering to one another before they became aware that he was awake. In his groggy state, he had the crazy notion that he would overhear the Gypsies discussing their use of black magic. Maybe they would even disclose the incantation the dancer had used on him, and by knowing the secret he would be freed from her evil spell. As his mind began to clear, however, these imaginings seemed a little foolish. Although he still did not dismiss his belief that they dabbled in witchcraft and other liaisons with the devil, he seriously doubted that they would talk openly about their wicked endeavors.

His shoulder still throbbed without mercy, but he was surprised to feel the heavy bandages that covered his upper body and were wrapped around his cut hand, especially since he had been certain that when the Gypsy had finished with him, he would be a dead man. Of course, he reminded himself, as long as he was in her presence, he still was not a free man.

"I don't think he had anything to do with the attack," Tasmin said, leaning close to Nanna so that she could keep her voice low. Although she had determined that he was innocent, until Nanna confirmed it, Tasmin still worried that he might have been involved with the men who had ambushed their camp.

"He wasn't," the old woman said flatly. She heard the young woman breathe a relieved sigh, but she did not offer further comment. It occurred to Nanna that perhaps she should tell Tasmin the truth, but her visions about the *gajo's* association with the outlaws were not clear in her aging mind. Somehow this man was connected with the ones who had attacked the Gypsy camp. Yet she was certain he had not ridden with them, and did not wish to bring harm to the Gypsies. Beyond these revelations, though, everything else concerning this stranger was a mass of confusion. As Persia had discovered last night when she had read his palm, this *gajo's* past was a mystery that was not easily unraveled, and without delving into the events that had made him the man that he was now, it was difficult to predict the exact course of his future where certain areas of his life were concerned. However, parts of his future were much more simple to decipher, such as the direction his heart line traveled.

When Nanna studied the fan of tarot cards she

had spread facedown on a tiny table, her old face screwed up with curiosity as she stared at the faded colors on the back of the cards. "See here," she finally said, pointing to the pair of cards which she had pulled away from the rest of the deck. "A queen of clubs and an ace of diamonds!"

Tasmin scooted forward as her interest peaked. When Nanna read tarot cards, she was seldom wrong. "What do the cards say?"

The old fortune-teller raised her dark gaze to the face of the young woman. A mild look of surprise flashed through her expression as she looked back and forth between Tasmin and the *gajo*. "Two love songs you will hear," she stated, motioning to both cards. Pointing first to the queen of clubs and then to the ace of diamonds, she added, "A kiss of fire that will tell you which to choose, and a lover's knot that no man can untie."

A frown creased Tasmin's beautiful face as she studied the cards Nanna held in her withered hand. "What does all that mean?" Because she did not want Nanna to think she doubted her, she tried to keep skepticism out of her voice. Since she had only one love, Romalio, it was foolish for Nanna to talk of two love songs.

A poignant smile crossed the old lady's lips as she turned toward the unmoving *gajo* again. "This you must learn for yourself." She reached out and gently touched Tasmin's smooth cheek with her rough fingertips. Her mouth opened as if she wanted to say more but did not know how to put her thoughts into words. Her weathered face hosted such a strange expression, a mixture of gladness and regret, that Tasmin grew almost leery of the old woman's predictions. She thought of asking to hear more about the unexplained visions the old woman could see in her dog-eared cards, but she could tell that Nanna had no intention of divulging more on the subject of her love life.

"The *gajo* listens," Nanna said matter-of-factly. She leaned back in the chair where she sat and studied the man with a sly grin upon her lips.

Tasmin glanced at the man with a look of apprehension, but from her viewpoint he appeared to be still unconscious. Anger flared in her breast when she saw one of his eyelids raise slightly, then clamp shut again. "You pretend to sleep, but Nanna knows you are a fake," she spat as she leaned toward him. Though she still had a distinct European sound to her speech, she had mastered much of the English language in the past two years. But when she became excited, or angry, as she was now, her speech became heavily accented once again.

Like a little boy who had been caught stealing candy, Blayde felt his cheeks grow hot with embarrassment. Slowly he opened his eyes and focused his still-foggy vision on the beautiful but enraged face that loomed over him. He wondered how he could still think about her beauty when she had just tried to kill him. Even more, he wondered what it was about her that could arouse these foreign feelings of desire in him whenever she was near, or even when he conjured up her image. He was completely baffled that he could dwell on these thoughts when, for the past three years, he had been so convinced that he would never want another woman again after Emma.

He blinked, hoping that when he looked at the Gypsy again, these unwelcome feelings would be gone. But Fate had something else in mind, and when Blayde reopened his eyes, he had the irresistible urge to kiss those soft lips that were only inches from his own. Witch! he screamed inwardly. His insane thoughts had to be the invention of her black magic. Once again his green gaze was drawn to her raven one for a time that seemed suspended, and as before, neither of them appeared to have the power to look away. Blayde felt the small amount of energy he had regained drain from his weary body as he fought against her evil hold. How unfair for her to weave her wicked spells on a man who could not fight back, he told himself in defeat.

Finally, it was Tasmin who found the will to pull herself from the magnetic hold they seemed to have on one another. Even when she looked away, though, their encounter left her feeling as if she was about to embark on a road she had never before traveled, but her destination was a mystery that frightened her. The *gajo's* eyes were as green as two emeralds; however, they lacked the shimmering luster of precious jewels. Instead, the many facets of his piercing gaze were shadowed with grief and anger. She longed to know his innermost thoughts— to know everything there was to know about him, or at least to have a bit of the rare insight that Nanna and Persia possessed, so that she might have a glimpse of his deepest thoughts. "I—I'm glad you're better," she said in a hoarse voice as she tried in vain to calm the fluttering in her stomach. She sat back in her chair, hoping that putting more distance between herself and the *gajo* would also restore some semblance of her sanity.

Blayde swallowed hard and licked his dry lips before testing his own voice. He was not any better, because he had to get away from here—from her—if there was ever any hope for him to get better. "I have to go," he said, while he attempted to push himself up to a sitting position. His head seemed to spin on his shoulders, but determination kept him upright. He heard the old woman give a loud huff, but he focused his attention on the young one . . . the evil one who had used her sorcery to bewitch him.

Tasmin sighed. She still felt guilty for misjudging his intention with regard to Danso and Cyri, but by tending to the wounds she had inflicted on him, she had also spared his life. She thought she should be glad that he was eager to leave, because then she could put him out of her mind for good. Then, too, her beloved Romalio would be the only recipient of her sensuous longings. "When you are able to travel, you will be free to go," she answered as she realized that she had known the king all of her life, but poor Romalio had never conjured up the types of wanton imaginings that the *gajo* had managed to do in less than a day's time.

"I have to go now," he repeated with a defiant toss of his auburn head. The motion made his head feel as if it was going to spin off of his body. He closed his eyes for a moment in an effort to regain his composure and to try to halt the rapid waves that swam across his vision. "I—I will rest for a moment, then go," he added in a more timid tone of voice. His eyes opened once more, and he glanced at the old woman. He was overcome with the odd sensation that she was looking right into his soul, just as the young fortune-teller had the night before, when he had been leaving the Gypsy camp. Were all Gypsies witches? he wondered as an icy shiver ravaged his weak body.

"Are you cold?" Tasmin asked with concern when she noticed his trembling motion.

"He's afraid," Nanna answered in a taunting voice. She leveled her dark gaze on his face, almost daring him to disagree with her.

A look of disbelief crossed Tasmin's countenance. "Afraid?" she repeated, also turning to stare at the *gajo*. "But you are safe now. I am sorry that I—"

Nanna's snide chuckle interrupted Tasmin's apology. "He thinks we are evil." The old woman pulled herself up to a standing position in the low-roofed *vardo* and waved her arms animatedly as she leaned toward the man. "He thinks we're—" She paused, then added in a menacing tone, *"witches!"*

Blayde cringed as another cold chill worked its way down his spine. He was more convinced than ever that he truly was in the company of the devil's companions. The old lady had just read every thought in his mind, and he had no intention of staying in this den of corruption for one moment longer. "Let me the hell outa here!" he demanded, throwing the sheet off his quaking legs. When he noticed he was clad only in his underwear, anger joined his fear. "Where the hell are my pants?"

Each woman looked at the other, then back at the *gajo*. His outburst had stunned them into silence, but Nanna promptly recovered and began to chuckle to herself. "Give the *gajo* his pants," she said to Tasmin, "and let him be on his way."

"But—but Nanna," Tasmin dropped her arms to her sides in defeat. "He is not well enough." Nanna's hunched shoulders shrugged, but she did not speak. Tasmin dared to dispute her once; she knew the girl would not repeat her rebuttal. Without another word, Tasmin reached for the *gajo's* denim pants, which she had folded and placed at the foot of his bed when she and Nanna had undressed him, a thought which made her blush with the memory, even though they had left him clad in his underwear. Still, even with his drawers still on, he was the closest thing to a naked man that Tasmin had seen in all her eighteen years. She hesitated for a second as she stared at the pants she held in her hands while shamelessly recalling every minute detail of the *gajo's* muscled body, which had not been concealed from her inquisitive eyes. The heat which enflamed her cheeks was scorching and served to increase her embarrassment as she prayed Nanna would not guess the *marime* thoughts that controlled her mind. With a nervous glance at the old woman, Tasmin suddenly tossed the man's pants in his lap. With her eyes downcast and a fiery blush blazing a trail of shame across her cheeks, she headed for the *vardo* opening to make a quick retreat. "I'll gather some food for him." She hoped she had only imagined her voice sounded several pitches higher than normal when she spoke.

Blayde stared after her until she had disappeared from view. Her flustered state had not gone unnoticed, but since his own thoughts were in such an uproar now that he was free to go, he did not dwell on the reasons behind her strange behavior. Although he wanted nothing more than to get away from these heathens, he worried that he was not strong enough even to climb out of his bed. His shoulder burned with an intensity that made him wish he could lose consciousness again, and just the thought of standing up made his insides knot into a tight ball. Still, when he looked at the smirking face of the old woman, he decided that he would be better off dead than to be at the mercy of this coven of witches. With this thought in mind, he reached for his pants and slowly rose to a standing position. The *vardo* was not tall enough for his six-foot frame, so he had to hunch over. His head spun and he noticed his hands trembling visibly as he gingerly pulled on his bloodstained pants. The shirt he had worn was nowhere in sight, and as he glanced around for the garment, the old woman spoke to him as if she was reading his mind again.

"The shirt was ruined, but here is another." She opened a small trunk which stood along one wall of the *vardo* and took out a folded white shirt.

Blayde paused, then took a deep breath before he

reached for the clothing she held out for him. Sheer determination was the only thing keeping him upright, and worst of all, he knew the old woman was aware of how terrible he felt. That she was letting him leave was all that mattered, though, and the sooner he was out of here, the better he would feel. With this giving him a bit of strength, he forced himself to continue to dress. But the shirt the old lady had given him was not the type he was accustomed to wearing. Rather than a button-down front, this shirt had a vee neck which he had to slip over his head. Blayde studied it with a perplexed expression as he wondered how he was going to get this contraption over his bandaged shoulder. He gave a startled gasp when the old woman grabbed the shirt away from him.

"See?" she said as she gave the garment a quick shake to unfold it. "It is loose and will fit over the wounded arm." Not waiting for his reaction, she tossed the shirt over his head and pulled it down until it was bunched up around his neck, then chortled to herself when she saw the horrified expression on his pale face. Her insight told her this *gajo* was usually a very brave man, so she found his tremendous fear toward the Gypsies quite humorous.

Although his senses were still off-balance, Blayde wasted no time in donning the shirt without further assistance from the old Gypsy. Just having the hag so near was almost his undoing; he certainly did not want her to touch him again. "My gun," he said as he slipped into his tall boots, hoping he sounded more capable of leaving than he felt. Pretending was a wasted effort with this witch, he reminded himself, because it was apparent she was not fooled by his act. He looked away from her wrinkled countenance and knowing ebony gaze while he cursed himself once more for having come into the Gypsy camp last night. By now he would be halfway to San Francisco, and maybe closing in on Ben McCalister and his gang. Because of his bad judgment—and bad luck—the McCalister gang would once again leave a cold trail for him to follow.

"Your weapons are hanging outside," Nanna said in her foreign-sounding voice. She motioned toward the door at the end of the wagon. Then, as if she was finished with the *gajo,* she sat back down in her chair and began to study her tarot cards once more.

Blayde exited from the wagon as fast as his shaky limbs would carry him. He didn't care that he had to hang on to the wall for support, nor did it matter that he was so wobbly by the time he had climbed out of the wagon that he had to lean against the rough planks of the sideboard until he was able to take a full breath. All that was important was that he was out of that witch's presence, and soon he would be free of this whole den of demon worshippers. Once the thudding in his chest calmed, he took a deep breath and closed his eyes tightly until his head stopped spinning enough so that he could fetch his gun from the hook where it hung. The weapon was like a soothing ointment for his agonized body and mind. Unless the six-shooter was close at hand, he no longer felt complete. But his bandaged hand made it almost impossible for him to fasten the belt around his waist.

"I have fed and rubbed down your horse."

The sound of the girl's voice made Blayde jump as his gunbelt and holster hit the ground with a dull thud at his feet. He felt fire spread through his cheeks again, making him feel even more foolish. He couldn't remember the last time someone had caused him even a slight embarrassment, but this raven-haired witch was arousing all kinds of emotions he had forgotten he was capable of feeling.

"Th—thanks," he managed to stutter as he took the reins in his still-trembling hands. "And . . . thanks for tendin' to my shoulder and—"

"I am truly sorry," Tasmin interrupted. She motioned towards his injuries as she took a step forward. She noticed how he tried to step away, but the side of the *vardo* halted his escape. His fear amazed her, especially since his people were the ones who caused so much pain for the Gypsies. "Are you sure you're able to ride?" Her gaze lowered to the ground, where his gunbelt lay in a heap.

Another rush of crimson flooded Blayde's face as he glanced in the same direction. A fleeting thought occurred to him that it was amazing he had not shot his foot off with his stupidity—then he would have had no hope of escaping. He plastered his body against the wagon when the Gypsy girl leaned down and scooped up the belt and gun. Was she going to use his gun to finish the job she had started earlier with her knife? In breathless silence, Blayde watched as she took another step forward. Paralyzed by her

83

nearness, he felt her arms slip around his waist. He closed his eyes, trying to avoid looking at her again. But when his mind began to paint a vivid image of her lithe form dancing around the campfire, bronzed skin glistening naked in the moonlight, his eyes flew open once again. Had she used her sorcery to produce that immoral thought in his mind, he wondered?

A tremor of unknown origin raced through Tasmin's veins as she fastened the buckle on the *gajo's* gunbelt. The memory of helping Nanna undress him this morning waltzed before her eyes, but this time embarrassment did not steal away her senses. She allowed her hands to linger longer than necessary, while she imagined what it would be like to strip his muscled body of all its clothes. O Del! her mortified mind cried. Forgive me! But how could she forgive herself for her mind's sinful indulgences? Her knowledge of what occurred between a man and a woman when they made love was limited to gossip from the married women and the brief instruction Nanna had given to her and Persia about proper conduct when they were in the presence of men. To Tasmin, it seemed that nearly everything about this ritual was *marime,* so why would her thoughts be so utterly consumed with something so wicked, and why would her body react to these thoughts with such unabashed enthusiasm?

Her cheeks burned as a scarlet stain colored her complexion. Even so, her brazen eyes refused to look away from this man—this man who was solely to blame for her mind's rapid decline from the rigid path of righteousness that she had been taught to follow. For their hungry gazes to lock once more was inevitable; for them to halt this obsessive habit was impossible. In the span of time that passed while their motionless bodies stood rooted to the spot and their eyes continued to seek answers to questions that had not yet been asked, Tasmin realized that if he rode out of the Gypsy camp now, she might never see him again.

"I don't even know your name," she said as a deep-seated fear clutched at her breast. She would spend the rest of her life yearning for caresses she would never know, remembering a face that would tantalize her every dream, and cherishing emerald green eyes that would haunt the darkest crevices of her shattered heart . . . and she did not even know his name.

Chapter Seven

Tasmin pulled her hands from the man's belt buckle and backed away as if she was afraid the fire emitting from their bodies would ignite and set them both ablaze. The *gajo's* emerald gaze darkened with unspoken thoughts that made Tasmin's blood boil like hot molten lava, and when he did say his name, his voice sounded as though it could barely escape from his hoarse throat.

"Chandler . . . Blayde Chandler." He coughed, then cleared his throat loudly and drew in a deep breath. It felt as if he had been holding his breath ever since she had first approached him. With the trance that had imprisoned them now broken, Blayde tore his eyes away from her face, adding, "I must go."

Tasmin nodded her head in a slow manner and glanced down toward the ground. *Blayde Chandler*. A shiver rippled down her spine. Why couldn't she just be grateful that he had not died from her rash attack, and that soon he would be out of her life for good? Her concentration ought to be on Romalio's return, she reminded herself. But the thought of her beloved's return did not fill her with the joy she knew she should feel, and this realization cloaked her in guilt. A worried frown overtook her beautiful face as she fought against these conflicting emotions. But, she told herself, once the *gajo* was gone, and Romalio returned with Persia and the others, everything would be back to the way it should be. Blayde, her mind repeated, Blayde Chandler. Another shiver raced down her spine and throughout her entire body, leaving her trembling in its wake.

In his mind, Blayde repeated his words with a firm inner voice. If he didn't go now, he was certain the tiny bit of sanity he retained would be gone forever. The reins he had held in his hand a moment ago now dangled limply from Eclipse's halter. He reached down and clasped them tightly, then straightened up slowly. Every movement left him dizzy and weak, but determination to leave made his actions more cautious. When he glanced around, he got his first glimpse of the burned campsite. His shocked gaze returned to the girl as he muttered, "Dear God!"

Though Tasmin was certain he had nothing to do with the attack, she was even more relieved to notice how surprised he was by the destruction of their camp. "Remember, I told you that we were ambushed early this morning. That is why I had hidden the children in the thicket." She repeated the explanation she had given to him after she had attacked him with her knife, while she nervously picked up the corner of her *jodka*—an apron with numerous pockets inside and out, worn by all Gypsy women so they could carry the various necessities they needed for their daily chores. The aprons were always made of Italian silk, and now Tasmin twisted the shiny black material between her fingers in a nervous gesture.

Though he vaguely remembered her telling him about the ambush, he had not realized the extent of the ruination until now. It was no wonder she had attacked him so viciously when she had spotted him with the children on his horse. When he looked at her troubled face again, he no longer saw a crazed witch whose intent was to destroy him. A sheepish expression crossed his whiskered face as he realized how crazy he must seem to her. He would always be convinced that she was using black magic to arouse his male desire, but he also knew that the attack on this small caravan, which included mostly women and children, was an inexcusable act of violence. "Who did this?" he asked, glancing at the ghostly skeletons of the burned wagons. Several children were poking sticks into the debris scattered around the campsite. He recognized two of them as the ones he had taken out of the thicket that morning.

Tasmin also looked at the youngsters as an exhausted sigh shook through her slender form. "Someone who does not like Gypsies."

"You did not even know who it was who attacked you?" Assuming that they had done something treacherous to provoke the attack, Blayde's voice held a disbelieving tone.

His insinuation did not go unnoticed by Tasmin. She returned his accusing look with narrowed eyes that flashed with silvery lights. "We did nothing to deserve this attack," she spat, then rushed on in a breathless voice that had grown heavy with her European accent. "We have to hide in the forest like criminals because we are afraid of being accused of something we did not do. But our only crime is that we are different from your kind, and because we are Gypsies, we are kidnapped and slaughtered like wild animals." Her anger at this injustice lit her dark complexion with a reddened flush as she gave her head a defiant toss. From beneath the scarf, which attempted to bind her thick tresses, a heavy profusion of raven hair was flung over her shoulder with the quick motion of her head. She flipped the long strands back with an angry sweep of her hand and raked her eyes toward him with another enraged glare. Even this man, this one who made her heart skip a beat every time his green gaze settled upon her, could not make her forget the pain her people suffered every day of their lives just because they were Gypsies.

Her proud attitude caused Blayde to doubt some of the rumors he had always heard about these people, but it did not erase all his suspicions. His encounter with the Gypsy fortune-teller last night had proved to him that they were thieves. This recollection reminded him of the reason he had decided to return to the camp today, and after all he had suffered because of this decision, he figured he might as well claim his property. "I do not care to judge the entire Gypsy race, but I do know first-hand that y'all are a bunch of thieves." He noticed a scarlet flame streak through her cheeks with the fury that his statement provoked, and he cursed at himself for noticing also how beautiful she looked when she was this enraged. Before she could make a retort to his accusation, and before his mind could dwell on the way she made him feel, he added, "Last night, as I was leaving here, I was robbed by some——"

Infuriated by his words, Tasmin cut in sharply, "You lie! I watched you leave the camp last night, and no one came near you." How like his kind to lie about the Gypsies! Still she could not understand why he felt it necessary to invent this tale. She had actually thought he might be different from most of the *gajo* they encountered. Now she knew he was one of the lowest of his kind.

Blayde's whole body throbbed with the pain that radiated from his shoulder, making him weaker and more impatient to leave with every second that passed. However, he was not going to leave without Emma's picture, and he might as well get his five-dollar gold piece back while he was at it. "When I went to get my horse, there was a girl 'bout your age waiting in the trees," he motioned in the direction of where he had tied Eclipse last night. "She wanted me to pay her so she could give me some cock 'n' bull about my fortune, but I refused, so she stole the money I had in my shirt pocket." Telling the story increased Blayde's anger, and when Tasmin opened her mouth to dispute him, he did not give her a chance to speak. "I'm not makin' this up, and I want

90

my money back. But mostly I want back the picture she stole out of my pocket when she took my money."

The deadly look that emanated from his green eyes as he leaned toward Tasmin did not invite dispute. A sick feeling washed over her as she realized that he probably was telling the truth about being robbed, and even worse, she knew who he had met in the woods last night. She loved Persia and Nanna dearly, but unfortunately, they both had a weakness when it came to stealing, and she was aware of their habit of slipping trinkets and coins from unsuspecting victims. Worse, she had seen Persia emerge from the woods shortly after the *gajo* had left the night before. "I—I," Tasmin searched her English vocabulary for the right words, but her mind was a complete blank. His fury, and her own feelings of guilt over Persia's actions, had left her feeling mute. "I believe you," she finally said, and was relieved to see some of the rage drain from his face. She also noted the pained expression his anger could not disguise.

Since Blayde already knew what a wildcat this Gypsy could be, he was surprised that she accepted his accusation without a rebuttal. Obviously she could not dispute what she knew was true: that her people were all thieves. Now, however, Blayde just wanted his belongings so he could leave. He took a labored breath, then asked, "Where is the girl? I'll confront her myself."

"How I wish you could," Tasmin said sadly. She made no effort to hide the sorrow she felt toward her friend's fate as her eyes became rimmed with tears.

Her apparent despair was not lost on Blayde. But his own agony consumed his energy and left him with little sympathy. "Look, she can keep the damn money! I just want the picture back!" His voice filled with anger again as he took a step forward, but his steps faltered when a wave of dizziness overcame his waning senses. He staggered back against the suppoort of the side of the *vardo* in an effort to remain conscious.

Tasmin was instantly at his side, and her eyes were drawn to the circle of fresh blood that was soaking through the top portion of his clean shirt. "You should not be up yet. Please," she pleaded, "Give your wounds a chance to heal for a while longer."

With a determined shake of his head, Blayde forced himself to stand upright again. He glared at Tasmin with the most indignant look he could manage in his weak state, which immediately made her turn loose of the hold she had on him. "Take me to the girl," he demanded once more, knowing that his strength was about spent.

"I can't," Tasmin retorted, returning his patronizing stare. "Your people kidnapped her this morning for reasons I can not even bring myself to say out loud. But that should make you happy, eh, *gajo?*" Her face contorted with unbridled wrath as she added, "Because, after all, she is a thief—and a Gypsy—so she is no better than a dog." The tears that sprang from Tasmin's eyes burned fiery trails down her cheeks as she spun around and stomped away from him. The events of the day had worn her nerves to a frazzle, and she could no longer tolerate the *gajo's* contempt and demands. She needed to be alone . . . to be away from him. Once in the shelter of the towering trees she stopped and dropped down to the ground on her knees in exhaustion. Let him bleed to death, she told herself. But just let him be gone when I return, and please, she added to her silent prayer, make his memory go away too . . .

Blayde stared at the fleeing girl until she had disappeared into the oaks, but he made no attempt to go after her. He did not trust Gypsies, and though he was still furious that the young fortune-teller had stolen from him last night, he was not happy to learn about the girl's fate, nor did he like the idea that the Gypsies lived in fear of being attacked. This was something he had never been aware of until now. He reminded himself that the Gypsy dancer could be lying to him, too. He glanced around at the forlorn campsite, wondering once again just what had provoked this attack. A shooting pain in his shoulder reminded him of his own problems, so before another wave of nausea and dizziness overpowered him, he pulled himself onto his horse's back. Eclipse did not make a move until his master was secure in the saddle, but the excursion had stolen away most of Blayde's energy. With the last of his strength he directed Eclipse in the opposite direction from where the girl had fled. He struggled to keep his senses clear, but each time the horse put down a hoof, the pain in Blayde's shoulder grew more intense.

He kept telling himself that he would not rest until

dark, but it was not even dusk. Blood that refused to clot had his bandage and shirt drenched in red, and his vision was blurred. Eclipse led them along a trail that bordered Chico Creek, although Blayde was not aware that they were even on a trail or in what direction they traveled. The searing pain from his shoulder had consumed all of his senses, and the last thought that passed through his mind as he lost his hold on reality was of the raven-eyed witch who had caused him this unbearable agony.

Chapter Eight

Unlike many Gypsies who feared the darkness, Tasmin loved nighttime, when the fires blazed and she did not have to see beyond the glow of the firelight. She imagined the world did not exist beyond the hazy circle of firelight and in her private Gypsy kingdom only good prevailed. But even more than her dream of peace for her people, Tasmin found herself excited by the night. The fiery fingers that reached out from the blaze seemed to summon forth every ounce of passion her soul possessed, and the single release she knew for this ravenous hunger was to abandon herself to dance. As the music pulsated through her body, she became one with the spirits of nature and as free as the wind that whispered through the trees. She absorbed the haunting sounds of the Gypsy violins and the passionate cords of the dulcimer as naturally as the air she breathed, and the riveting melody of the guitar increased her pulse until she felt as though she had climbed to the highest summit of desire.

The evening of the attack, however, the lonesome melody played on the violin by one old Gypsy made Tasmin feel more forlorn than ever. She prayed constantly to O Del that Persia and the other two girls were not suffering at the hands of the kidnappers, and that Romalio, Soobli, and the rest of the men would return unharmed. After the events of this terrible day, though, she held little hope that all her prayers would be answered.

Soobli's wagon was one of the *vardos* that had been spared, and after tucking tiny Danso and Cyri into one of the beds they shared in the wagon with their father, Tasmin gently kissed each of them. She gave another prayer of thanks to the Gypsy God for not allowing their home to be destroyed today. It seemed those two *chivvies* had already lost far too much for ones so young.

They were locked in their own private dreamland, and their cherub faces were as innocent as the day they were born. Tasmin smiled to herself as she left them to their innocent musings, where she hoped they would not encounter the nightmare that had occurred this morning. A light drizzle of rain had begun to fall by the time she made her way to Nanna's *vardo*. Soft snoring echoed through the thin walls of the old woman's wagon. Content that Nanna was sleeping peacefully, Tasmin headed back to Soobli's *vardo*. Because of the trauma they had endured today, she did not want to leave the *chivvies* alone tonight, although she needed the comfort of being near them as much for her own sake as for theirs.

The violin chords of the lone musician no longer

filled the night air, and the camp was now as quiet as a tomb. The rain was dwindling down the last of the flames in the large fire which burned in the middle of the camp, and the entire area had a sense of desolation. Tomorrow they would put to rest the Gypsies who had been killed in this morning's raid. The bodies, as well as all the belongings of the dead, would be burned at daybreak. An icy chill invaded Tasmin's bones as she tried not to dwell on tomorrow's bleak beginning, especially since the funerals of those who died by an act of violence were also accompanied by a grave sense of fear. Roms believed that Gypsies who died unexpectedly, by hostility or with resentment toward the living, would return from the other side, because ghosts of murdered Gypsies would not be able to rest and would haunt the living forever. But if it was believed a Gypsy was about to die and there was time to conduct the sacred ritual, there would be no fear of that ghost returning. The ritual, usually overseen by Nanna, would consist of the old woman attempting to chase the Death Spirit away by shaking smoking sticks and shouting curses. When death was imminent, Nanna would throw up her skirts and threaten the Death Spirit with *marime* and tribal defilement. If the Death Spirit was not dissuaded by this last resort, then the rest of the tribe would pass before the dying person and beg their forgiveness so that he would not be tempted to come back and haunt them. The poor souls who had died in this morning's raid had bestowed no forgiveness on the living, so their ghosts would not find peace on the other side and would wander endlessly, just as they

97

had in life.

The *gajo* had been gone but a few hours, and Tasmin had hardly thought of anything else. He had not been well enough to travel, and the profuse bleeding in his shoulder when he had left earlier this evening was proof. As the night closed in around the secluded campsite, Tasmin imagined him lying somewhere among the trees, or facedown in the creek, lifeless and drained of blood. Not able to shake these morbid images when she stretched out on her brother's quilt, Tasmin found it impossible to sleep. She tried to tell herself it was only the guilt she felt over stabbing the *gajo,* though she couldn't deny that it was something much deeper. She wanted—needed—to see him again, if for nothing else, to know that he was all right. If she could be sure of this, then she could put him out of her mind for good.

After a long, sleepless night, Tasmin was certain of what she had to do . . . she had to know that the sad-eyed *gajo* was not lying somewhere near death, or perhaps already dead. When the first hazy streaks of dawn began to filter through the dark sky, Tasmin kissed her sleeping niece and nephew, then quietly slipped out of her brother's *vardo.* It pained her to think that she would not be here to care for them when they awoke, but she was secure in the knowledge that they would be taken care of by all the good people in the camp. Everyone was considered *familia* among the Gypsy tribes, and no one was ever left to fend for himself unless he was branded as *marime.*

This thought made Tasmin rethink her decision to

go after the *gajo*. Since *marime* meant one was shunned by the rest of the tribe because of some impure act or lack of modesty, Tasmin wondered about the venture she was about to undertake. *Marime* could be brought about by something as innocent as a woman permitting her skirts to brush against the legs of a man, or for a deed as sinful as adultery. To go alone to seek the *gajo* would surely bestow the dreaded affliction of *marime* upon Tasmin. Still, there was something much stronger than herself compelling her to go, and she could only hope that everyone would understand why she felt that she must do this. If only she could explain it to herself . . .

The rain, which had fallen most of the night, left the ground soggy, and there was a chill in the air that did not feel natural for this time of year. Tasmin wondered if her own gloomy state of mind made it seem as though the seasons had become confused, making the day seem more like a bleak winter dawn instead of a summer morning in June. Only a few horses remained at the camp since the men had taken most of the mounts when they had gone in pursuit of the kidnappers. Tasmin grabbed the nearest hobbled horse, and after releasing the leather straps that held his back legs, she swung up on his back. Even the threat of *marime* could not make her change her mind once she had determined that she must go in search of the *gajo*. She would deal with the consequences later, she told herself as she glanced back at the circle of *vardos* once again.

After a few minutes of indecision, Tasmin decided not to go to Nanna's *vardo* before she left. She wanted to tell the old woman where she was going, but if Nanna should forbid her to leave, Tasmin knew she would go anyway. It was better that she did not talk to anyone, she determined as she led her horse away from the quiet Gypsy caravan. Once she was convinced that the *gajo* was not lying suffering somewhere nearby, then she would return to the camp and try to make amends for her rash behavior. Perhaps she would have to ride only a short distance before she would be satisfied. If his shoulder had stopped bleeding, and if he had camped somewhere in the vicinity, then hopefully by this morning he would have regained some of his strength. Tasmin decided that if she came across a fresh campsite close by, and even if the man was nowhere in sight, this would be all the evidence she would need to satisfy her concern about his condition. Still, there were other possibilities to consider, but she did not want to dwell on the negative things she might discover when she went in search of the *gajo*.

She reasoned that this journey would dispel the guilt she could not shake for having stabbed the man, and she tried to convince herself that she really did not want to encounter the *gajo* again. Yet just the idea of being close to him once more made her pulse race with a yearning for things she could not comprehend, and a nagging voice somewhere deep inside her kept taunting her with the true reasons for her impulsive decision to go after the dangerous stranger. The idea of never seeing him again was more than her impassioned heart could bear, but as the inner voice shouted out this truth, Tasmin stubbornly denied her feelings. She wanted only to know that he was alive—nothing more. When she returned, and once Romalio and the others returned, everything would be as it should again. She would dance in the moonlight, beneath the Gypsy sky, and all the sadness of this time would be nothing more than a dull memory. As their dwindling caravan once again wandered on the endless road that all Gypsies traveled, her dear friend Persia could help her prepare for her wedding to the king, and their lives would once again be filled with sunshine and promise. But today dark, threatening clouds made the horizon of the future appear to be very foreboding.

Chapter Nine

Blayde remembered this feeling, but he had not experienced it for such a long time that he had almost forgotten how comforting it was just to be near her. Secure in the knowledge that she would be here whenever he opened his eyes, he did not try to force himself to awaken. Emma . . . dear, sweet Emma. How he loved her, and he'd no doubt she loved him equally as much. Her surface beauty was obvious: hair the shade of cornsilk and eyes as blue as the midday sun; still, her inner beauty was just as rare. Blayde had loved her from the first moment he had set eyes on her at the church social. Courtship, marriage, and a son followed in rapid succession, and with his flourishing career, Blayde's life seemed perfect.

Emma . . . she had come back after all this time. A poignant smile came to rest on Blayde's mouth as his heavy lids slowly began to open. *Emma,* his hazy mind called out, but when his eyes focused on the face above him, his senses were thrown into turmoil.

He had felt her gentle touch, but could he have been mistaken? His eyes drowsed shut again as his mind drifted back to the past. He would sleep a while longer, his foggy mind determined. Then, when he awoke the next time, he would be able to see clearly his dear Emma's face, instead of the dark image that he had glimpsed just now.

Tasmin drew in a tired breath, and, as she had been doing for most of the day, swabbed the *gajo's* brow with a cloth she had dug out of her apron pocket. She shivered from the cold that had settled over the rain-soaked ground and warily peered out through the opening in the huge tree trunk where she had taken refuge from the storm. Darkness would soon close off the forest from the rest of the world, and she worried that if she did not attempt to make a fire, the *gajo* would not survive the night. It amazed her that he had managed to travel this far before collapsing. Earlier in the day, when she had first glimpsed him lying at the hooves of his loyal horse, he had lost so much blood that she was certain he was already dead.

He was unconscious, barely alive, and soaked to the bone from the rain that had begun the night before and still continued to fall. The Gypsies had been in Northern California long enough for Tasmin to know how unpredictable the weather could be. They were too far from the Gypsy camp to make it back before nightfall, especially in a cloudburst as relentless as this one. After she had come upon the *gajo,* it was all she could do to hoist him onto his horse and get him to the shelter of the nearest clump of trees before the wind and rain made traveling impossible. A huge tree which, during some previous storm, had been struck by lightning and left hollowed out at the base, provided a meager escape from the horrendous weather.

With the rain endlessly pelting down, Tasmin wondered how much longer either of them could survive without warmth, nourishment, and especially more protection from the destructive storm. With an uncertain glance at the *gajo,* she realized she had to venture out in search of a better refuge, and before nightfall reached the forest. She had propped the injured man up against the rough wall of the burned-out tree trunk, and it was obvious from his labored breathing that he needed to be able to stretch his tall form out in order to be made more comfortable. His shoulder had stopped bleeding, but he had acquired a fever which left him sweating profusely in spite of the freezing air in the darkening forest.

Once Tasmin had finally convinced herself that she had to go out into the downpour, she wiped the *gajo's* face once more. Then she laid her hand for a moment against his hot cheek in a gentle caress. The compassion she felt for this stranger was so overwhelming that she could not even begin to understand the enormity of her feelings.

"Emma?"

Tasmin pulled her hand away from the man's face. Startled by his hoarse voice, she waited to see if he was regaining consciousness. But the name he had muttered was his sole admission, and Tasmin soon realized he was too ill to speak coherently. As she crawled out from the tree, though, she found herself wondering who Emma was, and why, when he was so racked with fever, her name was the one thing that would penetrate his pain. When the velocity of the storm hit her full force, Tasmin did not have time to ponder over it. All her energy and concentration was needed to fight the force of the violent gales of wind and rain.

Although it seemed a hopeless task, Tasmin pushed herself through the raging torrent in her quest to find a better place to move the injured man. The ground was like a sponge beneath her feet, with water splashing up around her bare ankles as she trekked between the drooping branches of the waterlogged trees. She wished she had worn her tall leather boots, but this morning her thoughts had not been on her footwear, and now the flimsy leather sandals she wore provided no protection for her feet and legs. She thought that if she could get the man out of the forest and head toward the rolling hills on the opposite bank of the creek, she would be able to find a cave, or at least an alcove in the hillside that would be high enough to get them out of the water that was accumulating on the ground. But as she reached the edge of the forest she was horrified to find that the once-peaceful waters of the lazy creekbed now rushed over their banks like a surging river. If the rain did not stop soon and the creek continued to rise, even the forest would be flooded before the night was through.

Panicked, Tasmin turned and began a rapid retreat back into the meager protection of the trees. As she trudged through the soggy grasses, the realization that she and the wounded *gajo* were trapped here increased her panic. If the rising water from Chico Creek began to flood through the trees, there would be no place for them to go. She thought about tying the man onto the back of his horse and heading in the opposite direction from the creek, but the rain made visibility difficult, and even finding her way back to the hollowed-out tree was not easy. Besides, without using the creek for guidance, Tasmin was not certain which way to go. If she set out blindly, there was a chance they would end up going in circles. As she crawled back into the sparse security of the old oak she reminded herself that the *gajo* was too sick to move until she had a specific destination anyway. She glanced at his pale face and was filled with empathy, now accompanied by a growing sense of doom.

She must have been insane to come looking for him, she told herself again, regardless of the fact that she was to blame for his condition. There was nothing she could do to help him, and because of her rash decision, she had placed her own life in peril. If the ferocious storm did not wash them both away, and even if she were to return to the Gypsy camp, her behavior would undoubtedly make her an outcast among her own people. Tasmin closed her eyes and leaned back against the rough bark in defeat. She did not attempt to stop the tears which escaped from beneath her eyelids. How could everything have gone so wrong? As she allowed herself to wallow in self-pity, she also realized that she alone was to blame for her predicament. She knew that by coming after the *gajo* she might have to risk everything, and because of the storm, she could not go back to rectify her actions. Perhaps if she had been able to return to the camp before night had fallen, as she had planned, she could have made the others understand why she had felt so strongly compelled to help the *gajo*. Even though he could die, that she'd been alone with him throughout the night would be enough to brand her *marime* for the rest of her life.

"O Del, what have I done?" Tasmin asked of the Gypsy God, while her tears continued to mix with the rainwater which had drenched her clothes and soaked into every pore. The guilt she had felt over stabbing the *gajo* was now transferred to the agony she felt over leaving the camp. Danso and Cyri had needed her and she had deserted them. Her heart twisted in her breast as she thought of the two tiny *chavvies*, all alone, wondering where their aunt had gone. She was the closest thing to a mother that either of them knew, and if Soobli and the others had not yet returned to camp, they would feel completely deserted.

She realized now that she had been too consumed with her own selfish needs to think about all the people who would suffer when they discovered that she had left the camp. Even a woman as brave and wise as Nanna needed her now that Persia's fate was so bleak. When Romalio and the other men did find Persia, Savana, and Vilo, the women would probably be in need of medical help, as well as support from their families and friends to help them through the horrible ordeal they had endured at the hands of the outlaws. Tasmin would not permit her thoughts to dwell on the extent of abuse her friends might have suffered during their captivity, because she

107

could not bear the thought that they might all be *marime* as a result of the awful circumstances of the past few days. An agonized maon escaped from Tasmin as she realized what a drastic mistake she had made—again. It seemed that she just kept making the wrong decisions lately, ever since the *gajo* had entered her life.

"Emma," the man's weak voice whispered again. Tasmin barely heard him above the pounding of the rain, but knowing that he was still fighting for his life diverted her thoughts back to the reason she was here. Leaning forward, she laid the back of her hand against his cheek and was surprised to feel that his soaring fever had subsided. His skin was clammy, but no longer felt as though it was on fire.

"*Gajo?* Blayde?" she called out, using his name for the first time. She had never called a *gajo* by his name before, but saying this man's name did not seem the least bit odd. "Can you hear me?" In the close confines of the hollowed tree trunk their bodies were forced to touch. Still she pressed even closer to him and spoke into his ear, hoping that the sound of her voice could coax him back to full awareness. Tasmin noticed that his eyelids fluttered slightly, giving her a bit of hope that he might regain consciousness. "Please, Blayde, don't give up now," she pleaded in a desperate tone as she once again touched the side of his face with her palm.

Blayde's body begged for release from the pain that radiated from his shoulder and consumed his every fiber, but his determined mind refused to give in to the acute agony. Emma's gentle touch and the sweet sound of her voice were drawing him away from the release that death could grant him. As he began slowly to pry his heavy lids open, Blayde was struck by the revelation that the only way he could be with Emma again was if he was allowed to stay asleep forever. Yet he was certain that Emma was coaxing him back to the world of the living, and though his weary mind thought it was strange that she would lead him in this direction, he did not have the will to fight against her.

Night was stealing away the little bit of light which filtered through the jagged hole where the tree had been ripped open by lightning. In the waning light, Tasmin could barely make out the *gajo's* face, but she could tell that his eyes were finally open. "So, have you decided to rejoin the living?" she asked, although she did not expect an answer. It was apparent, even in the dim light, that he was barely conscious and still not able to focus on his whereabouts. He took a deep breath, then emitted a painful-sounding groan. In these close quarters Tasmin felt his body shiver with the cold that she, too, now found impossible to ignore. Without a second thought she slid an arm under his head and embraced him tightly against her. If they were going to make it through the night without freezing, she knew they had to depend on the only warmth they had, which was their own body heat.

Blayde was too weak to resist her tight hold, and to Tasmin's surprise, the tenson in his taut body seemed to relax after she held him in her arms for a few minutes. His breathing grew more even, and though he had lapsed into sleep again, Tasmin could tell he was resting much easier. Inside the tree it grew dark long before the last of the gray daylight had faded from the rest of the forest, but fortunately the rain was dwindling down to just an occasional sprinkle. Still, every so often a roar of thunder would roll across the heavens, or a fleeting spear of lightning would illuminate the forest for a brief instant, permitting Tasmin a glimpse of their eerie-looking surroundings. The boughs of the tall trees hung almost to the ground from the weight of the moisture which had accumulated from the rain, and among the gnarled roots and waterlogged grasses, deep puddles of water surrounded the jutting tree trunks.

The air in the tiny refuge where Tasmin and Blayde waited smelled of a musty, burnt odor, and the ground was soggy and made squashing sounds beneath them whenever they moved slightly. Tasmin almost envied the *gajo* for being too incoherent to realize how awful their situation was on this black, wet night. If she could only force herself to fall asleep, maybe she could escape from this nightmare for a short time, too. But she was too miserable to sleep, nor would her tortured thoughts allow her to lapse into slumber. Combined with the indescribable discomfort of their situation, Tasmin's concern over being labeled "unclean" by her family members and friends also burdened her troubled thoughts. She tried to put this degrading possibility out of her mind, but as the night wore on, she could hardly concentrate on anything else. There had been other women—most of them guilty of adultery—who were considered *marime* in her tribe, and Tasmin remembered how she would go out of her way to stay away from them for fear that their impurities would somehow rub off on her.

The man sighed in his sleep and snuggled closer against her breast in search of the warmth and softness he found there. The darkness did not allow Tasmin to focus her sights on him, but even without light, she could see him as clearly as if the sun was illuminating the face that rested so close to her heart. It was the face she had not been able to escape from ever since the night Romalio had asked her to dance for the stranger. Nor could she dismiss the way his unforgettable green eyes had penetrated directly to her soul and left her questioning heart in complete confusion. What was it about this man that had stolen away her senses and awakened yearnings that even her devotion to Romalio had not yet brought forth?

Chapter Ten

The seven men who had kidnapped the three girls were scattered in various locations and positions around the one-room shack. A couple of the outlaws had managed to find their bedrolls, but the rest had passed out on the hard dirt floor, although in their drunken state it was doubtful that they would care. They had satisfied their bodies with their vile needs, and their thirst had been quenched by the large quantity of whiskey they had consumed.

Persia held her breath as she listened to the disgusting array of noises emitting from the men as they slept. The pounding of her heart sounded like thunder to her ears, and it surprised her that the loud thudding was not noticeable to anyone else. She pressed the back of her hand against her swollen lips in an attempt to stifle the scream she felt well up in her throat when her mind flashed over the events of this terrible day and night. Gypsy language did not contain words that could describe the hatred she felt towards the *gajo* dogs, and the anger she felt at the unspeakable things they had done to her and her friends.

A loud snore came from one of the men, making every nerve in Persia's aching body stand on edge. The disturbance did not seem to affect any of the men, but then all seven of them had consumed so much whiskey after they had each taken their turn violating the three Gypsy girls that Persia thought it would be a miracle if any of them ever woke up again. Savana, however, drew in a sharp breath when the man snored unexpectedly. A cutting pain shot through Persia's breast when she thought about young Vilo's fate, but the memory only fueled her determination to get Savana and herself away before they met with the same violent end. Then, there would also be time to grieve for poor Vilo and to pray to O Del that her battered soul receive sanction for the brutal manner in which she had met her death. Even as badly as she wanted to give in to the sorrow that swelled in her breast, Persia reminded herself that it would do Vilo no good now.

"Savana?" she whispered, hoping the other girl was alert, and that none of the men would waken.

Savana's bruised face turned toward the voice as she quietly called back, "We have to get away." The dilapidated shack where they had taken cover when the storm hit was shrouded in darkness, and neither girl could see the other's face. Still, it was apparent to both of them that escape was their only hope of survival. The ruthless killers had not shown an ounce of remorse when their brutality had caused Vilo's death. If Persia and Savana did not succeed in their attempt to get away, they knew they would

113

meet the same end as Vilo. After being subjected to repeated rapes and beatings, though, they had nothing else to lose. Death would be far more merciful than to spend another minute in the presence of these *gajo* savages.

Persia did not answer Savana with words. Her reply was to push her aching body up from the hard floor where the killers had left them lying after they had grown tired of attacking them and had turned their concentration toward drinking. She choked back the cry which lodged in her throat, her battered body racked with pain from the numerous rapes. Her insides felt as though they had been crushed and mangled and her legs were almost too shaky to support her weight. Gritting her teeth against the acute pain, Persia limped the short distance to where Savana lay.

"Are you able to stand?" she whispered, reaching down to help her friend.

Though she was as weak as Persia, Savana forced herself up to a standing position and held tight to her friend as she fought against the pain which threatened to make her pass out. "Let's go," she whispered in a voice which was barely audible. Her effort to hide her pain was lost on Persia as each of them tried to keep their own sanity in the wake of this unbelievable madness.

Carefully making their way toward the doorway, they clung to one another with the fear that at any instant one of the men might wake up and catch them trying to escape. The old shack was no more than four shod walls and a thatched roof, yet when the violent storm had struck, it had provided a welcome shelter. However, once they were all contained in the tiny hovel, it also provided a den for the molestation of the Gypsy captives. Neither woman could cleanse her mind or her body of the abuse she had suffered on this terrible day. For now, they forced their minds to concentrate only on escaping with their lives. If they allowed themselves to dwell on the brutality they had endured, their shame would prevent them from caring whether or not they survived.

In their drugged state, none of the outlaws had thought to tie up his prisoners. By the time the outlaws had lost interest in the women, Vilo's young body had succumbed to the abuse. Her lifeless form still lay sprawled against the back wall, and Savana and Persia had both lost consciousness and no longer offered much excitement for the madmen, who had drunk themselves into oblivion. Not one of the seven outlaws made a stir as the two women fled from the shack.

Once out into the dark night, however, Persia and Savana found themselves disoriented and still as frightened as ever. "Which way should we go?" Savana asked as she continued to clutch the other girl's arm.

"It doesn't matter," Persia answered. She squeezed Savana's hand reassuringly and began to lead them away from the shack. All that mattered was that they were no longer in the company of the demon *gajo*, but Persia had already determined that it would not matter whether or not they ever located their tribe again. Though the abduction had not been their fault, that they had been violated by the *gajo* made them *marime,* and even their own people would not be able to offer them refuge from the eternal horror of this day.

The rainstorm was beginning to let up slightly by the time the women had made their way into a grove of trees a short distance from the old cabin. They welcomed the dark forest because not only did the looming trees provide a meager shelter from the weather, but it also hid them from view of the shack. Still, they knew that in the morning, the first place the outlaws would look for them would be in the forest. With this thought urging them on, the girls did not allow the wretched elements to slow their escape. Neither of them was wearing shoes, and their clothes were ripped and bloodstained, but they barely noticed the freezing temperature in the waterlogged forest as they pushed themselves to continue. Not even the sheer torture that each step caused for their pain-racked bodies could stop them in their quest to get as far away from the outlaws as possible.

"The only thing that keeps me going is the thought of seeing Teril again," Savana said without warning while they waded through ankle-deep water left on the forest ground by the cloudburst.

Persia did not answer her. Didn't she know that her husband would never want to look upon her face again? Had Savana forgotten the moral laws of the Gypsies that would mar their lives forever? A fleeting image of Tasmin playing on the creekbed this morning flashed through Persia's mind. "The old customs seem so silly," she had said. At that time, Persia had been filled with irritation toward her friend because of her disrespectful attitude toward their laws and beliefs. Now Persia would give just about anything if they could change at least one of those ancient customs. Being *marime* was the greatest fear of all Gypsy women, for once she was labeled with this degrading title, the rest of her life was worthless. Persia thought of all the dreams she had harbored in her heart for her future. But this cruel twist of fate was something that the cards had not foretold. Even her dear friend Tasmin would not be permitted to speak to her again. How stupid of Savana to think that Teril would be happy to see her—that is, if they were able to locate their tribe again.

"Teril is a good man, an understanding man," Savana began in a tone that suggested she was attempting to convince herself of her husband's virtues. "I know that sometimes it seems that he is too jealous, but he really is a good man." When Persia still did not answer, she began to rattle on again. "He will understand. He—"

"Stop it!" Persia interrupted as she twirled around and grabbed the other girl by the shoulders. "Just stop lying to yourself. We are unclean now. Do you really think that anyone, especially Teril, will be glad to see us again?" Persia felt Savana's shoulders sag beneath her tight grip and she wished she did not have to be so harsh. But she could not allow her friend to continue to fool herself about returning to the same life they had known before today. Everything was different now, and Savana had to face reality. She would still be Teril's wife, but he would never ask her to share his bed again.

117

A violent shiver shook through Savana. "Why," she sobbed, "Why do we have to tell them what they did to us?" Her voice trembled as much as her body as she added, "They don't have to know, do they?"

Persia hung her head and tried to draw in a deep breath, but even breathing hurt. How she wished she could agree with Savana and convince herself that what had happened today would never have to be known. But this was not possible. No one would believe that the outlaws had abducted three women merely so they could have female traveling companions. And how would they explain Vilo's death to her parents if they should see them again? This thought made Persia think again about Savana's words. Telling Vilo's family about how the young girl had died was one of the hardest things Persia had ever imagined having to do. Perhaps Savana was right—why did they have to divulge all the details of their abduction?

"For Vilo's sake, if we do find our people again, maybe we should not tell anyone what happened today," Persia finally reasoned. Though she felt guilty for using poor Vilo as the excuse for her decision, Persia felt a rush of relief wash over her quaking being. No one had to know that they had been raped, nor did they have to know that Vilo had died from the brutality of the numerous rapes her young body had been forced to endure. Lying was sometimes considered *marime*, but intentionally hurting others was also *marime*. Perhaps O Del would understand their desperation and would allow them to exchange one sin for another—just this once.

118

"We will find them, we have to," Savana answered with desperation in her voice. What would happen to them if they did not find their people again? They could not think that they could wander into the nearest town and begin a new life among non-Gypsies—that was not even a possibility. Their only hope was to find their people, although they both were aware of the fact that the campsite would have been moved by now. Once the Gypsies were on the move again, it could be days—even weeks—before they stopped for more than a day or two at a time. Lost, on foot, and in their weakened condition, both women realized how remote their chances were of locating their tribe again.

"Come, let's not stop for too long," Persia said as she began to lead the other woman through the dark forest once more. She did not want to stop long enough to lose her bearings and get turned around. Then they might end up heading back in the direction in which they had just come . . . right back to the devils who had kidnapped them. Once they had found a place to hide and could rest their aching bodies, they could try to figure out where they were and make a guess as to what direction they should take in their attempt to relocate their people. But now it almost seemed as if the sky had drawn a heavy blanket of clouds over the stars so that they did not have to gaze down at the sight of the shamed women, and the rain continued to sprinkle through the thick branches of the menacing-looking trees as if Mother Nature was trying to cleanse the two women of their impurities.

119

Chapter Eleven

"W—Where am I?" Blayde's weak voice broke the silence which had dominated the hollowed oak all through the night.

Tasmin jumped at the unexpected sound. He had hardly made a noise until now, and several times she had feared he was dead when his breathing had grown so faint it sounded as if it had stopped altogether. She had pressed her ear to his chest to determine whether or not his heart was still beating. When she was not worrying about the *gajo*, the rest of her night had still been terrible; she was lost to brief patches of sleep that offered no rest, and an alertness that had her imagining every sort of morbid possibility, from being washed away in a flash flood to having Romalio discover her here with the *gajo* wrapped tightly in her arms. Of course, the latter was not likely, since no man could travel in this storm, but that did not stop Tasmin's mind from running rampant with this sort of wild fabrication.

"Are you awake?" she asked in a voice that was almost as hoarse as the man's. She tried to sit up but found that the cramped position in which they had spent the night had left her muscles too sore to move. The man groaned when her effort disturbed his still-throbbing shoulder. "I'm sorry," Tasmin gasped when she realized that she had caused him more agony. Throughout the long hours they had spent in this hellhole she had come to only one solid conclusion: she had not come after this man and placed herself in *marime* just so that he could go and die.

"I—I," his eyes traveled up to her face as he tried to focus in the dim light that flooded through the forest with the break of a new dawn. "Where am I?" he repeated in a daze.

Tasmin glanced out at the soggy forest and sighed. She had no idea where they were. One grove of oaks was the same as another, and since they had entered during the worst of the storm, she did not even know from which direction they had come. "I'm not sure," she replied honestly. She loosened the tight hold she had kept on him most of the night and permitted his limp body to sag against the rough bark of the tree trunk.

Blayde leaned his head back against the trunk and closed his eyes for a moment in an attempt to clear his groggy senses. Tasmin was certain he had passed out again, and she wondered how much longer she could bear to sit here and do nothing while he remained unconscious. Much to her relief, his eyes reopened, and when he looked at her again, she could tell he was beginning to come to his senses. He stared at her for only a second, then his gaze rolled up and around as he looked at their strange surroundings.

"It was the only shelter I was able to find when the storm became so bad that we could no longer travel."

He focused his attention back on Tasmin but did not make an effort to speak. All he could remember since leaving the Gypsy camp was his relentless dreaming of Emma. He had even imagined that he would be joining his dead wife soon, and now he wondered why God had played such a cruel trick on him.

When he remained silent, Tasmin continued to fill him in on the past twenty-four hours. "I came after you yesterday morning. You must have passed out, because I found you beside the creek a short distance from here. By then it was raining so hard I was barely able to get us into the forest. This burned-out tree was the best I could do." Her voice had grown apologetic, which matched her guilty expression.

Blayde cleared his throat and gave his head a weak nod. "You did good." Actually, he was surprised to learn that once again she had made an attempt to save his life. "Why did you come after me?" he asked as this curious thought occurred to him.

Tasmin shrugged in response. She had asked herself that same question at least a hundred times since she had left the camp. "I guess I still feel responsible for y—you," she said in a voice that held no certainty. "After all, I was the one who stabbed you."

"Yep, you did do that," Blayde agreed with an apparent lack of compassion toward her remorse. Still, it was useless to dwell on what had already happened, and he was not one to waste time pondering over the way things should have been. He winced with pain when he raised himself to an upright position. The look of concern on the Gypsy's face left him even more confused about her true motives. Her sincerity seemed genuine, but she had to have an ulterior motive for coming after him. Could it be that she still intended to use more of her witchcraft on his weakened mind?

Tasmin saw the strange look overcome his face as he stared at her. Why did he seem so leery of her? Nanna's taunting reference to his belief that they were witches flashed through her mind. Surely he did not really believe such nonsense. The idea seemed so ridiculous that she did not even want to mention it to him for fear that he would confirm Nanna's insinuation. Instead, she leaned forward and glanced out through the jagged opening in the trunk, then tilted her head back so that she could gaze up at the patches of sky that peeked out from between the treetops. The California weather was a constant mystery to her. Yesterday it had seemed as if the black clouds would never empty themselves of rain, but this morning the sun was beginning to shine a glorious spectrum of rays over the drenched land. "There is not a cloud in the sky today. If you are able to travel, maybe we can try to find my people's camp."

"I can travel on my own," he replied in a

determined voice. The pained expression on his face belied his stubborn statement; but he had no intention of returning to the Gypsy camp.

An aggravated sigh emitted from Tasmin as she narrowed her dark gaze at him. "You are in no condition to go anywhere alone. Why do you resist my help when I'm trying so hard to make up for what I did to you?"

Her anger was apparent in the way her black eyes flashed with bolts of shimmering lights, and the last thing Blayde wanted to do was to arouse her ire and cause her to cast another spell on him. "Look," he began in his slow drawl, "I forgive you. Stabbin' me was a mistake, and I do appreciate your help." He glanced at the waterlogged ground outside the scanty sanction of the hollowed-out tree and added, "I would have died out there without your help. But now we are even, and we both need to be going our separate ways."

Part of Tasmin knew she should agree with him. Yet there was still the unexplainable affinity that had drawn her to him from the first instant they had set eyes on one another, and this feeling had become stronger with each moment they spent together. She could not willingly agree to part company with him, not now, not until she knew she would be free from his memory as well. "You are not well enough to go on alone," she said in defense of her heart, which knew she could not guarantee its release from this green-eyed *gajo*. Besides, it did not appear that he was ready to travel, since she could not help but notice the dark circles which rimmed his eyes and the

124

pallor of his complexion beneath his scraggly auburn beard.

Blayde drew in a ragged breath and leaned his head back against the tree trunk once more. Did he dare argue with her? Perhaps he would be wise to consent to her wishes. When he had won her trust, he could make his getaway. All at once, Blayde realized how frightened he must seem. He did need to get away from her, but not just because he believed her to be a sorceress. His determination to leave on his own was also because of how her presence summoned up so many emotions he refused to confront. Even now, just being so near to her was driving him even more insane than his fears of her witchery. But, her reminded himself, he would never be feeling these forgotten sensations if it were not for her evil spells.

"My horse?" he said in a cracking voice, which caused a red flush to move across his pale complexion. "Is my horse out there somewhere?"

Everything about this *gajo* perplexed Tasmin, but she was too exhausted to try to figure out why he insisted on acting so strangely toward her. Though he could not remember yesterday, or the long night he had just spent wrapped in her arms, Tasmin could not dismiss all that they had been through together since their first meeting. But it appeared all that concerned him was his horse.

"Your horse is safe," she replied in an irritated voice. The horse she had been riding had disappeared during the stormy night and she had no idea where he had wandered, but the *gajo's* silver roan

125

had stood beneath the branches of a nearby oak all night long. "I will go fetch him if you promise not to try to run off as soon as I bring him here to you."

Had she read his mind too? There was no escaping from these Gypsy witches if they always knew what he was thinking. He glanced at the woman and could tell she saw the guilty blush rise up on his face once again. At that moment he made a silent vow that she was not going to beat him at this mind game, regardless of the wicked powers she possessed. Right now, he might be in a weak state of mind and body, but he would heal, and then he would show her who was the more strong-willed. "I'm not a fool," he said as he leveled his green gaze on her. He could tell she was surprised by the way his voice had stopped breaking and now acquired a sound of determination. "I need you, don't I?" he added without allowing his piercing stare to waver.

Tasmin was caught off-guard by his coldness, uncertain once again of his motives. Yes, he did need her because he was definitely not well enough to travel alone. But, didn't he understand that they needed one another. Now you're being foolish, Tasmin told herself, how could he be expected to understand what destiny had in mind for them when she was still seeking the answers for herself? "I'll get the horse," she said as she pulled her gaze away from his icy stare. She scooted through the narrow opening in the tree trunk and rose up slowly on her shaky limbs. The cramped position in which she had spent the night left her so stiff that it was several minutes before she could make her legs function. As the circulation began to work its way through her body, it sent waves of pain through her entire body and brought stinging tears to her eyes. She bit her bottom lip to keep from crying out until the sharp, prickly sensations began to recede and she was finally able to attempt to walk on her wobbly legs.

The air still held a slight chill, and since her clothes and body were soaked through from rainwater, she was racked with cold shivers that cut into her like icy shards. She could not remember ever being so miserable, but just as she was drowning herself in self-pity, she remembered Persia and the other two girls who had been kidnapped by the outlaws, and her own situation did not seem so bleak anymore. The silver roan whined softly as she approached him, but he did not shy away when she reached out and clasped the reins that dangled from his halter. He still wore his saddle, and Tasmin knew she would have to unsaddle him and dry him off before the man could ride him again.

While she lugged the wet saddle and blanket from the horse's back, she was amazed at how well trained the animal appeared to be. Gypsies valued their horses, and much time was spent training them to be mounts worthy of their prized position among the tribe, but Tasmin had never thought that *gajo* treated their horses with much respect. More than once, the Gypsies had acquired a horse who had been mistreated by a *gajo* and had nursed the animal back to health. Of course, this habit contributed greatly to the Gypsies' reputation for horsesteal-ing. The Roms, however, felt they were only being

127

humane and that their thievery was based on an act of kindness.

To Tasmin, though, it was apparent that this horse had been well cared for by his master, which made her smile to herself as she untied one of her long silk scarves from around her neck and proceeded to wipe down the animal's back. The slick material was not ideal for this sort of job, but at least the horse would be a bit more comfortable when she resaddled him. Her concentration was broken by the feeling that she was being watched, which made her gasp and swing around. Although she had no idea what had drawn her attention away from the horse, she was not prepared to meet with the intense, emerald gaze of the *gajo*. She found herself frozen to the spot, unable to move or look away. As always, his stare made her feel as though she was stripped of her senses and no longer had a mind of her own with which to think or reason.

Blayde had dragged himself out from the hollowed tree, but he found that he was still too weak to stand on his own. He positioned himself against the outside of the tree trunk and proceeded to watch the girl as she worked with his horse. His first thought had been that she was probably thinking about what a prize Eclipse would be to steal. But the loving way she had tended to the animal surprised him. Even the expresson on her face seemed so innocent and caring that his mind had been purged momentarily of all his bad opinions of the Gypsy. He was consumed with the unwelcome feelings of passion once more as his eyes hungrily drank in the way her wet clothes clung to her ripe curves. Though the early morning sun still shone sparsely through the tall treetops, the rays that cloaked the forest ground offered enough light to make her thin, damp garments almost transparent. Little was left to Blayde's imagination, yet his selfish mind envisioned her dark, satiny skin bare and within his grasp.

Even as she swung around and caught his shameless appraisal of her lithe form, he did not attempt to look away. Her beauty had him possessed, and if she had truly placed him under her evil spell, at this instant he was ready to cast his soul to the devil and succumb without resistance. He was too weak to deny his wanton desire for this raven-eyed witch, and his only regret was that he was also too feeble to make these ravenous yearnings a reality.

The look on his face was undeniable, but in her innocence Tasmin did not know how to react. Another cloudburst could have poured down from the sky, but even that would not make Tasmin's eyes shift away form the *gajo*. His look provoked the same intense feelings that she experienced when she danced around the campfire, except that now these emotions were stronger and more potent.

Tasmin could almost imagine the passionate chords of the dulcimer whispering through the trees. The sound seemed to echo through her spinning mind until she began to wonder if the music was only in her imagination, or if a Gypsy musician had magically appeared to serenade the magic of this moment.

Tasmin was the first to summon the will to break the hold this man had over her, but only because she could not bear another second of this suspended agony. Every pore of her trembling body ached for release; she could feel her breasts straining against the thin material of her white blouse as if they were about to burst with yearning for his touch. An indescribable ache inched through her legs and settled in her throbbing loins, making it almost impossible for her stand on her quaking limbs, and even her wanton lips burned for his kiss. *A kiss of fire* . . . Nanna's prediction came back to haunt Tasmin. *Two love songs you will hear* . . . but it was not possible for her to fall in love with a *gajo* . . . not possible!

Tasmin forced herself to turn away before she could no longer deny what her body threatened and what her mind and heart were too fragile to resist. She had to lean against the side of the horse until she had stopped shaking enough to stand on her own again. Thinking coherently, however, was a wasted effort. Nothing made sense. Until she could fathom why this man had entered her life and why he had such a profound effect on her, there was little use to feign sanity. When she felt ready to face him again, she prayed that he would no longer be watching her, or that at least his expression would be void of the impassioned beckonings. But O Del had no intention of answering her prayers, and when she braved another look in the *gajo's* direction, his penetrating stare was still focused on her with the same unmistakable desire.

When she felt her body begin to repeat the same

shameless performance, Tasmin began to fill with rage. This man was nothing compared to Romalio. How could she allow herself to react so immorally when he merely glanced at her? As her anger strengthened her mind, she fought a frantic battle with her fevered body. She would not let these *marime* desires overwhelm her again.

"A—are you ready t—to go?" she stammered in a voice that sounded miles away to her ears. To make her shaking limbs move toward him was one of the most difficult tasks she had ever had to do, but she managed to walk to where he sat without crumpling into a heap at his feet. "A—are you—" She started to repeat her previous question, but her words were cut off when the *gajo* reached out with his good arm and grabbed onto her hand. Before Tasmin realized what was happening, he had pulled her down into his lap and was engaging her lips in a devouring kiss that wiped away any lucidity she might have retained. Her mouth had taken control of her mind, returning his kiss as if they had been deprived of this delicacy for an eternity. To her shock, she felt his tongue slowly pry apart her lips, then begin to engage her own tongue in a taunting seduction that sent tremors of excitement racing through her body. Her reaction to this new invasion was timid only for an instant before her tongue enthusiastically began to imitate his bold entwining action. Her entire essence became a fiery mass of anticipation as their lips and their bodies molded together, and tied her heart into a knot of love that could never be untangled.

There was no reason to Blayde's unexpected actions; he was sure he had shocked himself worse than her when he had pulled her into his lap. Moments ago, he had felt too weak to stand, but when she had stepped so near to him, he had gained more energy than he had known possible. All the years of deprivation seemed to make him crazy with an urge that he could not control, and he could not halt his aching need to hold this dark wildcat in his arms and to kiss her sensuous lips . . . just once. Because once he had fulfilled this relentless need, he told himself with renewed determination, he would get away from her and never permit himself to think of her again. After just this once . . .

Chapter Twelve

The impulsive kiss left both Tasmin and Blayde too stunned and breathless to speak for a few seconds after they were forced to pull away from one another. Blayde's arm, which held Tasmin's waist in its tight embrace, went limp, but she made no attempt to get away. The dark flush of color that each wore told of the fevered effect the kiss had left on both of them.

"That shouldn't have happened," Blayde said at last. He knew he could not retract his actions, yet part of him was not sorry that he had kissed her. Even now, he had to fight with himself to keep from drawing her close again. His hand yearned to entangle itself in the wild disarray of her long hair, which was no longer encumbered by the scarf she usually wore, and his throbbing lips longed to kiss every inch of her luscious body.

"But it did, and we've both known that it was meant to happen ever since the night when I danced for you."

Her admission was something Blayde found he could not argue with, but it surprised him that she would be so bold. If it had been feasible on the night about which she spoke, he would have scooped her into his arms then and kissed her as passionately as he had a moment ago. But then or now, this unexpected turn of events could not change the obvious, that there could never be any more between them than this one overpowering kiss. "It shouldn't have happened," Blayde repeated, as if he was trying to convince himself. Why didn't she get up? Her nearness was whittling away the last of his resistance. When she still made no attempt to move, he tried another approach. "We'd better get going. I reckon your man is mighty worried about you." The odd expression that overcame her face hinted that he had touched upon a subject that troubled the girl a great deal, and also reminded him of the attack on the Gypsy camp. When he had been at the old woman's wagon yesterday, he had not seen the Gypsy king anywhere.

"Has any harm come to your king?" Though he knew his question had been asked too bluntly, especially if the man had been slain in the ambush, Blayde was curious to know why the Gypsy was acting so remorseful.

"He was safe the last time I saw him, and I pray that he is still safe and has returned to the camp."

The sorrow in her voice confused Blayde, and the look on her beautiful face was even more baffling. If her man was safe, why was she so sad? "Then we should go. No doubt he'll be happy and relieved to see you."

A deep sigh shook through Tasmin's slender form as she glanced at the *gajo's* puzzled face. His people did not live by the rigid customs that ruled the Gypsies. Would he laugh at their beliefs if she attempted to explain to him how, even though he had been racked with fever and she had been attempting to save his life, the fact that she had spent the night with him would mean her people would consider her unclean? "He will not be happy," she replied as her eyes dropped down in an ashamed manner. "He will never want to look at me again."

A rueful chuckle emitted from Blayde. He couldn't imagine that there was a man alive who would not want to gaze upon this beautiful creature. "That's ridiculous. I saw how he looked at you that night when you danced around the fire. That man worships you." Just the memory of her sensuous dance made Blayde's weak body tremble with desire again. How he hoped she would not notice.

"I saw how you looked at me that night, too," Tasmin said softly, allowing her gaze to raise up again and settle on his lips. The memory of his recent kiss caused her lips to part slightly. She felt a tremor shoot through his taut form, and like a chain reaction, her own body shook with unspoken longings.

Again time passed without meaning as each one's gaze bespoke the inner passions which yearned for release. Blayde was acutely aware of the way the curves of her firm young body molded into his lap, a realization that provoked his inner thoughts to materialize as he felt his desire for her swell against the restraint of his jeans. He noticed a shocked expression filter across her face as she became aware of his unleashed passion pressing into her backside. Mortified at his own loss of control, Blayde cleared his throat in a loud manner and attempted to break the spell that she was once again weaving around his vulnerable heart. But his defenseless body was more resilient and longed to answer the invitation he was certain flashed from her dark gaze once her shock had begun to fade. In spite of his defiant loss, Blayde knew that he could not give himself to a woman just because she was willing and available. He would not disgrace Emma's memory in this manner. There was only one way in which he could make love to a woman again, and that would be if he loved her in the same manner that he had loved Emma . . . and that would never happen!

The look of shame which drew a shadow over the *gajo's* face made Tasmin realize her own immoral behavior. How could she permit herself to forget the strict code of virtue by which she had been raised? She was reminded that even allowing her skirts to touch this man's legs was considered a sin; sitting here in his lap and experiencing these lustful sensations was definitely taboo. She jumped up from the *gajo's* lap and stumbled backward in an effort to put herself a safe distance from him, but no amount of distance was safe where this man was concerned.

"You're right, we shouldn't—" she paused as though she wished she did not have to agree, though she knew there was no other choice. Her mind screamed at her that she shouldn't have permitted him to kiss her, that she shouldn't be here, that they shouldn't have even met one another. Why had O Del brought them together if he was only going to cause them so much heartache?

Blayde struggled to stand, but he was still too weak and only managed to raise up on his knees before a bout of dizziness washed over him. He cursed under his breath at his inability to fend for himself. The last thing he needed was to have the Gypsy girl help him. He didn't want her near him for fear that she would try to cast her spell on him again and he would be tempted to draw her into his arms for a second time. Should this happen, he knew there would be no stopping either of them.

Tasmin watched as he fought to stand, and though she longed to offer her help, she was afraid to approach him. She could not chance losing the fragile hold she had on her emotions. Thank goodness the *gajo* had made her realize how disgracefully she was behaving! If at this instant he took her into his arms once more, she knew she would not have the power to stop him. Much to her humiliation, her body trembled with anticipation as she found herself praying that he would grab her again. Inwardly she told herself she would not approach him again, but when he made another futile attempt to stand, Tasmin's reserve disappeared and she rushed to his side.

"You are not as strong as you think," she scolded as she wrapped her arms around his waist and helped him struggle to his feet.

Though Blayde did not say it, he thought it was

ironic that he was strong enough to pull her into his lap and kiss her with such intensity, yet he could not even stand on his own two feet by himself. Obviously, this witch had him completely in her control, and if he didn't get away from her soon he would not have any will of his own. Once, on his feet, Blayde was relieved to discover that the dizziness had just about faded, and although he was a little weak-kneed, it was only a few seconds until he felt as if he could stand on his own without the girl's support.

"I think I'm going to be fine now." He took a cautious step and when he did not falter, he used his good arm to push the girl away from him in a not-too-subtle manner. "I could probably ride without any problem too." He looked at his horse and motioned with his head, "Thanks for carin' for him, and—for me," he added. When he glanced back at the Gypsy girl, her stricken expression filled him with a sadness that he did not understand. "Look," Blayde added, while trying to dislodge the sudden remorse he felt over the idea of leaving her. "I—I do think it would be best if we parted company here. You have to return to your people, and I," he sighed as if the weight of the world had suddenly settled on his slumping shoulders. "I have things I have to do."

"Please, let me go with you," Tasmin asked. The stunned expression on the man's face was apparent, but her sudden request surprised her even more. She knew he was probably thinking the worst: that she was a loose woman who only wanted to be with him for wanton purposes. How could she tell him that she had nowhere else to go?

Blayde shook his head in a negative gesture. "That's not possible. You have a man waiting for you back at the camp, and I can't have no woman taggin' along with me, it would be too dangerous." Having this particular woman anywhere he was would be dangerous in more ways than one, Blayde told himself as he turned away from her sorrowful stare.

Choking back the lump she felt rising in her throat, Tasmin also turned so that she would not have to see the *gajo*. It was too painful to look at his face when his haunting expression was filled with so much disapproval. Had she really expected that he would allow her to go with him? She had made herself look foolish just by suggesting it, and now he was twice as anxious to get away from her. Without another word, Tasmin began to walk across the soggy grasses toward his horse. When she had finished resaddling the animal, she turned back towards the *gajo*, but she avoided meeting his emerald gaze.

"I saddled him for you, since you are in no condition to lift anything yet. I only pray you will be able to ride without tearing open the wound in your shoulder again." Since it was obvious to Tasmin that he was thinking about how all his recent misfortune was solely her fault, she decided that the sooner she left, the better it would be for both of them. "Good Luck, *Gajo*, and—" She paused, glancing back at him, even after she had warned herself not to look in his direction again. He was the most perplexing man she had ever encountered, for a dozen conflicting emotions flashed across his face and from his piercing gaze, yet all of them were as unreadable as if they were written on a tablet of stone. "I am truly sorry for all the pain I caused you," she added before turning to leave. Even being *marime* among her own people could not hurt as badly as leaving this man, she realized as her reluctant feet began to move across the waterlogged ground.

Blayde made no effort to stop her as he watched her go. To part company now, before anything else happened that neither of them could control, was their only chance. There were too many unexplainable emotions that each aroused in the other, and it was not possible to think they could ever fulfill any of these cravings. Blayde knew he was not capable of releasing any of the rekindled desires this fiery Gypsy witch had summoned forth, yet he felt a strange twitching in his chest as she disappeared from his view. Free at last, he said to himself, while attempting to shake off the uninvited feelings that accompanied her leaving. He permitted himself to acknowledge the gnawing guilt he felt over making her set out on her own in the rain-drenched forest. But it was the sense of overwhelming loss that he could not understand, nor would he allow himself to try to unravel these alien feelings. She was gone now, and that was all that mattered.

Just making his way the short distance to Eclipse was a chore for Blayde's battered body. By the time he had managed to climb into the saddle, he was drenched in sweat, and in more agony than he had thought possible. He had to admit that the Gypsy was right, he was not ready to travel yet. Still, he hated to agree with anything she said, even if she wasn't here to see that her prediction was coming true.

"Damn," Blayde muttered to himself as he fought to remain upright in the saddle. It was useless to think that he would be able to get anywhere in the shape he was in. That damn witch had fixed him good; even now that she was gone, her wicked spell still held him in its tight grip. In a determined attempt, Blayde urged Eclipse to start walking, but the horse had only gone a few feet when his rider knew it was useless to continue. Bringing Eclipse to a halt, Blayde uttered a defeated sigh. He was too wobbly to hold himself upright in the saddle, and if he pushed himself to keep going, he would end up the same as he had before—unconscious and helpless. He glanced at the jagged opening of the hollowed-out tree where he had spent the night with the Gypsy. It had afforded a shelter during the worst of the storm, and it was the nearest thing to a refuge Blayde could find.

He directed the horse to the burned-out tree trunk and with a painful groan slid back down to the ground. Before he could crawl into the meager shelter, he knew he had to unsaddle Eclipse again. If the horse was forced to wear the rigging for another day, he would develop sores under the wet saddle and blanket. As he slowly forced his aching body to go through the motions of tending to his horse, he grew more and more annoyed with himself for being

141

so stupid. He could have been spared all this additional torture if only he had listened to the Gypsy. But then he reminded himself that if he had avoided the Gypsy camp the other night, none of this would have happened. When at last he had finished caring for Eclipse, he dug a small knapsack of food out of his saddlebags along with a flask of water and settled back against the inside of the hollowed tree trunk.

The sun was quickly drying out the forest ground and Blayde knew that before long the humidity would make this hole an unbearable oven. Until he was strong enough to attempt traveling again, however, he had nowhere else to go. He took a piece of hardtack out of the knapsack and began to nibble on it with little enthusiasm. He realized that he had sent the Gypsy off without anything to eat, then with a rush of irritation wondered why he was so concerned. In an effort to ease his own guilt, he decided that the Gypsy camp was probably close by and that she would be with her own kind soon. He reminded himself once again that if it wasn't for her, he might have caught up to Ben McCalister and his gang by now. Through the years there had been many times that he had almost caught the outlaw, but it seemed that something or someone had always interfered. He had been close to catching up with the gang just last week, but he had recklessly gone into the Gypsy camp, and now he was still suffering the consequences, while McCalister was probably in San Francisco by now. But Blayde was freed from that witch's curse now that she was gone, and he did not intend to be so foolish again. Someday soon, he knew McCalister would make a mistake, would linger for too long in one area, and then Blayde would finally have the revenge he had been seeking so diligently for the past three years. Then Blayde knew he would be a free man in every sense of the word . . . free to join his beloved Emma and Timmy.

Chapter Thirteen

As Blayde had predicted, the aftermath of the storm produced a smoldering day that had the ground completely dry by noon. The humid air was so thick that breathing was a labored effort, and the hollowed-out tree offered no comfort from the heat; even the towering trees afforded little shade. By eating, drinking, and resting, though, Blayde felt strong enough to make another attempt to ride by mid-afternoon. He hoped to travel some before nightfall, then get a good night's rest so that by tomorrow he could make up for lost time. He wanted to be in San Francisco by day after tomorrow, and if he didn't encounter any more bad luck, it was possible. The Gypsy passed through his mind again, as she had continuously throughout the day, summoning up images of long, raven hair entwining around her sensuous body as she danced before him—and only for him—in the beckoning glow of the campfire. His lips yearned to say her name out loud, but he fought against the urge to be this familiar with her memory. Still, his disobedient mind allowed the lyrical name to echo through its tormented passages over and over again. Tasmin . . . Gypsy Witch.

Annoyed, Blayde drug himself out from the burned tree trunk and tried to concentrate on getting as far away from this area as possible. He only hoped that he could also escape from the lingering effect of the beautiful witch's spell. His shoulder was stiff, but the acute pain had dimmed considerably, and saddling Eclipse was not as difficult as unsaddling him had been this morning. Before long, he had the rigging back on the animal and his attention focused on getting to San Francisco. The Gypsy witch hardly entered his mind . . . well, hardly!

Once Blayde led Eclipse through the dense grove of oaks and out into the open, it did not take him long to locate Chico Creek. The creek still carried some of the burden left from the rainwater, but it no longer flooded over its sandy banks. Since the creek was close to the spot where he and the Gypsy had spent the night, and Blayde could not recall how far he had ridden before he had passed out yesterday, he figured the girl was probably back at her camp by now. His deduction, though, did not ease any of the nagging guilt he felt over making her leave on foot without food or water this morning.

Blayde eased himself from Eclipse's back and was relieved when he was not overcome with another bout of dizziness. Apparently, he had been right; once he was away from all of those witches, he would have no trouble recuperating from his wounds. At the edge of the creek, he removed the bandage from his hand to discover that the wound was healing better than he had hoped. The Gypsies had packed the cut with some thick concoction which was a mystery to Blayde, but it obviously worked and that was all that mattered to him. Cautiously, he worked his fingers back and forth, with little pain accompanying the movement. A sigh of gratitude emitted from his dry lips with the knowledge that he could draw his gun with this hand if the need arose. Of course, until the cut was healed completely, his speed would not be as swift as before—his aim, however, would still be deadly accurate. His confidence in his ability was not exaggerated, and those who had dared to challenge his skill with the six-shooter had learned a hard lesson in dying.

As if to prove to himself that his well-honed aim had not gone astray, the bounty hunter focused his sights on a tiny black rock that shimmered in the sunlight on the opposite side of the creek bank. He gingerly drew his Colt .45. Then with his good hand, he cocked the hammer. Without any time to take aim, his lean body tensed and a bullet whizzed over the top of the water. When the dust cleared from the distant bank, the spot where the gunman had pointed his gun was nothing more than a sandy hole and no trace of the black stone remained. It left his hand feeling weak and shaky, but he was satisfied with the result as he slid the weapon back into the holster which hung at his right thigh. Some men in his profession found it necessary to wear a gun on each hip; Blayde thought this a weakness. One bullet was all it took to kill a man if you were good. His .45 held six bullets, so why carry the extra burden of another weapon?

With his mind at ease about his gun hand, Blayde pulled off the bloodstained shirt the old Gypsy woman had given to him and began to unravel the bandage that bound his shoulder. He hoped his shoulder was healing as well as his hand as he splashed creek water on the cloth until the dried blood began to loosen its hold on his skin and he was able to ease the bandage away from the knife wound. In spite of the ordeal he had been through in the past couple of days, Blayde was once again amazed to see that his shoulder, which was coated with the same thick brown packing, was also healing without any sign of infection. He wondered if Gypsy medicine also contained some sort of black magic potions?

After washing the soiled bandages in the creek, Blayde then hung them on a nearby bush to dry. A soft, sandy area at the edge of the water looked like an appealing place to rest while the bandages dried, so Blayde stretched out on the ground and let the sun also drench his wounds with its healing rays. The heat upon his stiff shoulder felt like a soothing ointment, and before long Blayde slipped into a peaceful slumber. For once, no nightmares of the past haunted his sleep, and luckily, the raven-haired witch who had invaded his dreams lately also left him alone on this humid afternoon as he dozed beside the creek.

"Is—is he dead?" Savana asked as the two girls

approached the man sprawled at the edge of the water. Their eyes were drawn to the wounds in his hand and shoulder, but as they walked closer, they could also see the gentle rise and fall of his muscled chest. "He's the *gajo* who visited the camp," she added in a whisper.

Persia stared at the form of the injured man in a stunned silence. Though she had known that she would see the *gajo* again, finding him in this condition was a complete shock. However, an inner voice told her that Tasmin had something to do with his injuries, and this revelation caused Persia even more concern. If Tasmin had found it necessary to resort to such an act of violence, then this man must have committed a terrible deed. With this thought in her mind, Persia grabbed Savana's arm and whispered in a panicked voice, "Do not go any closer. He might be dangerous."

Savana halted her steps and glanced at Persia in confusion. "But he is badly injured. How much harm could he do?"

A heavy sigh emitted from Persia as she continued to stare at the sleeping *gajo*. He did look harmless in this vulnerable position, but she could not dismiss her uneasiness. Besides, there was not a *gajo* alive whom she would trust again after what they had just been forced to endure at the hands of the outlaws. Her eyes were drawn to the gun that he wore on his hip. The holster rested on the ground, but she knew it was not feasible to think that they could get the weapon away from him without waking him. She glanced at his horse, who stood close to his master, and noticed that a shotgun hung from a scabbard that was attached to the saddle. To retrieve this weapon seemed more logical, if she could only reach the animal and still not disturb the *gajo*.

"His horse!" Savana gasped, her voice almost rising above a whisper. "We can take his horse." Just the idea of being able to rest her cut and bloody feet caused her to tremble with anticipation. On horseback, they would find their tribe in no time, Savana's soaring thoughts determined, and she could be reunited with Teril sooner than she had dared to hope.

"Yes, we'll steal his horse," Persia whispered with a nervous glance toward the *gajo*. Her gaze then focused on the shotgun again as she added, "But first I'm going to get that gun, then we'll wake him and find out what he did to Tasmin!" Though she heard Savana gasp with shock at her insinuation, she did not give the other girl a chance to question her motives before she started to creep toward the horse. As she tiptoed past the man he let out a deep sigh, which made her afraid to take another step until she realized that he was only making noises in his sleep. When she could make her feet move once more, she quickly closed the rest of the distance to where his horse stood. The silver roan whined softly when the girl approached him, but Persia gently rubbed his neck and gained his trust in no time. Confident that the animal would not protest her nearness, Persia carefully undid the latch that held the shotgun in its carrier. After she had the weapon in her hands, she took the first easy breath that she had taken since they had come upon the man. With the shotgun in her hand, at least, she did not feel defenseless. Never again did she want to feel as she had when they had been at the mercy of the murderous *gajo* dogs who had violated her and her friends.

Moving to within a couple feet of the *gajo*, Persia steadied the gun against her shoulder and aimed the barrel at the man's head. "Hey, you—*Gajo!*" she shouted at him, then when he did not waken immediately, she leaned down in a bold manner and nudged him in the ribs with the gun barrel. This action made his eyes fly open at once, and to her horror, his injured arm moved with an unnatural speed to the top of his holstered six-shooter.

"Don't move, *Gajo*," Persia screamed in alarm. Her entire body jumped as if a rattlesnake had just struck at her feet. But then, this *gajo* moved as swiftly as a snake and was twice as deadly, Persia reminded herself. His gun was already in his hand, but due to his wounds, he had not yet been able to cock back the hammer. "Drop that gun," she commanded as she tried to calm the explosive thudding of her heartbeat.

For a moment Blayde was sure he was having another vivid nightmare, because surely his luck could not be this bad. His blinked his eyes to clear the haziness of sleep and in an effort to regain his sanity. As awareness began to settle in his disbelieving mind, he realized that his injured hand held his pistol in its stiff grip. His nightmare had seemed so real that he had even drawn his gun against the imaginary demons that traipsed through his slumbering soul. He shook his head in an irritated manner at his own foolishness while cursing the Gypsies under his breath. His nightmare had distinctly taunted him with the accented voice of a make-believe Gypsy witch, but when he also became aware of the looming shadow that shielded him from the sun, his annoyance turned to dread. A moan of disbelief echoed through his throat as he stared up into the barrel of his own shotgun.

"Drop the gun," Persia repeated. Her voice shook almost as violently as her hands, but she managed to hold the gun to his head in spite of her terror.

For an instant, Blayde was certain his foe was the Gypsy dancer, but the strange tone in her voice threw him off-guard. When he was able to focus clearly on the girl who held the weapon, however, he was surprised to see that it was not Tasmin. Yet this girl's appearance left him speechless with shock. He recognized her at once as the fortune-teller who had stolen Emma's picture and his money, but her disheveled and battered condition made a chill run down his spine.

"Do not move too much, *Gajo*," Persia warned, making her position clear by glancing at the shotgun in her shaking hands.

A wry grin turned the corners of Blayde's lips as he let the gun slip from his hand. The six-shooter rested in the sand and was still within reach, but since he could not cock the hammer without using his good hand, it would be a wasted effort to grab for it again, especially when she held a weapon that was prepared to blow his head off in less than a heartbeat. "No problem," he said in a sarcastic tone as he wondered if she was blind to his injuries. Since her fear was so obvious, he contemplated making a grab for the shotgun with his uninjured hand. With the metal of the barrel close enough that he could smell the hot iron, though, he was not prepared to take such a gamble. Besides, the girl's battered appearance tore at his heart and brought back a flood of recollections from the past that he had never wanted to recall again. What was it about these dark-eyed people that continuously reminded him of the awful events of those bygone times?

"Sit up, but slowly," the Gypsy cautioned, nudging the gun to his forehead.

The feel of the metal against his skin made Blayde's mind snap back from the distant memories and reminded him of his present danger. Although a raging anger washed through him at the realization that he was once again facing death at the hands of a Gypsy wench, another snide smile claimed the man's lips as he pushed his stiff body to an upright position. Long ago he had learned to hide his emotions when dealing with an opponent. This was a skill that had been valuable when he had been an ambitious young lawyer in the courtrooms of Texas, but it proved even more invaluable now that he walked a precarious line that hovered on both sides of the law.

From his new viewpoint, Blayde was now able to see both women, which made a noticeable tremor shake through his body when he saw their pitiful conditions. He recalled Tasmin's remarks concern-

152

ing the devastating fates of the girls who had been kidnapped by the men who had attacked their camp. Once again his mind was flung back through time to a day he thought he had sealed in a crypt that could never be reopened. Emma's body, beaten beyond recognition, twisted and bloody, lying beside the colorful flowerbed she had so lovingly tended. Looming behind her was the smoldering carcass of the home they had built with their own hands, ghostly wisps of smoke still trailing up from the ashes and debris. And Timmy, somewhere . . . somewhere . . .

No! No! his frantic mind screamed. He felt as if his sanity was balancing on the brink of this horrible image. For three years he had succeeded in eluding the awful details of that last day for fear that he would not be able to cope with the agony. Until he had foolishly wandered into the Gypsy camp, his sole consolation and recollection of that day had been the revenge he vowed to seek. Now, suddenly, as if someone had pried open the rusty nails that he had painstakingly hammered into the coffin in which he had buried these memories, all the horror of that day returned to him as vividly as if the clock had turned back time.

"Gajo?" Persia called out as she took a step back. The expression that had washed over his face and the ghastly pallor of his complexion had caused an icy chill to whip through the fortune-teller's veins. How she wished she had the power to unlock the dark secrets of his haunted green gaze. But ever since the night when she had read his palm, she had

153

known that this man had already suffered far too much and for too long a time for his heavy heart to withstand any more pain. She only wished Tasmin did not have to be the one who had been chosen to help carry his burden, because the road her dear friend would have to tread to ease his torment was as long and endless as the road her people had forever traveled.

Chapter Fourteen

As the hinges began to creak shut on the past, Blayde slowly dragged himself from the edge of the madness which threatened to claim him. If he had not been so hell-bent on revenge, maybe he would not have been able to overcome the torment of remembering that horrible day when his wife and son had been slaughtered. But his strength was revived by the fact that his mission had yet to be completed. He turned his glazed eyes toward the frightened Gypsy fortune-teller as he was struck with a realization that sent his senses reeling once more.

"Th—the men who attacked you—do you know who they were?"

The strange expression which had overcome the man's face also affected Persia in an odd way. For one brief second she was afforded a glimpse into this man's mind, but the images of flowers and smoking ruins that flashed before her eyes were so disoriented that she was even more confused than before. Still,

Persia was certain that whatever had happened in the *gajo's* past had left such a profound effect on him that at times the memory threatened to steal away his grip on reality. Since it was obvious to her that his mind had just taken an unexpected sojourn back through these painful recollections, she worried that he was about to slip into some sort of a trance, or to lose consciousness. She was relieved to hear that he was still coherent, but the question he asked surprised her. Her head moved from side to side in a negative gesture. How could he expect her to know who they were when she could not even remember what they looked like? There was nothing about their hideous faces that her mind had wanted to retain for future reference. For the rest of her life, though, she would remember the vile things they had done to her.

Even without her answer, Blayde knew who had ambushed the camp, and he did not need an explanation as to what had taken place while they had been the outlaws' captive. The horror of their experience was written on their harrowed faces, and their bloodstained skirts told him what they could not. His sympathy went out to them, but his anger exploded like dynamite as his determination to find Ben McCalister reaffirmed his three-year-old vow. He had known the McCalister gang was somewhere in the area, but he'd no idea they were this close. If he had not ridden so far away from the Gypsy camp the other night in his frantic attempt to get away from the unwelcome desires the dancer had aroused, perhaps he would have been nearby when they had attacked the camp. And maybe his chance to avenge the murders of his wife and son would have been presented to him at long last. It seemed he was always in the wrong place at the wrong time where the ruthless McCalister gang was concerned. But then, it had been this way ever since the beginning, since the day when McCalister's gang had broken their leader out of the El Paso jail shortly after his trial. Blayde had been celebrating his court victory at a local saloon when he should have been home protecting his family.

"Th—there were seven of them." Savana's quiet voice broke the permeating silence that had followed the *gajo's* inquiry. "The cruelest . . . he—he was strange-looking," she pointed toward her left eye, "and they called him—"

"Red Eye," Blayde finished saying for her. Ben McCalister's unsavory right-hand man, Red Eye, was so nicknamed because his eye had once been gouged with a hot poker by an unfortunate woman who had been fighting off the outlaw's unwelcome advances. Savana nodded in reply, then lowered her gaze as if she was too ashamed to meet the *gajo's* eyes. Blayde did not push the issue, because it was plain that neither of them wanted to divulge any more of the details about their recent captivity. Besides, what he needed to know had already been said.

"What happened to you?" Persia motioned to his wounds with the barrel of the shotgun. Her jet-black eyes flashed with an arrogance that suggested she knew the answer to the question she had just asked.

Blayde returned her direct stare with his own unwavering gaze. "Your friend the dancer, she reacts before she thinks." A humorless grin taunted the corners of his mouth as he added, "As seems to be the habit among most of you—you—" He stopped himself from saying anything that might infuriate her enough to set off her trigger finger.

"You must have done something to her first."

With a defiant shake of his auburn head, Blayde retorted to Persia's insinuation, "The only thing I'm guilty of is being a fool for wandering into your camp the other night. Must been outa my mind, and I'm still paying the cost for tryin' to befriend a bunch of heathen!"

His outburst left both Savana and Persia with the distinct feeling that they had been insulted. Although they had no idea what a heathen was, it was apparent by his contemptuous tone that he thought they were not worthy of his friendship. "Where is Tasmin?" Persia demanded. She enforced her request by stepping close to him again and placing the gun inches from his face.

"She's back at the camp, safe and sound," he retorted without a blink of his eye. If this thievin' Gypsy was also a witch, he figured she would know that he was saying whatever was required to save his own hide. But she only continued to watch him with an intense stare as though she was trying to determine whether or not he was telling the truth.

"Do you know where our camp is?" Savana asked in an excited tone.

Blayde hugged his injured limb with his good arm and shrugged. His shoulder was beginning to throb again, and he wished he could wrap the bandages around the wound to prevent him from moving his arm unnecessarily. "Not far," he lied again as he motioned upstream with his head. "Just follow the creek." When he glanced up at the girl who had asked the question, he caught her eyeing Eclipse with an anxious expression on her battered face. "Don't go thinkin' about stealin' that horse," he blurted out, heedless to the gun that was still hovering dangerously close to his nose. These thievin' wenches will have a real fight on their hands if they're thinking along those lines, he told himself angrily.

"You forget who holds the weapon," Persia replied in a haughty tone.

"And you can forget about stealin' my horse." He was reminded of Emma's picture and the money she had already stolen from him, although he had already given up all hope of reclaiming his possessions. His eyes narrowed, then settled on the face of the girl with a deadly intent that invited no dispute.

Persia swallowed hard as she stared back at the *gajo*. True, she was the one with the gun, but she had no doubt that if they attempted to take his horse, he would retaliate without mercy. She glanced at Savana, then back at the *gajo* with a nervous flutter of her eyes. "Perhaps, if the camp is nearby, we do not need the horse."

A loud gasp flew from Savana. "But I can not walk another step!" She motioned toward her bloody bare feet, then turned toward the man with her mouth open as if she was about to tell him that her friend was crazy to suggest that they did not need his horse. Her words were halted before they could escape from her mouth. His dark green gaze was now fixed on her and provoked the same unsettling reaction that they had aroused in Persia. She looked to the other girl in defeat. They really did need his horse, but Persia was wise when it came to making important decisions. Maybe she had seen some impending event with her insight, and perhaps there was a good reason for her quick reversal about stealing this *gajo's* horse. Savana gave a meek shrug and remained silent.

Persia yearned for a clue that would explain this stranger's hypnotizing aura, but the fragmented visions that had flashed through her mind only served as fuel for her curiosity. For a reason she could not fathom, she knew this *gajo* had to be allowed to go on his way. There was something he must do . . . something so devastating that her mind could not grasp the enormity of his desperate mission. His quest was somehow entwined with the events of the past few days, and the outcome would affect all of them, but beyond this tangled profusion of knowledge, Persia's insight was lost. Of course, there was one fortune she could tell that had no perplexing twists, even though it broke her heart to foresee, because it also meant she would lose her dear friend forever.

With a heavy sigh, Persia gave in to defeat. "Point us in the direction of our camp, and we'll be on our way." She allowed the shotgun to drop away from the *gajo's* face, but she made no attempt to return the gun to its scabbard. "We might need this, so we'll be taking it along with us," she added, waving the weapon through the air.

160

Blayde held his breath until she had swung the gun back down and released the hammer. She had been smart enough to give up on their notion of stealing Eclipse, but the horse would do him little good if the fool woman shot his head off with her stupid escapades. He gave his relieved head a nod that was a bit more enthusiastic than necessary when someone was about to steal a man's shotgun. But then he was reminded that he had done nothing rational in the past few days. "Your camp is in that direction," he answered, then gestured to the north. He figured his guess was close to accurate, since he knew he had been heading south—towards San Franciso—when he had lost consciousness.

A look of gratitude was evident on both girls' faces, but their weariness was more noticeable. They had been walking nonstop since last night, and it was late afternoon now. Both knew they had to get some rest, but fear of being recaptured by the outlaws was greater than their need to sleep. Persia gave the *gajo* one last look before she turned away from him, a look that left Blayde shaken to the core. Her sorrowful expression had held more than just the pain of the past few days, and as he watched her walk away with the other Gypsy girl, he had a fleeting notion that he would see her again in the near future. "That's ridiculous," he said to himself aloud. He would never see any of them again . . . except for the dancer, whom he suspected would taunt his dreams every night.

"Gypsy Witch!" he said from between clenched teeth. He would not permit her memory to remain with him any longer, and he made another firm vow that he would not even allow himself to think about her again. With this settled momentarily, he struggled to his feet and carefully rebandaged his wounds once more. His shoulder was better when it was bound tightly and could not be jostled around, and by the time he had begun to ride Eclipse southward, he felt as if his strength was beginning to return. With an enraged growl, he glanced down at his empty scabbard. He would need to buy himself another shotgun as soon as he reached the next town, then he would have to cut down the barrel—a necessity for a man who needed a shotgun that was easy and fast to handle. A sawed-off twelve-gauge also provided a gunfighter with a broader blast pattern at any target a short distance away. Blayde thought it unlikely that the Gypsies would need his gun to fend off the McCalister gang, because he had no doubt the outlaws were headed toward San Francisco by now and would not bother to come looking for the Gypsy girls. They had already served their purpose for the men, but Blayde was amazed that they had escaped with their lives. The idea that only a couple of days ago he had been so close to Ben McCalister made his blood boil and added to his increasing energy. Everything would be over soon; he could sense that the end was drawing nearer with each step of Eclipse's hooves.

Briefly, he let his mind inch back through time again. But he was cautious not to dwell on the images he had recalled earlier and instead summoned forth the recollections of the man he had so diligently sought for all these years. Ben McCalister—the lowest scum of a man he had ever known.

Though Blayde had never seen him in action, the outlaw was rumored to be one of the fastest guns in the West. Three years ago the murderer had been less than twenty-four hours from a hangman's noose, and he had had Blayde Chandler to thank for his misfortune. With the odds stacked in McCalister's favor, it had almost appeared as if the outlaw would once again walk away from the latest charge of murder and robbery for which he had been incarcerated in the El Paso jail. But a cocky young prosecuting attorney was determined to see to it that Ben McCalister never killed again. Blayde Chandler had expertly stripped away all of McCalister's false alibis, until the jury was finally able to see each of the facts without a shadow of a doubt. They sentenced the ruthless killer to hang the very next morning, but McCalister had a few tricks of his own up his sleeve.

Blayde could still remember the elated feeling that had accompanied him when he had walked into the saloon after the trial that hot August afternoon. He had won many cases since his career had begun several years earlier, but none had given him so much satisfaction. There was something about Ben McCalister that had raised Blayde's ire from the first time he had seen his mug on a Wanted poster. When he finally had the misfortune to meet the killer face to face, the two men had an instant dislike for one another from the start. It went beyond the fact that Blayde was almost obsessive in his determination to prove McCalister's guilt—it was something more personal, but even now Blayde did not understand why he had been so driven to see McCalister hang. Perhaps it was a premonition of what would happen if the outlaw did not die; maybe Blayde had sensed from the first moment he had glimpsed the cold image on the Wanted poster that someday this man would turn his entire world inside out and cause him more agony than he'd ever imagined possible.

Three years ago come August, Blayde had thought of nothing besides than celebrating his victory. Several rounds of drinks later, his whiskey-laden mind clumsily listened to the distant sounds of a passerby who had just discovered the dead bodies of the sheriff and the deputies who had been guarding the murderer. To this day Blayde was mystified as to how McCalister's gang had managed to kill the four lawmen, then break the prisoner out of the El Paso jail without arousing suspicion. Enough time had passed for the gang to ride to the home of the man who had caused so much aggravation for their boss. They made sure the prosecutor would never forget the McCalister gang for as long as he lived, and now Blayde was determined that he would live long enough to see to it that justice was finally served.

He had not allowed himself time to grieve for his family and had set about on his new task immediately after the burials. Blayde knew how to handle a gun, since it was a required skill in a land as untamed as Texas, but he spent months honing his fast-draw until he was confident that he could move as swiftly as his bullet flew through air. Ben McCalister would meet his match when he faced "The Prosecutor" as he and his gang had come to re-refer to the man who had relentlessly dogged their trail for three years. In the beginning, when the gang had found great mirth in leading Blayde on wild-goose chases, they had made a game of his plight. But when word of The Prosecutor's expertise with a six-shooter spread, McCalister and his men began to develop a sense of foreboding toward the man who shadowed their every move.

The road Blayde now traveled was laden with lowly sorts, an endless score of outlaws who, like McCalister, committed deadly crimes and evaded punishment for their evil deeds. A personal commitment to rid the world of this type of scum had provoked Blayde's career move and had gained him wide acclaim because of his dedication toward his new profession as a bounty hunter. His efficiency with a gun was becoming legendary, but his fearless disregard for his own life made him the most dangerous of men. The Prosecutor had now become a threat to McCalister's gang, whose games had grown deadly. Still, their attempts to dispose of the cunning gunman had failed. Now Blayde derived a great sense of satisfaction in knowing that they constantly looked over their shoulders, wondering . . . fearing the day when they would turn around and their Maker would be in sight. He had no plan for the rest of the gang, but when he did catch up with Ben McCalister, the killer would wish that he had died by the hangman's noose, because it would have been a much more merciful death than what Blayde Chandler had in mind.

Chapter Fifteen

At the creek, Persia and Savana scrubbed themselves and the tattered garments thoroughly in preparation to rejoin their tribe. No visible traces of blood remained on their torn skirts which to arouse suspicion as to the extent of the abuse they had suffered during their captivity. Their bruises and cuts, they reasoned, could be blamed on their frantic escape through the forest after sneaking away from the outlaws. They had rehearsed their story over and over, and though they each feared O Del's punishment for their lies, they dreaded a lifetime of *marime* even more.

The *gajo's* directions had been accurate, even though Persia had sensed that he was only guessing about knowing where their campsite was located. Shortly before darkness had claimed their vision, while following a scarcely-worn path, the young women had come across a scattering of twigs alongside the trail. Wandering Gypsies always used this form of communicaton when it was necessary to leave messages for absent members of their tribe. With the knowledge that they were so close to their people, they decided to rest for the night and ready themselves for the deceitful life on which they were about to embark. They took turns sleeping, however, because they still worried that the killers might be looking for them. This possibility was less likely now; they were certain that if the outlaws had wanted to come after them, they surely would have found them by now.

The girls did not disturb the discreet markers which had been left alongside the trail, since they had no way of knowing for whom the signs had been left. They did know, though, that not long ago their tribe had traveled this way. Each band of Gypsies used a secret code, and Romalio's tribe always arranged their roadside messages in the shape of a long snake, with a rock as the head. At whatever end the rock was placed was the directon in which the caravan was traveling. Except for the scatterings of barely-noticeable twigs, great efforts had been made so that the trail appeared as though no one had journeyed this way recently. Many times, after the caravan had passed through an area and found a campsite farther down the trail, the Gypsies would return on foot and wipe out whatever traces were left by the horses' hooves and the wagon wheels. After an attack on their camp, they always took this precautionary measure before stopping at another campsite.

"It is for Vilo that I have agreed to do this, but I

don't think it will work." A troubled frown lined Persia's bruised face. She had spent her waking hours in deep concentration, hoping for a glimpse of her bleak and uncertain future. This insight was not available, however, and she had been granted only the horrible recollections of the past few days. Her greatest worry now was that Nanna would know immediately that they were lying. Her grandmother had an uncanny way of unveiling the truth, and because of this, Persia had never attempted to lie to her about anything.

"I know that you are also doing this for me, and I thank you from the bottom of my heart." Savana reached out and lightly touched the other girl's arm, halting their steps for a moment. "And I know how difficult this is for you because of Nanna."

"She'll know we're lying."

"But will she tell the others?"

Persia's shoulders sagged as though she could not carry an invisible burden that had been placed upon her back. She didn't know how her grandmother would handle her deceit, but she'd no doubt that Nanna would immediately know the truth about what had happened while they had been captives of the *gajo.* "Nanna will do whatever she thinks is best," Persia answered.

They continued on their way in silence. Each step taken by their cut feet was more painful than the last, yet neither of them suggested stopping. Occasionally they both thought of the *gajo's* horse, and how much easier their trip would be if they had taken the animal. Still, neither of them voiced her thoughts, nor did they speak of the *gajo* again. But as the day wore on, each began to wonder if she had the stamina to take another step. Just as it seemed the night would close in on them again, the faint odor of smoke reached their nostrils, while the smell of Gypsy fires led them home. They walked into the camp in late afternoon, just as the women were beginning preparations for the second meal of the day.

Supper, which was usually served before five o'clock in the afternoon, was the only meal the Gypsies ate other than breakfast first thing in the morning. The barking of an alert dog signaled their arrival as all eyes were directed toward the unexpected sight of the two young women. Yet it was several minutes before the shock of their sudden appearance wore off enough for anyone to speak. Vilo's mother was the first to approach the girls, and the expression on her face needed no words. That her daughter was not with them was already more than she wanted to know.

"I'm sorry," Persia said in a choked voice as she reached out to console the woman. Nura stared at the outstretched arms for an instant, then a silent sob shook through her body before she turned and ran to her *vardo* without uttering a sound. Giorgo, Vilo's father, made his sorrow more vocal as his anguished cry rang out through the hushed camp.

"How?" he asked when he was finally able to speak again. He approached the two girls slowly, using a tree branch to aid his steps. During the ambush, he had taken a bullet in his leg. Much to his

169

dismay, he had not been able to go with the other men who had pursued the outlaws. He stopped before Persia and Savana, who still had not moved, and repeated his simple question: "How?"

Savana spoke up almost too quickly. "The outlaws did not stop until nightfall, and as they tended to their horses, the three of us escaped into the forest. Shots rang out, and Vilo was hit." Savana took a deep breath, and making sure her eyes did not focus on any of the faces who loomed around her, she rushed on. "We all continued to run until we found a place to hide. It was dark and the *gajo bengs* could not find us. But by morning, Vilo was—the gunshot wound was worst than we thought." A trembling sob racked Savana's body as she tried to hide the disgrace she felt for telling such an outlandish lie. But to those who listened to her and watched her stricken performance, it appeared that her agony was due to her mounting sorrow for young Vilo's fate.

Giorgo remained quiet as his mourning heart digested his beautiful young daughter's death. For fourteen years he had cherished her, and now he would never see her shining face again, never witness the way her raven eyes twinkled with mischief when she played pranks on him, and never watch her complete the transformation she had only just begun from that of his little girl to that of a young lady who had just stepped up to the threshold of woman-hood. As he had witnessed the way she had changed in the past few months, he had found himself dreaming of the day when he would bounce his grandchildren—Vilo's children—on his knee. Now this was something else he would never do, but the thought raised questions that he did not know how to ask. Taking score of the girl's battered appearance, Giorgo let his eyes travel from Persia to Savana. When the girls noticed his pleading look, they both knew the moment they had dreaded most had arrived.

"Was she—" Giorgo could not finish his question as his voice cracked from the emotion that had welled up in his chest.

Persia's attention was drawn away from the heart-wrenching figure as she noticed her grandmother slowly approaching. She rushed forward without hesitation and threw her arms around the old woman's neck. "Grandmother, I never thought I'd see you again!" Persia's embrace was returned unashamedly as Nanna hugged the younger woman to her breast. The old fortune-teller's thoughts were filled with relief and joy that her granddaughter was still alive and had been returned to her. She, too, had believed she would never set eyes on the girl again. For two days she had studied the tea leaves and read the tarot cards, and then, when all else had failed, she had made a fire and attempted to see the future in the wispy trails of smoke. But still the future had evaded her, and it made her wonder if her ability to foresee impending events was no longer so powerful.

"Come with me to the *vardo,*" the old woman said in a quiet voice which shook with emotion. She turned toward Savana, adding, "Both of you, come. I will tend to your injuries."

"I must go to Teril," Savana replied, scanning the

171

camp for her husband.

"He is not back, and neither are Romalio or Soobli and the others," Nanna answered with a weary sigh. Her aging body gave a visible shudder as she thought of all the sorrow that had consumed their *familia* in the past few days. "And Tasmin is missing, too."

"Where is Teril?" Savana's panicked cry rang out.

"What do you mean, Tasmin is missing?" Persia clutched her grandmother's arm for support as she began to feel the last of her strength drain away.

The old woman glanced from one girl to the other before answering their question. She turned first to Savana. "Teril and the others went after the outlaws who took you." Before Savana could make more inquiries, Nanna directed her attention to her granddaughter. "Tasmin has followed the green-eyed *gajo.*"

Persia gasped in disbelief. "No, this is not possible. We saw the *gajo* late yesterday afternoon . . . he travels alone." Her gaze met with her grandmother's dark eyes, and for the first time Persia was saddened to see that a look of fear and confusion lurked in those ebony depths. "Grandmother," Persia cried, "What has happened to her?"

A defeated shake of her gray head was Nanna's sole reply. Every source of her power had indicated that Tasmin and the *gajo* would spend the rest of their lives together, but apparently once again her insight had grown dim. The obvious look of defeat that overcame the old woman's expression caused a pang of sympathy to shoot through Persia's breast,

172

and as she watched her grandmother she became aware of how old she truly was. Persia had never thought of Nanna dying; actually, she had believed her grandmother would live forever. At this moment, however, she realized how fragile Nanna had become. She almost looked as if she had aged twenty years in the past few days. Persia knew that her captivity had been greatly responsible for her grandmother's decline. How would she ever manage the added burden of the two girls' deceit?

"We'll talk in the *vardo*," Persia said as she wrapped her arms in a tight embrace around her grandmother's drooping shoulders. She glanced at Savana, motioning with a toss of her head for her to accompany them. Whispered murmuring throughout the tribal crowd told Persia that the speculation about whether or not they were *marime* had begun. Giorgo started to follow the three women, but he paused after taking several faltering steps. He did not want to know—not yet—if his precious little girl had been violated before her death. As he turned toward the *vardo* where his wife had fled, he decided that if she had been raped, then he never wanted to know the truth. Of course, even as he told himself this, an inner voice deep in his heart told him that eventually he would have to hear the entire story from Persia and Savana, but not yet. Now he just wanted to join Nura in their *vardo* and release all the pent-up anger he had tried to corral for the past few days. Then he could give in to the indescribable sorrow of knowing that his daughter was dead.

A strained silence hovered over Nanna's *vardo* as

she began to swab Persia's and Savana's cuts with a damp cloth. Several times her mouth opened as though she wanted to say something, but she would remain quiet and resume tending to the girl's injuries. Persia, however, could not suppress her worry about Tasmin's whereabouts.

"Where do you think she could be, Grand-mother?"

"Cei nosli," the old woman answered, but Persia gave her head a negative shake. "She is a runaway," Nanna repeated in a confident tone. "Why else would she take off without telling anyone that she was leaving?"

"But you said that she was with the *gajo.*"

Nanna stopped her diligent doctoring and met her granddaughter's troubled gaze. "You said she was not, so I guess I was wrong." Nanna's eyes shifted away from Persia's face as if she was ashamed of her admission. She had been wrong too often recently, and she was afraid to glimpse what lurked in her granddaughter's secret thoughts for fear that she would misunderstand something vital.

A stabbing pain inched through Persia's breast as she once again witnessed Nanna's confusion. While her grandmother continued to clean and dress their wounds, Persia and Savana sat in cautious silence. Savana worried that the wise old woman would ask them what had happened during their abduction, so she was afraid to say something which might provoke a discussion about the extent of their torture. Persia, however, was saddened by her beloved grandmother's frail state of mind and did not want to mention anything that would add any further burden to Nanna. The uneasiness that permeated the tiny wagon was almost suffocating. At last Nanna was satisfied that she had done all she was capable of doing for the two girl's wounds.

"You can rest now." Glancing toward Savana, she added, "Your *vardo* was burned during the ambush, but you can stay here."

Savana's hand flew up to her mouth to stifle the cry that suddenly rose in her throat. She was not sure how much more strain she could handle; first the horror of the past few days, discovering Teril was gone, and now learning that her home, along with her treasured belongings, had been destroyed. All this, combined with the excessive fear that they would be labeled as *marime* and Teril would reject her as his *bori,* was too much for her weakened and fragile being to handle. The sobs that racked Savana's body seemed uncontrollable, while she buried her face in her hands and gave into the massive agony that spewed from her heavy heart. Persia moved to her side and draped a comforting arm around her shoulders, but Savana's sorrow added to her despair, and before long both girls were yielding to the pressure they could no longer contain. Their sobs echoed through the tiny wagon as they clung to Nanna, who had gathered them both in her arms.

"It's all right to cry," she told them. "Cry now for Vilo, and for the sorrow her family must endure. Cry for all of them, but cry mostly for yourselves, because you and only you know the depth of your own anguish." The weathered hands of the old fortune-teller gently stroked each girl's hair as she closed her eyes, and her mind, to the vivid images that invaded through her thoughts; one would live a long and fruitful life, the other would succumb to the tragedy of this terrible time. But Nanna could not allow herself to see which fate belonged to Savana, and which had been predestined for her cherished granddaughter Persia.

Chapter Sixteen

Who was Emma? Tasmin asked herself for at least the hundredth time. Was it *her* picture the *gajo* had wanted back so desperately when he had accused Persia of stealing from him? She recalled the haunted sorrow that lurked in his emerald eyes, wondering if it was for Emma that he mourned so profoundly. Emma? A dozen questions converged on her tired mind, though she told herself that it was only wasted energy to continue to wonder about the *gajo*. A weary sigh slipped from Tasmin's dry mouth as she bent down beside the creek and scooped a handful of water up to her parched lips. It seemed as though she had been walking forever, but it had only been one day since she had departed from the *gajo*. She had spent the night in the shelter of an old dugout that had probably been used by a prospector panning for gold in Chico Creek during the time when gold had been abundant in this area.

Tasmin glanced down at the sandy banks of the

creek, taking note of the shimmering flecks of gold along the water's edge. Fool's gold . . . still, even a fool deserved a second chance, but she wondered if O Del had already decided she wasn't worth the effort. Maybe fools who could not seem to learn from their mistakes were not granted repeated opportunities to right their wrongs. Tasmin had no doubt that chasing after the *gajo* was wrong, yet nothing could have stopped her. Even now she was not certain that she was sorry for her actions; she was only saddened that he was gone from her life for good.

Kneeling at the creek, Tasmin was granted with a hazy reflection of her haggard face. Long ago she had lost her scarf, and her hair hung in dirty strands down her back and past her waist. The grime that coated her face was streaked by tears which had a habit of springing from her eyes without notice, and her black *jodka* apron, skirt, and blouse were torn and filthy. The flimsy sandals she had worn on her feet had broken their leather straps; she had discarded them along the way, so her feet were as battered as the rest of her weary body. Unexpectedly a loud growl emitted from her stomach, her first indication that she was growing hungry. Until now her thoughts had been too consumed with the *gajo* to make room for thoughts of her own misery. But with the realizaton that she had not eaten for almost two days came a gnawing hunger that made her nauseated and weak.

She sat down on the bank and glanced around at her surroundings. The landscape looked exactly the same as it had yesterday, when she had first began her long journey back toward the Gypsy camp. There were long stretches of rolling hillsides, where lizards and rattlesnakes dominated the area while sunning themselves on the smooth rocks. Thick woodlands of gnarled oaks, impenetrable chaparral, and the steady presence of Chico Creek with its deep, clear waters and dense profusion of thickets ran at the base of the foothills. Scattering of wildflowers dotted the hills and open meadows, and thick patches of ferns in a dozen or more varieties carpeted the forest. Tasmin did not know how she would ever find her people again, and at times she wondered if she was destined to wander this strange land alone for the rest of her life, now that her true fate with the *gajo* had gone astray.

As she stood up on her aching legs after quenching her thirst, and attempting to ignore her hunger, Tasmin tried to convince herself that she should continue to search for her caravan. It seemed useless to go on when she could simply lie down here at the edge of creek and never get up again. Just as she was about to give in to the defeat which was rapidly claiming her exhausted being, the sounds of horses' hooves captured her full attention. The sense of panic that washed over her was so unnerving that she felt as though her feet had grown roots and would not allow her to move. But when she surveyed the area once more, she realized there was nowhere to run anyway. Still, her first thought was of the outlaws who had ambushed their camp and kidnapped her friends, which left her too terrified to think

179

straight. She twirled around in a frantic circle, debating which way she should flee. The creek offered no refuge, and there were no forests close by to which she could run for cover. Before she could make her mind function clearly, however, the riders had rounded the bend of the creek and were in clear view.

"O Del, Tasmin!" Romalio yelled when he spotted her standing mutely at the edge of the creek. His horse did not have a chance to halt its steps as he sprang from his saddle, then ran to stand in front of her before Tasmin could even begin to compose her fleeing thoughts.

Her mouth opened, but no sound escaped. Was Romalio here? It didn't seem possible. Could she be hallucinating? she asked herself. Romalio—right before her eyes. His trailworn face was shadowed with disbelief as he stared at her with his shocked gaze.

"What are you doing here?" The question was an angry demand, and the furious sound of Soobli's voice whipping through the stillness snapped Tasmin and Romalio out of their stupor.

Tasmin's eyes flew back and forth between the enraged glare of her brother and the sensitive face of the man whom she thought she would love for eternity. "I—I—am lost," she stuttered in a hoarse voice.

"But how did you get separated from the others?" Romalio's request was filled with concern, and his worried expression creased his dark, handsome face with deep lines that made him appear older than his thirty-five years. The past few days had left him completely drained of energy, and the only thought that had kept him from going insane was the idea of being reunited with his beautiful Tasmin. But now, standing face to face with her, he sensed that their reunion would not be as he had hoped. "How?" he repeated, his intuition telling him that her feelings towards him had changed drastically.

"Romalio, I—" She glanced again at her brother as an icy wind invaded her body. His dark expression was so overcome with rage that she found it hard to talk with him standing so near.

Grabbing her by the shoulders in a moment of panic, Romalio begged, "Please, what is it?" His eyes darted over her head and around the area as if a new fear had suddenly entered his mind. "Are you the only one left? The others . . . are they—" His voice also faltered as though he could not bring himself to speak the thoughts that had just occurred to him. When she shook her head in a negative gesture, Romalio closed his eyes and inhaled a relieved breath.

"This is foolishness, Tasmin!" Soobli growled as he approached the king and his sister. "What curse has brought you here?" His fury caused Tasmin to cringe, and only the support of Romalio's hands upon her shoulders kept her from falling backward onto the sandy bank.

"Give her time," Romalio commanded without a glance in Soobli's direction. His troubled eyes watched only Tasmin, for a sign that he hoped would disperse of his growing sense of foreboding.

181

But the anguished look on her face told him that there was no alternative. "Princess, come with me." The Gypsy king threw a threatening glare at Soobli when the other man started to protest. Without looking at the rest of the men who still remained on their horses, Romalio began to lead Tasmin away from the group and toward a dense growth of chapparal that bordered the creek several hundred feet upstream.

Tasmin stumbled along beside him while a dozen disoriented thoughts spun wildly through her head. What could she say to this man that would make her disgrace any less of a burden to him? To lie would be an insult to his intelligence, for Romalio would somehow learn the truth eventually. Tasmin herself would have to tell him about the *gajo*, because a man as kind and loving as her king deserved only honesty from the woman he loved. Even now, the love that emitted from his raven gaze as he patiently waited for her to speak was crushing to her fragile soul. How could she look into his gentle eyes and tell him that he had lost her forever?

The whiskered face of the green-eyed *gajo* blocked Romalio from her vision for an instant and caused a knot to form in Tasmin's stomach. She had no clue as to why this man continued to interfere in the course of her life, even when he was gone. But in the brief time that she stood before the king she became aware of how deeply the *gajo*—Blayde Chandler— had settled himself in her heart. She had believed that he was out of her life for good and that he would never come back to her, but a glimpse of the future had just opened itself to her inquisitive gaze, and there she had seen the quiet *gajo* again and known that it was she who must go to him.

Tenderly she reached up and touched Romalio's cheek. The lower portion of his face was covered with a rough growth of whiskers, and dark circles hovered beneath his troubled gaze. His flat-brimmed hat still shaded his face, but the thick black curls that tumbled to his shoulders were matted and tangled. Tasmin could see how much he had already suffered, and she hated herself for what she was about to do. Indecision tore at her insides and made her head spin like a whirlwind, causing the words she was about to say to stick in her throat. She would tell him the truth—part of the truth—but she could not tell him everything . . . not yet.

"I have much to say to you, my king," she began. She felt his jaw tighten against her palm as he prepared himself to listen to the words he knew he would dread hearing. Drawing in a deep breath, Tasmin dropped her hand down and nervously began to twist the corner of her tattered silk apron between her fingers. "I will start at the beginning, with what happened after you left the camp to go in search of Persia and the others, and when I went to get Danso and Cyri from the thicket." She studied the corner of her torn apron as though she expected to see a revelation within the silky folds.

No longer able to bear the suspense, Romalio pulled the material from her shaking fingers and raised her chin up with his cupped hand. He made it impossible for her to move her head, so Tasmin was forced to meet his demanding gaze. "Whatever it is, it will not make me love you any less. You're my princess, and soon you will be my *Phuri dae*. Nothing—nothing can change this!" The determination his tired voice had gained surprised Tasmin, and the tight grip in which he held her chin was even more unsettling. "Tell me," he added in his strained tone, "Tell me that nothing will prevent you from becoming my Gypsy queen!"

A tight lump formed in Tasmin's throat as Romalio continued to hold onto her chin so that she could not look away from his face. Never had she seen him lose his patience, but it was obvious now that he was on the verge of his breaking point. "No . . . nothing can change what is in the cards, or that which is written in the tea leaves," she replied in a trembling voice as she allowed her tearful gaze to lock with the pleading eyes of her king.

Chapter Seventeen

"I demand to know what is going on!" Soobli said as he stomped to where Romalio and his sister stood. His raven eyes flashed with indignation when he stopped before them, and his scathing glare was leveled at his sister.

"And you shall find out what is going on, as will I, when Tasmin is ready to tell us." Romalio's eyelids narrowed as he turned toward the other man, making it apparent that he had no patience for this interruption. When he looked back at Tasmin, though, it was also obvious that he did not intend for her to prolong her silence, either. He still held her tightly by the shoulders, and she could feel his grip grow stronger as his anxiety increased. The time had come, Tasmin realized, to face up to her rash and foolish venture to chase after the *gajo*.

She stumbled over her words, quickly relating the events that had led to her stabbing the stranger, and to his rapid departure in spite of his injuries. "I could not live with myself after he left." She lowered her gaze to the ground, adding, "I knew he was not well enough to leave, so I went looking for him."

"How could you do something so stupid? Why should you care whether or not the *gajo* lived or died?" Soobli's words escaped from between clenched teeth, and even Romalio's look of warning did not detour him as his flashing black gaze drilled into his sister. "And who is caring for my *chavvies* while you are on this wild-goose chase?"

Tasmin sank back against Romalio's embrace as her brother's face came within inches of her own. "It was foolish of me—I know this now. But—"

"And did you find the *gajo?*" Romalio cut in, his tone low and melancholy, as if he already knew the answer.

Once again Tasmin glanced toward the ground, her head dropping shamefully. She did not want to see the accusations she knew would fill her king's ebony eyes when she admitted to her error. "I did." Her simple reply did not offer any further explanation, but Romalio did not ask for more.

Abruptly, he turned loose of her and took a step backward. A dozen questions filled his mind, but none that he could force himself to ask. Her obvious disgrace told him more than he wanted to know, but still his defiant heart kept crying, It doesn't matter! He would love her regardless of what she might have done.

"We'd better get going if we are going to catch up to the caravan soon." Romalio's voice was controlled, yet a noticeable tremor accompanied his words. "There is an extra horse," he added as he sidestepped Tasmin and Soobli in a hasty retreat.

Since she had not looked up as he walked away, Tasmin gasped, startled, when Soobli grabbed her arm and yanked her forward roughly. "What a stupid little pig you are!" He shoved her away as if he had decided that she was dirty, his lips curling into a snarl as his ebony eyes raked over her disheveled appearance. "You'd better go after him and beg for his forgiveness, and," his eyes drew into narrowed slits when he leaned toward her, "no matter what happened between you and the *gajo,* you make sure that Romalio is convinced that you are still *wazho*— untouched and pure!" His tone of voice had acquired a threatening quality which caused a chill to race through Tasmin, especially when she raised her eyes up to his dark, glowering face.

"I will tell him the truth," she retorted, tossing her head back in a defiant manner and meeting the cold stare of her brother's eyes, eyes so much like her own in shape and size, yet so different in the way they viewed life.

Soobli's complexion darkened to a deep crimson; his face was masked with rage. In his veins ran royal blood, and his foolish mother had deprived him of his heritage when she had taken him away from his father's people. Now another stupid woman was trying once again to steal away his claim to power. He did not intend to allow it to happen this time. He was a prince, he reminded himself as anger overtook what remained of his rational thoughts, and if not for his mother, he undoubtedly would have taken his

187

father's place as king. His only chance to regain a bit of his royal heritage was through the marriage of his sister to Romalio.

For a long time he had been composing a plan in his mind; Romalio had no family, and when he married Tasmin, her entire family would assume positions of authority among their tribesmen. However, if something happened to Romalio before Tasmin could bear him a son, the next logical person to step into the position of king would be a member of her family. As king of the Gypsies, Soobli intended to lead this dwindling tribe back to their homeland of Romania. Once in *Puro tem,* he could concentrate all his efforts toward locating his father's people, over whom he would also claim leadership. In his dreams of power, Soobli imagined himself as king over the largest band of Roms in the world. He would not permit his foolish sister to destroy this ultimate goal for him!

"You will tell him whatever it takes to win back his trust and faith," Soobli commanded as he reached out to grab a handful of his sibling's long, tangled hair. He yanked on the raven mane in a violent gesture, drawing sadistic pleasure from the pained expression that overtook his sister's face. "Because if Romalio decides that you are not a worthy *bori,* I will make it my personal pleasure to see to it that Danso and Cyri are never permitted to speak to you again, or even to look in your direction for the rest of your miserable life!" Satisfied by the stricken expression on Tasmin's face that his threatening words had had a lasting effect, Soobli let the clump of hair drop from his hand, then twirled around and left her standing mute and alone behind the grove of chapparal.

A stabbing sensation pierced Tasmin's breast as the depth of her brother's fury claimed her spinning thoughts. He knew precisely how to hurt her the most, and she had no doubt that he would use his innocent children against her if he did not get his way. She turned her tear-streaked face up toward the azure blue sky, wondering what the gentle spirit of their mother must be thinking as she looked down from the heavens to witness the deceitful and hostile path that her son and daughter were traveling. "Forgive us," she whispered as her raven gaze scanned the cloudless sky in expectation, almost as if she hoped to see her mother's dark visage hovering high above her. Only the flawless blue expanse greeted her pleading eyes, yet without any visible change Tasmin was overcome with the feeling that she was not alone. She took a deep, cleansing breath and closed her eyes as she recalled the last words her mother had spoken to her five years ago . . . "You are a *tacho rat*—a true-blooded Gypsy—and because of this you will forever follow the *Drom,* the road of life that leads to freedom. But never forget to follow your heart first, even if at times the road seems impassable. For this, my precious Tasmin, is the true *Drom,* and will lead to eternal happiness."

Follow your heart, Tasmin repeated to herself as she opened her eyes again and squared her shoulders in a determined manner. Without hesitation, she walked out from behind the chapparal and headed toward the spare horse Romalio had mentioned. In complete silence the men watched her with inquisitive eyes, but Tasmin refused to be intimidated by their bold stares. She purposely sought her brother's face, however, meeting his icy gaze with her own unwavering look of determination as she passed by him. Swinging herself up on the bare back of the horse, she haughtily glanced at the men in an impatient manner as she waited for Romalio to give the command for them to be on their way. The king, however, did not turn in her direction when he mounted his horse and began to lead them northward again. Tasmin sighed with relief once they were moving and she no longer had to contend with her brother's enraged face or the sideways glances of the other men. Her brave and uncaring charade was taking a toll on her exhausted being, and the only thing she could concentrate on was finding a way to fulfill the vow she had just made to herself.

Darkness had claimed the California landscape once more before the weary band of riders decided to rest for the night. They were no longer worried about locating the caravan, because the first of the stick markers had been spotted shortly before nightfall. By midday tomorrow they knew they would be reunited with their families and kinsmen. A supper of dried meat and bread was eaten with barely more than a word or two spoken by anyone. Except for Romalio and Soobli, none of the other men knew why Tasmin had been separated from the rest of the tribe. Her unexpected appearance at the creek bank, though, had increased the feeling of doom which had already accompanied the men on their journey back to the caravan. They had discovered the cabin where the outlaws had taken their captives during the storm, and had also buried the violated body of Nura and Giorgo's young daughter, Vilo. No trace of Persia and Savana had been found, however, and after the violent rainstorm the Gypsies had not been able to pick up the outlaws' trail again. It was assumed that the other two girls were still the killer's captives, and with saddened hearts the Gypsy men were now returning to tell their people the devastating news.

Immediately following the evening meal, the men began retiring to their bedrolls. Neither Soobli nor Romalio had made any attempt to talk to Tasmin, but it was Romalio who handed her a piece of hardtack and a chunk of bread. Briefly he permitted himself to look into her dark gaze, but it was long enough for Tasmin to realize that he still loved her in spite of her rash actions of the past few days. She also knew that he would be fair in his assessment of her fate, so the king was who she approached when the rest of the men had grown silent and still.

"You found no trace of Persia and the others?"

Romalio jumped at the sound of her voice. He had tossed his bedroll several dozen yards from the other men and was sitting cross-legged on the makeshift bed. When Tasmin approached, he was staring into the darkness as if he was in a trance. The stars were just beginning to glow in the black sky and the moon was shrouded by a hazy glow that lent an eerie feeling to the night. He glanced in Tasmin's direction but made no comment that would invite her to stay.

Tasmin halted at the edge of his bedroll, attempting to decipher his expression, then giving up this task when she realized it was too dark to determine his mood. His silence bespoke his temperament, though, since she had never known him to intentionally ignore her. A wind whipped through the small glade where they had stopped for the night, causing Tasmin to shiver, even though the breeze was warm and balmy.

"Tsinivari," Romalio said quietly.

Again Tasmin shivered, but this time the cause was the icy chill of fear that inched down her. *Tsinivari* were the evil spirits who inhabited the night fog. Until now she had never let the thought of *Tsinivari* cloud her images of nighttime. But on this foggy eve, her usual perception of the perfect world, which was concealed by darkness, was replaced with visions of hovering ghosts and red-eyed demons lurking in the shadows.

"Vilo is dead."

His unexpected, low-spoken words sliced through Tasmin as if he had screamed them into her face. O Del! Poor Vilo. Once again she recalled the last time she had seen Vilo during the ambush, when the young girl had been tackled by the murderous *gajo*. A mournful sob racked her body as she gave in to the sorrow she could not contain. "Per—Persia?" Her voice was barely more than a choked whisper, yet Romalio heard.

"We found neither Persia or Savana. We assume they are still in the captive of the *gajo.*" He remained

192

seated on his bedroll, but now he turned to gaze up at her through the faded night. Her slender form, hunched over with sorrow, tore at his breast. He yearned to hold her, comfort her, in his arms. Yet the memory of the long-haired *gajo* invaded his soul— the *gajo* whose eyes had spoken of desire when he had gazed at Tasmin dancing in the firelight. Tasmin belonged to Romalio, and had always been his from the first moment he had seen her toddling around the campfire . . . She had been two years old and he a young man of seventeen. Even then her charm had been undeniable, her impending beauty evident. The young prince had been old enough to claim a bride, but an inner voice told him that patience would reward him with a treasure beyond his wildest imaginings. Watching Tasmin Lovell grow into womanhood had fulfilled this prophecy. He had worshipped her for sixteen years and had waited far longer than was customary to make her his *bori*. She could have been his *Phuri dae* for at least four years by now, but foolishly, he had waited for her to tell him that she was ready to become his wife. He had wanted her to fulfill all her childhood desires so that when she was prepared to become a woman he could unleash all the fire he knew simmered within her passionate being.

But she had made him wait much too long. Now he wondered if there had been an unknown force keeping them apart. Could it be that O Del had something else in store for his princess? Why had the *gajo* suddenly appeared in their camp the other night, and what was there about him that had prompted the king to invite him to stay? More important, why had he asked Tasmin to dance for the stranger, when he knew how profoundly her dance could affect a mortal man? On that night she had danced like never before, a nymph exploding with sensual invitation, a mystical enchantress inspiring all who watched her to fall under her bewitching spell. Thinking back even now, Romalio felt his rapacious fantasies fueled; it made him weak with longings that he could not acknowledge, at least not until he knew the truth about the time she had spent with the *gajo*.

For the fates of her friends, Tasmin wept unabashedly. She did not care that Romalio sat wordlessly at her feet. Nor did her own future matter to her at this time. Nothing seemed as horrendous as the suffering Persia and Savana must be enduring—unless, as with Vilo, their torment had already come to an end. All the heartbreak of the past washed over her with the news of this latest tragedy, making her tears sound even more remorseful. The wandering ways of her people commanded a high price, and since arriving in America, their tribe had decreased by half. If this continued, soon there would be none of them left. Because they were Gypsies, because freedom and independence meant more to them than life itself, was their very existence doomed?

Without warning, Romalio was pulling her shaking form into his arms, his own pain forgotten for the moment as he thought only of easing her agony. Holding her close, though, added more burden to his traumatized heart. He could not deny his love for her, he realized, and regardless of her association with the *gajo,* he would somehow find a way to forgive her.

"I love you, Princess, and together we will overcome all this sorrow," he whispered as he gently stroked the thick mass of her long hair.

As his soft-spoken words reached Tasmin's unsuspecting ears, her misery expanded. If only she could return his love, if only they could be together. But if she told him that she loved him and that there was still a future for them, she knew she would be lying. She started to shake her head. "Romalio, I—"

Her words were interrupted by Romalio's sudden kiss, a gesture that was meant to convince her that he had not spoken lightly about his love for her. His mouth crushed against her lips with a savagery that surprised even Romalio, but it was a hunger that he could not deny. He had to prove to her, and to himself, that the terrible events of the past few days had not destroyed all the hopes he harbored for their life together.

Tasmin sensed his desperation, and as if she too hoped they would each find a refuge in this fevered moment, she began to return his kiss with a frantic urgency. She felt his embrace tighten around her trembling waist as she raked her fingers through the thick black curls that curved around his face. Please, O Del, she cried inwardly, let his kiss ignite a fire that will extinguish the flame in my heart that was lit by the *gajo*.

As Romalio's lips played with hers, she allowed her tongue to dart forward in the bold manner in which the *gajo* had taunted and tantalized her during his unyielding kiss. And though Romalio's tongue eagerly entwined with hers, it did not produce the sweet taste of forbidden ecstasy that the *gajo* had evoked. A pang of disappointment shot through Tasmin's breast. Still she pressed harder against Romalio's taut body and deepened her ravenous kiss in an effort to recapture just a little bit of the magic induced by Blayde Chandler.

As quickly as he had attacked her lips, Romalio pulled away and gasped for breath. "You'd better get some sleep," he said in a choked voice, then glanced down at the ground, as if overcome with embarrassment.

It was too dark for Tasmin to make out his expression, and his tone of voice told her nothing about the effect their kiss had left upon him. Only the intense disappointment that washed over her own heart was evident as she nodded mutely and began to move away from him.

Unable to speak because of the lump that had formed in his throat, Romalio watched as she was swallowed by the darkness of the night, and with her went the last of his dreams. At first, when she had begun to return his kiss with such devotion, his hopes had soared. But then reality had closed down upon him as if the sky had just collapsed and he had become filled with such a feeling of loss that he had thought he might pass out. It was then that he had halted the deceitful kiss and pulled away from her. If only she had not tried so hard, he told himself, but in her blind desperation to cleanse her own conscience, she had unwittingly crushed the last of Romalio's hopes that their love still thrived. When he had kissed her for the first time a few days ago, he had kissed an innocent young maiden. But tonight her kiss bespoke a passion so fierce that Romalio knew someone had already accomplished what he had only dreamt of doing; someone—the *gajo*—had kindled the simmering fire in her soul and unleashed a wild blaze that Romalio knew he could never hope to contain.

Chapter Eighteen

The duration of the trip was much the same as the day before, with none of the men speaking to Tasmin, and few even glancing in her direction. Romalio's sullen disposition had increased the other men's suspicions about the princess's motives for leaving the rest of the tribe. Since he had not made any mention of her recent activities, however, the men were curious as to why she had been so far from the caravan. Soobli's mood was so foul that no one dared approach him with questions, but his hostility toward his sister caused the men to suspect that she had been attempting to run away when they had come upon her at the creek. *Cei nosli*—a runaway Gypsy girl—was not uncommon, but usually a girl did not run away unless she had been cast out by the rest of the tribe. Speculations ran rampant in the men's minds about what the king's intended *Phuri dae* had done to prompt her to run away.

Before they had broken camp this morning, Tasmin had tried to convey her sympathy to

Savana's husband. Teril had acted as if she had been trying to infect him with the plague and had purposely ignored her gesture of kindness. Tasmin kept to herself after his rejection, an easy task, since no one, not even Romalio, had made any attempt to associate with her. Riding along the discreet trail marked by sticks and rocks, Tasmin had plenty of time to mull over her situation and the options she had for her future. She agonized over leaving Nanna now that Persia was gone. But it was Danso and Cyri about whom she worried the most. What would happen to them if she was not around to care for them, or if Soobli followed through with his threat and banned her from seeing them? Soobli's violent temper and brooding bouts of depression did not make him a stable parent. Tasmin knew she could never pursue her own goals until she was certain that her niece and nephew would be taken care of by someone other than their father. She also knew that this was a vague possibility since their tribe was rapidly dwindling in population, and there were only a few couples who would be able to care for two small *chavvies*. Though Soobli did not give much attention to his offspring he was selfish and hateful, and Tasmin worried how he would react to her suggestion that he allow his *chavvies* to be raised by someone else.

The Gypsies at the caravan had just finished packing up the cooking utensils used for the morning meal, and were about to begin the day's journey when the weary travelers rode into camp. Their arrival was hailed by a round of shouts, which immediately brought everyone to the edge of the

199

camp to greet them. Since Persia's and Savana's return yesterday, the rest of the tribe was growing anxious to know the whereabouts of their menfolk. Their appearance now was grounds for celebration, especially since the Gypsies had feared their men might have encountered the outlaws once more after the girl's escape. Only Vilo's fate cast a dark cloud over the joyous reunion, and a tense atmosphere quickly ruled over the entire camp once the initial excitement had died down enough for everyone to become aware of the strange turn of events that had brought them all back together again.

Savana rushed toward her husband without hesitation as he dismounted, but his shock at seeing her made him shrink back against his horse, and caused the rest of the men to gasp in surprise at her appearance here in the camp. "Teril, thank O Del, you are back!" she cried as she reached out to him, unaware of his strange reaction toward her.

For a moment he could only stare at her as if he had seen a ghost. "H—how did you g—get here?" he finally managed to ask in a halting voice. He made no attempt to touch her and remained plastered against his horse with a horrified look on his face.

A perplexed expression overcame Savana's countenance as she dropped her arms to her sides. "We escaped," she replied, motioning to where Persia and Nanna stood. Then, returning her puzzled gaze toward her husband, she added, "What is wrong? Aren't you happy to see me?"

"Vilo—" Teril glanced briefly at the young girl's parents, who stood among the onlookers. "Why didn't she escape?"

His unexpected question threw Savana off-guard. "What do you mean?" she asked, innocently. He knows! her inner voice screamed, though she tried to appear calm. She threw a furtive glance in Persia's direction, but the other girl was staring at Tasmin with a stunned look.

"We found Vilo's body in the cabin." Teril looked at Giorgo and Nura, then toward the king as he grew solemn and silent.

Romalio cleared his throat and turned toward the couple in slow deliberation, dreading the news he believed he would have to relate to Vilo's parents.

"We know," Giorgo said, hugging his wife close to his side. Nura appeared to be in a state of shock, pale and withdrawn as she slumped against her husband's burly form. She was garbed all in white, as was the Gypsy custom during mourning. "Persia and Savana told us what happened to our lit—little girl." His brave facade began to crumble, and he was helpless to halt the tears that sprang into the corners of his eyes.

Romalio gave his head a slight nod and glanced toward the ground as if he was unsure of how to handle this situation. He had questions to ask both Savana and Persia about Vilo's death and their escape, but they would have to wait. His weary mind did not want to think anymore today; he was worn out from trying to decide how he was going to deal with his own decisions concerning Tasmin. Even if her association with the *gajo* had left her impure, he could not bear the idea of casting her out of the tribe. In his tired state of mind, he told himself that he would go against all customs, if necessary, but he was not ready to give up on his dream of making Tasmin Lovell his *Phuri dae*.

"We will stay at this campsite for a few days and rest." A heavy sigh accompanied the king's announcement. Then, without another word, he began to lead his horse to the area where the rest of the herd was hobbled. The other riders followed suit after greeting their families, but no one dared to mention what was foremost on everyone's mind: what had the men discovered when they had found Vilo's body, and where had Tasmin been for the past few days?

Tasmin slid from her horse and immediately sought out Persia. Her joy in seeing that her friend was alive and safe was obvious on her dirt-streaked face. Persia rushed forward at once, needing no more of an invitation to embrace her friend. Oh, how she wanted to tell her about all the horror of their captive. To relieve herself of just a bit of the burden that weighed so heavily on her conscience would make such a difference in the recuperation of her battered spirit. But she could not confide in anyone, not even her dearest friend, and this was the most difficult of all.

"Are you all right?" Tasmin asked after they had embraced. Her gaze moved slowly over her friend's face, noting the swollen bruises that marred her complexion. Though her concern showed in her worried expression, she made no comment about Persia's battered appearance. "We thought you were still with the outlaws."

"And I thought you were lost to us forever," Savana replied, not wanting to think or talk about her kidnappers. She gazed into the confused eyes of the princess, adding, "Savana and I encountered the *gajo* a couple of days ago. Nanna thought you would be with him, and when you weren't, we all feared for your fate."

A scarlet flush rose up in Tasmin's cheeks and did not stop until her entire face was feverish and reddened. "I was with him," she answered, unable to hide the intense feelings his memory aroused. "And I still believe that I will be with him again someday. But first, there are things I must tend to here."

Persia studied the kaleidoscope of emotions that haunted her friend's dark eyes. Tasmin's future was so easy to foretell. She was correct in her belief that someday, in spite of all the hardships they must first encounter, the Gypsy princess and her sad-eyed *gajo* would be together again. It saddened Persia to think that Tasmin had to leave again—to rejoin her *gajo*— but this knowledge also gave her the insight to realize what she must do. She reached out and clasped ahold of her friend's hand. "I will help," she said quietly.

A mild look of surprise crossed Tasmin's dusty countenance. Persia was the one person she could never deceive, but her offer to assist her in her plans filled Tasmin with relief. She had expected to be reprimanded for her rash behavior, and had thought that her announcement to go after the *gajo* again would be met with a barricade of objections. A smile curved the corners of her trembling lips as the tears she had tried so hard to control began to roll down her cheeks like timid raindrops. *"Nais tuk,"* she whispered in a voice choked with emotion.

203

"You do not have to thank me. I am your friend, and though our time together on earth is limited, I want you to know that I will always be with you in spirit no matter where the *Drom* leads us."

Persia's odd speech caused a chill to work its way through Tasmin's being. She did not like the fortune-teller's talk of spirits, and limited time. They would always be friends for as long as they lived . . . and that would be a very long time! She tightened her fingers around Persia's hand. "I will not allow you to talk of anything sad. Today is a new beginning, not an end." She blinked back the last of her tears as a visible strength overcame her features. "Together, you and I will see to it that destiny does not go astray again."

A slight nod of her head was all of Persia's reply, but the twinkle that suddenly lit her dark gaze was apparent. If her last mission was to help her friend fulfill her destiny, then Persia knew she could depart from this world without regret.

"It is good to see you again," Nanna said as she stopped beside the two girls. Her eyes traveled up to the face of the princess with a loving gaze. She never thought of her as not being her own flesh and blood, and the love she harbored for the girl was as strong as that which she held for Persia.

"Nanna, oh Nanna," Tasmin cried as she released her hold on Persia and threw her arms around the old woman's neck. "I'm sorry if I caused you to worry, but I—"

"Had to go," Nanna finished for her. "And you will have to go again." Her blunt statement caused Persia and Tasmin to glance at one another in awe.

Nanna always knew these things . . . always! The old woman smiled as she wrapped her arms around each girl and began to lead them toward her wagon.

"Wait," Tasmin said as she halted their steps and glanced around the camp with a panicked gaze. She did not have to look for long, however, because she spotted Danso and Cyri at once as they waited patiently for the adults to acknowledge their presence. When they realized their aunt was looking for them, both children rushed forward and were scooped into her waiting arms. Squeals of happiness filled the air when Tasmin lavished their smiling faces with kisses as she hugged them close to her breast. She loved them so, and holding them now, made her wonder if she could go away again and leave them behind.

"I will care for them while you rest." A woman's soft voice cut into Tasmin's joyful reunion with the *chavvies*. She glanced toward the source and was stunned to see Nura. Her white garments seemed so stark against her dark skin, and the emptiness in her raven eyes was equally as startling. Tasmin looked to Nanna for an answer and received it when the old woman gave her head a definite nod. But before Tasmin could utter a word, Soobli's cruel voice sliced through the air.

"Release my *chavvies* at once!" he shouted as he stalked toward his sister. The handsome lines of his face were distorted into an ugly mask of rage, and for an instant Tasmin hardly recognized her brother. He stopped directly in front of her, and before another word was spoken, he viciously tore the children from her embrace and roughly dropped them to the ground. In Romanian, he ordered them to go to their *vardo*. The frightened youngsters scurried off without chancing another glance in their aunt's direction. The small group who had clustered around Tasmin gaped in shocked silence at Soobli's contemptful countenance. He ignored everyone except his sister, at whom he pointed a threatening finger as he said, "Never touch my *chavvies* again. And if you defy me, I will see to it that you never set eyes on them again!" He twirled around on the heels of his tall boots and stomped away from his sister and the rest of the clan, who still stared at him with horrified expressions upon their faces.

When Persia exchanged glances with her grand-mother, they both knew they had each had the same premonition. Persia shivered as an icy wind whipped through her veins, while she noticed that Nanna clasped her arms around her frail form as if the same chilling sensation had also invaded her body. Turning to the stricken girl at her side, Persia was filled with sympathy toward her friend, and with rage toward Soobli. He could not get away with punishing his innocent children—and Tasmin—because of a grudge that he had harbored for most of his life, and Persia determined that she would see to it that the terrible vision which had just unfolded in her mind would never come to pass.

Tasmin could not move nor talk; even thinking coherently was impossible as she stared at her brother's *vardo*. The thought of Danso and Cyri huddling together inside the walls of the wagon, frightened and confused because of their father's rude ouburst, tore through her breast and made her feel as if an invisible hand was ripping out her heart. She yearned to go to them despite their father, but she knew this was something she could not do. His threats were not idle; she was aware of the range of her brother's hatred. Worse was that she also knew Danso and Cyri were the ones who would suffer the most if she dared to challenge Soobli's threats.

In a moment of panic, Tasmin's eyes flitted around the camp and came to rest on the man who had watched the entire scenario from a short distance away. Romalio's troubled gaze locked with hers, and in the brief time their eyes met Tasmin realized how much he still loved her. His abrupt departure after their kiss last night and his silence toward her during the ride to the camp this morning had made her think that his feelings toward her had changed. But there was no denying how deeply he still cared by the obvious expression of love which he wore upon his face at this moment. Tasmin knew that if she went to him, there was nothing he would not do for her. He would even challenge Soobli's threats, if Tasmin asked him to . . . but she could not continue to play with Romalio's heart, and if she went to him now, she knew she would only be giving him false hope that she did care as deeply for him as he did for her. Instead, she forced herself to look away from him, though it was one of the hardest things she had ever done.

"Come," Nanna prodded as she draped her arm around Tasmin's waist. From the opposite side, Persia also wrapped an arm around the girl's quaking form as they began to lead her toward Nanna's *vardo*. Tasmin did not resist their gesture, because the thought of curling up in the soft quilts in Nanna's *vardo* filled her with a comforting sensation. It was there that she had sought sanction after her mother's death; it was there that she had lain and dreamt of her future with Romalio after he had proposed marriage. Nanna's *vardo* was also where she had fled on the night when she had danced for the *gajo* . . . the night when she had reached the fork in the road of her life—the *Drom*—and had chosen the route that would change the destination of her life forever.

Chapter Nineteen

Teril took longer than necessary to tend to his horse, but it was his aversion to confronting his wife that made him extra attentive to the animal. Until he knew whether or not his wife had been violated by the *gajo* outlaws, he did not know how to act around her. He loved her, but he did not want a soiled woman who had been touched by another man— especially by a *gajo*. Just the thought made him sick to his stomach, but he had to face the possibility that his marriage might be over if he learned that she had endured the same type of abuse that had been evident when they had found Vilo's body.

"Teril, wait!" Savana called out as he walked toward the center of the camp, where the main fire had been rekindled so that food could be prepared for the men who had just returned. He turned and saw that his wife had been busy erecting a bender tent—a tent that was used when a *vardo* was not available. Since their *vardo* had been destroyed during the ambush, they would have to sleep in a tent until a new wagon could be purchased or built. Savana had already constructed the half-circle frame and was throwing blankets over the bent branches for protection from the elements. On the floor she would throw mats and rugs that had been donated by the *familia* for the makeshift house.

"Our new home," she said with a timid smile. Her husband's distant attitude was obvious, and though the men had not spoken of how or where they had found Vilo's body, she knew that everyone had questions which would eventually have to be answered. Somehow, she had to speak to Persia before the men had a chance to question them about Vilo's death. So far no one had asked them any questions about where they had been hiding when Vilo had died. They had made certain that everything the men had discovered would also be corroborated by the fabrication they had already invented. But first she had to convince Teril that she was still worthy of being his wife, a task that she realized would not be easy, judging by the way he was staring at her now.

"I will be finished soon and then you can rest in the tent," she added before quickly turning away from her husband. Although Nanna's administrations had managed to reduce most of the swelling from the bruises on her face, faint bluish discolorations still covered both of her cheeks, and one eye was rimmed with a dark purple smudge. Her lip had been split and was also swollen and bruised, so she could understand why Teril was looking at her in such a strange manner. That he had not even bothered to ask her how she was feeling, however, caused her more pain than any of her injuries. In an effort to ease herself of some of the hurt his callous attitude aroused, Savana busied herself with finishing the tent. Since it was customary for the women in the Gypsy camp to do all the menial work, she did not expect her husband to offer his help, but the way he watched her work all the while made her anxieties grow. By the time she was ready to enter the small tent to do the interior work, she was grateful for a chance to escape from her husband's intense glare.

She began to toss the assortment of braided rugs and mats around on the hard ground. Mattresses filled with straw would serve as beds, but as she attempted to make the barren tent feel comfortable, Savana could not help but to mourn the loss of her *vardo*. Teril had purchased the wagon in Denver, Colorado, shortly before their marriage, and there was no telling how long it would be before they would be able to purchase another wagon. To raise money for such accommodations, Savana knew they would have to go to a heavily populated area, where the women of the tribe would fill their hawking baskets with commodities that they would try to sell to the *gajo* women. Many hours were spent whittling wooden clothespegs, and dainty flowers, hairbrushes, and combs for these purposes. From assorted grasses, straw, and branches, the Gypsy women would weave baskets to sell door-to-door, while women such as Persia and Nanna would earn their pay by telling fortunes and selling bottles of potions and lotions, which they claimed had great healing or magical powers. The lure of the Gypsy magic intrigued most *gajo*, and the fortune-tellers

211

hardly ever lacked for willing clients.

While the women walked through the streets of the town with their large hawking baskets, the men earned money shoeing horses, or doing various other jobs for the *gajo* who were willing to hire them. There were times when the Gypsies encountered *gajo* who would gladly offer them work, then refuse to pay them for the services after the Roms had completed the job. Since they figured they deserved payment for their labors, though, the men would not go away empty-handed, and they usually managed to acquire another horse or two for their herd

When no work was available, there was always an opportunity for the men to earn money through horse dealings. Though some *gajo* shied away from buying horses from the Gypsies for fear that they were purchasing stolen property, many non-Gypsies did not care where, or how, the animals had been acquired. Regardless of the Gypsies' notorious reputation for thievery, their horse herds still were among the finest to be found, and a cunning *gajo* knew that he could purchase the best horseflesh at the cheapest price when dealing with the Romanians.

A rush of panic washed over Savana at the thought of being around the *gajo* again. She clutched her arms around her trembling body but was unable to halt the shaking in her limbs. The blanketed walls of the tent began to remind her of the dilapidated shack where the outlaws had taken them, and the memory caused a scream to well up in the base of her throat. She managed to clasp her hand over her mouth to silence herself, but still a pitiful cry escaped from her mouth. In desperation, Savana crawled toward the opening that served as a door. The air in the tent had suddenly become suffocating, and she felt as if she would choke if she did not get out into the open air again. She hurled herself through the door as if she were actually being chased; she was trying to escape from the imaginary demons who would haunt her for the rest of her life.

Outside the tent she gasped for air and struggled to regain her sanity. Every second that she had been the outlaw's captive had flashed through her tortured mind in the few moments that she had been inside the tent. When her senses began to return to a calmer level, though, her first thought was of Teril and what he must think of her crazy performance. He had already been looking at her as if she was abnormal; now he would probably think she was possessed by Beng—the devil himself! But her worries were unfounded at this time, because Teril was nowhere in sight. Much to her relief, it appeared that no one had witnessed her brief and unexpected act of insanity. Everyone had gathered in the center of the camp and was occupied with the men who had been chasing the outlaws. While Savana scanned the area in search of her husband, she could not help but wonder if they were all talking about what had happened to Vilo, and if they were already beginning to doubt Persia's and her story.

When she saw no sign of Teril, Savana decided to talk to Persia before she went in search of her husband. They had to synchronize their story, and then she had to convince Teril that they were telling the truth, a more complex problem now that Vilo's body had been discovered. As she hurried to Nanna's *vardo*, Savana had the feeling that everyone in the camp was staring at her, and whispering behind her back when she passed by. She told herself she was only being foolish; still, she could not bring herself to look anyone in the eye as she rushed towards Nanna's *vardo*.

She knocked briskly, then without waiting for an answer, stuck her head through the doorway. The three women who were inside did not seem surprised by her sudden arrival, but whatever it was that they had been discussing came to an abrupt halt.

"Come in. We've been waiting for you," Nanna said, then motioned for her to sit next to Tasmin and Persia on the narrow bed. She had told both Tasmin and Persia that the other girl would be coming soon, and she was grateful to see that her foresight had not gone astray again.

Savana's bruised face creased into a perplexed frown as she glanced from Nanna's aging countenance to that of the young princess. Then, turning away from them as if she was afraid to meet their eyes, she said, "I came to talk to you." She directed her sole attention toward Persia. "Could we go—" She paused as a heated scarlet blush mingled with the blue and purple patches which already colored her cheeks. What would everyone think if they saw the two of them sneaking off to talk privately? she wondered. She had probably made Tasmin and Nanna suspicious just by coming here and not including them in her conversation.

"There's no need," Persia retorted as she drew in a defeated breath, then exhaled heavily. "Nanna

214

knows everything, and so does Tasmin. I could never lie to them." She reached out and clasped Tasmin's hand as the two exchanged looks of understanding and trust, the kind experienced only by friends who were as close as these two had been through the years.

Savana felt excluded, but worse, she felt betrayed. "You told them?" she gasped, her dark eyes flashing with anger. "Don't you realize what you've done?" She still stood in the open doorway of the *vardo,* but she glanced behind her as if she was afraid someone had followed her. When she looked back at the three women, it was evident that fear was beginning to overcome her fury. "Teril will never want me back." Tears misted her gaze, then burned fiery trails down her battered cheeks.

Her pitiful outburst brought both Tasmin and Persia to her side in an effort to comfort her. Persia could not help feeling a stabbing guilt for breaking the promise she had made to Savana. But now that the men had discovered Vilo's violated body, she knew it would be useless to continue their farce. Besides, she could not live with herself if she lied to Tasmin and her grandmother. "What happened was not our fault. Perhaps—" Persia glanced at Tasmin, remembering the words of the princess, as she added, "It is time our people changed some of those old customs."

"The old customs are part of our heritage. They are too ingrained in all of us for them to be changed," Nanna retorted, destroying the fragile hope that had flared in the three young women for a brief moment. The old one stared at the tarot cards she had spread

215

out in front of her. Then, as though she had witnessed something in the cards that she did not want to see, she scooped them all into a pile and pushed them to the end of the table.

"Grandmother, what is it?" Persia asked, her voice tense and filled with dread. The other two girls wore expressions that echoed Persia's sense of foreboding as they all waited for the venerable fortune-teller's reply.

Nanna lifted her eyes from the cards and glanced at each of the young women in a slow, measuring calculation. "The old customs can not be changed," she repeated, her voice firm and unyielding. Then, making it plain that she did not plan to discuss the subject any further, she picked up her cup, leaned back in her chair, and began to sip her tea in silence.

Her strange expression left the girls in turmoil, especially since it was obvious that her insight had just granted her knowledge about the future. But whatever she had observed in the cards was not something she wished to share. As the trio of young women watched her, they each began to sense that perhaps this was one circumstance where they would be better off not knowing what was about to happen.

At last Tasmin summoned the courage to speak. "I will not allow the ancient laws to rule my life," she said with a defiant tilt of her chin. "I have done nothing wrong, and neither have you." She glanced at Persia, then at Savana. "You two especially should be comforted and embraced by our people for all that you have suffered. The idea that our beliefs would allow you to be banished from the tribe because of the torture and abuse you were forced to endure is savage and cruel." She swung around, facing the old woman. Her dark eyes were aglow with silver lights as her anger radiated through her face, leaving her complexion flushed in hues of scarlet. Yet when she spoke to Nanna, her voice softened, for her anger was not directed at the elder fortuneteller when she asked, "Surely you, of all people, can understand this?"

Nanna nodded her gray head and met the young women's fiery gaze. "Yes. I understand, but I cannot change the laws that were written a thousand years ago." She glanced at the other two girls, halting her gaze on the worried face of her granddaughter. "I am but one old woman whose days are numbered." She saw the objection rise up in Persia's expression, but she did not allow the girl to voice her rebuttal. "My wisdom grows dimmer with each passing day, but of this I am certain." Her old eyes moved slowly from Persia to Savana, then to Tasmin. Their weariness of her prediction was apparent in their expressions as they waited for her to speak again. She mulled over her next words in her mind, not wanting to confuse her thoughts or say something that could be inaccurate. The silence in the small confines of the *vardo* was deafening, until at last she began to speak again. "Three fortunes I have read in the cards. Only one is clear." Her gaze settled on Tasmin's beautiful, troubled face once more. "Many pitfalls still await you on the rocky road ahead, but you already know the *Drom* that you were meant to follow."

Tasmin drew in a quivering breath. The *Drom*— her mother's last words echoed through her mind again. "But what about—"

"The *chavvies* will be well taken care of," Nanna interrupted. "Soobli will soon follow his own *Drom* back to *Puro tem*, but his *chavvies* will remain here with the *familia*. Nura and Giorgo will take them into their *vardo*, and the tiny ones will help to fill the void left by their recent loss."

As the old woman's words sank into Tasmin's mind, she began to experience a deep sense of sadness. Soobli and his children were all who were left of her blood kin, and soon they would be separated from one another. But O Del had obviously predestined this plan, or he never would have led the *gajo* into the Gypsy camp on that sultry night which seemed so long ago.

"What about me?" Savana asked, no longer able to contain her growing anxiety about her own future. "Will Teril take me back?"

"Only one reading is clear to my old mind," she stated again. She looked at her granddaughter. A gentleness filled her wrinkled countenance, but because she was afraid that she would start to cry, she did not speak the words that hovered on her tongue. She had never shown weakness in front of anyone, and she did not want to give in to this urge now. Maybe there would still be time to say the words of good-bye before they were forced to part, or perhaps later, when she was not so tired and confused, she would read the cards again . . . Maybe next time she would see something other than doom in her dear granddaughter's fortune.

Chapter Twenty

Tasmin woke to the sound of crying, a low, mournful weeping that chilled her to the bone. For an instant she refused to allow her heavy lids to open, hoping that she would discover the noise had been something which had escaped from her dreamland. But she had not been dreaming, and this sound stemmed from a nightmare from which there was no escape.

"O Del!" she gasped when she was fully awake and realized that it was Persia whose mournful wail echoed throughout the *vardo*. "What is wrong?"

The other girl turned red, swollen eyes toward her friend. She knelt beside Nanna's narrow bed, where the old woman lay silent and still. "She's gone, Tasmin."

Though Persia's words did not register in Tasmin's groggy mind for a moment, she still sprang from her own bed as a sense of strangling panic washed over her. "G-gone?"

"I heard her calling to me." Persia's head dropped down, her long tangled hair falling over her tearstained face. A candle on the table burned low, lending an eerie, luminous glow to the dark *vardo*. A racking sob shook her body as her words stammered from her trembling lips. "She—she said she forgave us all."

"No, oh no!" Tasmin fell to her knees beside Persia. Her expression revealed denial and shock as she reached out toward Nanna. The old woman looked peaceful, as if she was just sleeping contentedly. When Tasmin lightly touched her cheek, Nanna's skin was still warm. It was not possible that she was dead. "She's only sleeping," Tasmin whispered. Tears began to trickle from her eyes in spite of her determined words.

Persia's head shook from side to side, and her hand clasped her grandmother's hand tightly. "She's not asleep, Tasmin. She's gone, really gone."

The permeating silence that engulfed the small *vardo* felt almost unnatural. Not a sound emitted from either of the girls for a few seconds, until at last Tasmin could not contain her sorrow any longer and a heart-wrenching cry tore from her lips. "Oh Persia, I am so sorry." She turned and embraced her friend as the two of them gave in to the deep torment they felt over Nanna's death. Kneeling beside the old woman whom they had both loved with such devotion, they cried until they had no more energy left for tears. Then the realization finally began to settle in Tasmin's mind as she began to think of what they had to do next.

"I must get Romalio."

Persia nodded in agreement as she took a quivering breath and wiped at the sheet of tears that blanketed her chapped cheeks. She did not utter a word when Tasmin left to fetch the king, but she was grateful for the few minutes she had to be alone with her grandmother. Once Romalio announced the old fortune-teller's death, Persia would not be granted any privacy in which to say her final good-byes to the woman who had been the only parent she had ever known. Persia did not remember her parents, since they had been killed in an accident when she was an infant. Her maternal grandmother had raised her ever since, so Nanna had been so much more than just her grandmother.

"Grandmother, how will I make it without you?" the girl whispered as she picked up the gnarled hand again. The heat of life was no longer evident in Nanna's body, and her hand felt cool in her granddaughter's fevered palm. Persia's swollen eyes filled with tears once again, but the hysteria of her grandmother's passing had subsided. A sense of calmness overcame the *vardo,* and Persia had a distinct feeling that her grandmother was finally where she had wanted to be . . . she was back in *Puro dem* again. As this thought passed through Persia's mind, the last of the candlewick fizzled out, leaving the *vardo* in complete darkness for an instant. Then, miraculously, the flame sparked again, shooting up several inches from the puddle of wax where just a second ago the fire had been extinguished. No fear invaded the girl when the strange phenomenon occurred, however, because she sensed this was her grandmother's way of telling her that she was now in a land where the flame of Gypsy fires burned eternal.

"Persia?" Romalio's tender voice broke into her quiet reverie. She glanced up at the king. A trembling smile rested on her lips and seemed misplaced on her swollen red face.

"She is in *Puro dem* now."

Through the glow of the flickering light that sparked from the candle holder where no candle remained to burn, Romalio and Tasmin exchanged sorrowful glances. Persia had been through so much agony lately, each of them worried that this latest tragedy would be more than she could bear.

"She is with Del," Romalio said in a quiet but firm tone as he reached down and helped Persia rise to her feet.

"Ei," the girl said. She could not disagree with the king, for she knew that her grandmother was with the Gypsy God. But she could not explain to anyone, not even herself, how she also knew that Nanna's spirit was back in *Puro dem*. As Romalio began to lead her out of the *vardo,* Persia glanced back over her shoulder at the candleholder. Only a tiny circle of wax remained in the bottom of the silver plate, yet a brilliant flame flared up from the ruins as if the candle had never burned away. She said nothing to the others; this was the last secret she would share with her grandmother.

Word of Nanna's death spread like wildfire through the small Gypsy caravan. By time the sun

222

had risen, a funeral procession was already under way. The knowledge that Persia had heard Nanna's last words of forgiveness, which had been meant for all those in the *familia,* relieved the fear that Nanna's ghost would return from the other side. Still, the passing of the beloved old fortune-teller was a heart-wrenching time for the Roms. As the oldest person in the tribe, she had attended the births of nearly everyone who belonged to this band of Gypsies, and she had also said the final rites at all the funerals over the past fifty years. The *Rawnie* would be greatly missed, and there was only one person who could possibly take her place as the tribal fortune-teller. But at this time, Persia's position among the tribe was still a matter of dispute.

A *diwanya*— a discussion between the males in the camp—was to be held on the day after Nanna's funeral to determine whether or not the two girls who had been held captive by the *gajo* should be branded as *marime*. The outcome of this important meeting would determine the course for the rest of Persia's and Savana's lives. Teril had avoided all contact with his wife, telling her that his strong devotion to their people's customs prevented him from touching her until he knew the decision, which would be made during the *diwanya*. The young bride had retreated into her bender tent, refusing to see or talk to anyone, especially Persia, whom she blamed for betraying their pact of secrecy.

Dressed in white, Tasmin and Persia sat in Nanna's *vardo,* awaiting the verdict of today's *diwanya*. They sipped tea from white china cups which Nanna had used only in times of mourning. The heat of the summer day was suffocating in the small quarters of the Gypsy wagon, but neither girl suggested going outside. Tasmin's tribal status was also being determined at the council, which was now in session in a specially-erected bender tent at the edge of the camp. Nanna's death had temporarily diverted everyone's attention from talk of the three young women temporarily, but the meeting could not be avoided any longer. Romalio understood Teril's anxiety concerning how recent events would affect his marriage, and he knew why Soobli was so eager to know his sister's status among the tribal members. Had it been left up to the king, however, the *diwanya* would not have taken place so soon after Nanna's death. He was tormented by his own conflicting emotions. Although he knew he could convince himself and the rest of the tribe that Tasmin had chased after the *gajo* only because she had felt guilty over the wounds she had inflicted on him, he also knew that he could not forget the way she had kissed him after she had been with the gunman. She had been taught how to kiss a man in a way that she had not learned from the king, and this realization enraged him. Yet at the same time, he yearned to forget about everything that had happened in the past few days and make a new start with Tasmin as his *Phuri dae,* just as he had always planned.

"Their decision today will not affect your future," Persia said nonchalantly. Her attitude since Nanna's death had taken on a strange aura of detachment, which worried and perplexed her friend.

"Of course it will," Tasmin said in defense. They had avoided talk of the last fortune Nanna had told, but it was inevitable that they would have to speak about it sooner or later.

"You will be gone before too much longer." She shrugged, then added, "Your life will not be guided by the Gypsy customs, so what will it matter?"

Tasmin stared at her childhood friend, feeling as if she barely knew the other girl anymore. She reminded herself of all the heartbreak and suffering forced upon Persia in the past few days. A weaker person could not have coped with so much tragedy, so Tasmin supposed Persia was entitled to act as cynical about the future as she wanted during this difficult time. "It is true that I must go after the *gajo*, but today's decision is still very important to me. I will always be a Gypsy, and I want to leave knowing that my people understand that I am not turning my back on my heritage. If they understand why I must go and do not hate me for it, then my leaving will not be quite as difficult." She reached out and laid her hand on Persia's arm. "Leaving behind those who I love will still be one of the most difficult things I will ever have to do. And you, my dear friend, will be the one I will miss most of all."

Persia shrugged once more, then moved her arm out from under the other girl's hand. She ran a white handkerchief over her perspiring brow as if Tasmin's words had not affected her in any manner. Then, without warning, her tough exterior cracked. She swung around and threw her arms around Tasmin's neck. "I can't bear the thought of being here without Nanna and you," she cried. "I don't care what the men decide today. Nothing will matter anymore once you are gone."

Tasmin clasped her arms around the other girl as relieved tears streamed down her face. She did not want to leave Persia behind thinking that their friendship had faded. "I don't want to leave you here," Tasmin said, her heart talking before her mind had a chance to digest this thought.

However, Persia immediately clasped the idea. "I'll come with you," she said as she pulled away from Tasmin. Her dark eyes glistened with tears and the excitement of the thought that had just occurred to her. "You should not travel alone, and I do not want to stay here. It is only logical that we go together."

Dumbfounded, Tasmin stared at her friend. The thought of traveling alone was terrifying, but she had complete faith in the fortune Nanna had foreseen. Someday she would be reunited with the *gajo,* and in spite of all the adversities in their lives, they would find happiness together. But what of Persia? Would she have any chance of making a life for herself in the *gajo* world? As this worry spun through Tasmin's mind, she hesitated in responding to Persia's suggestion.

"I guess it was a foolish idea," Persia said, a sound of rejection in her tone as her arms dropped away from Tasmin. "I would only be in the way once you find the *gajo.*"

"Oh, no!" Tasmin retorted, realizing that Persia

had misunderstood her uncertainty. "I would want nothing more than for us to be together. But once we leave here, we will also be leaving behind the only life we have ever known. I fear for my own safety in this strange land, and I also worry about yours."

For a second Persia did not reply. She knew Tasmin was sincere, and she understood her fears. The two of them, alone in the *gajo* world, was more terrifying than anything Persia could imagine. Recollections of the brutality she had suffered at the hands of the *gajo* flashed through her mind in vivid clarity and made her rethink her suggestion. But being in this *vardo* without her grandmother or her closest friend seemed almost as frightening.

"I can't stay here," she said in a hoarse voice. Her eyes moved away from Tasmin's face, traveling around the interior of the *vardo* that had been her home for all but the first few months of her life. The tiny home contained a lifetime of mementos from her grandmother, many older and almost as priceless as Nanna herself. Words could not describe how much it would hurt to leave behind all that was left of Nanna, but she would always carry her own memories of her grandmother in her heart, where nothing, or no one, could ever steal them away.

Before the young women had a chance to discuss the plan that had just began to form in their minds, a soft knock on the door diverted their attention. Their eyes met for an instant as the same thought passed through their minds; the *diwanya* was finished, and someone had come to relay the men's decision to them. The appearance of Romalio in the doorway confirmed their thoughts.

"It is finished?" Tasmin's voice was filled with apprehension as she moved toward him. Romalio nodded his dark head slowly at Tasmin, who felt a sudden need to be out of the suffocating wagon and back in the fresh air of the summer morning. Romalio backed out of the *vardo* and helped the princess down to the ground. As his hands encircled her tiny waist, a visible tremor shook through his body. He released her without meeting the eyes which he could feel gazing up at him and turned away quickly to repeat his gesture for the young fortune-teller who was about to climb down from the back of the *vardo*. He did both acts of kindness without a word, and his solemn expression caused both Tasmin and Persia to think the worst about the outcome of the *diwanya*.

"We have reached a decision, though it was not easy." His announcement increased the girl's fears, and when he glanced down at the ground as if he could not bring himself to look at them, they were both certain that they already knew what he was about to say. When his eyes lifted, his attention was directed at Persia. "I have already spoken to Savana," he said in a quiet voice. "She has accepted our decision better than I had hoped." He glanced away, his agony written clearly on his face. "The laws of our people are old and at times unfair. We," he motioned to the Gypsy camp that was spread out around him, "Are but a small *familia* whose very existence is threatened. All we have left is our heritage. If we lose this, we are nothing." Again he

228

lowered his gaze to the ground. His black, curly locks tumbled over his shoulders, shielding the sides of his face from view. The hat he usually wore on his head was absent, and his appearance lacked its meticulous grooming. The dark smudges under his eyes suggested that he had not slept throughout the long night that had proceeded today's *diwanya*.

"We are all *marime*," Tasmin stated in a flat tone of voice as her gaze traveled over the scattering of *vardos* and tents. She looked at no one in particular, even though most of the tribe had focused their attention on the king and the two young women. The decision made at the *diwanya* was already known throughout the small encampment, and a wide variety of emotions reined within everyone's thoughts. All of the young women whose lives were affected by today's events were loved by everyone, and there was not one person who did not wonder if the time had come to challenge some of the old Gypsy laws. Yet they all feared losing what was left of their people's traditions, which made the men's decision all the more difficult.

Romalio nodded, his words unable to escape from his dry lips. He kept his eyes to the ground, afraid that if he looked at the face of his beautiful princess he would lose the small amount of control he still possessed. Today he had fought the most vicious war he had ever encountered, and his heart had been the battleground. If he had decided to change all the laws, he knew his people would have consented. Soobli had pleaded with him to forgo the laws this time, but his sense of loyalty toward past generations of Roms guided his conscience and made the choice for him. At this moment, though, he despised all that he stood for, and as the pain of his decision washed through his aching being, he wished that he was strong enough to go against everything that his position represented. Yet there were others to consider, he reminded himself, others who had nothing but their pride toward their heritage left to sustain them in this cruel and selfish land.

The image of the promising future he had once envisioned for himself and the princess haunted Romalio's thoughts for a moment, but he forced them from his mind as he inwardly vowed that he would find a way to block those pictures from his mind . . . someday. Now, though, he needed to be alone to sort out the myriad of tormented thoughts that whipped through his overloaded mind. Most of all, he needed to get away from her, so that he could convince his shattered being that he had made the right choice for all his people, even though it was a choice that had torn him in two. He turned away, feeling as though the fragments of his broken heart were about to erupt from his chest.

Tasmin watched him walk away from her as a hundred different emotions pounded through her mind and body. Though she had known that their engagement had ended on the night of the *gajo's* arrival, she still held a special spot in her heart for the man whom had first claimed her devotion and love. Romalio would always remain in this special place in her heart, and now, as the reality of knowing their love was gone forever settled in Tasmin's burdened essence, she experienced such a sense of loss that she wondered if she would ever be able to recuperate from this pain. Still, she could not forget that Del had charted the *Drom* that she was to follow, and that this time in her life was merely a fork in the road. Someday this heartbreak would be only a painful memory, for soon she would take the first step that would begin her journey along the pre-ordained path that would lead her back to the green-eyed *gajo*.

Chapter Twenty-One

"Are you sure we have everything we need?"

Tasmin nodded her head, but still took the time to glance around the *vardo* once more. Their tapestry baggage and leather saddlebags were loaded with blankets, cooking utensils, food, and the few clothes they could stuff in along with the necessities. Outside, the last rays of the sun had just faded from the distant horizon, and as soon as the camp was deserted, the girls intended to begin their journey.

"Are you sure you're feeling up to traveling?" Tasmin asked her friend one more time. She worried that Persia had not recuperated long enough from her kidnapping ordeal and that all the riding they intended to do might be too much for her battered body. Although Gypsy medicine was strong and reliable, it had its limitations, too. Persia's outer bruises and cuts were healing rapidly, but Tasmin knew the wounds that were not visible were Persia's most serious ones.

The young fortuneteller gave her head a firm nod

and patted the heavy pouch that dangled from her saddlebags. "I'm fine, and I am taking all of Grandmother's secret ingredients with us in case either of us takes sick." She clasped her hand over her heart and shuddered. "But there is still much I have to learn about Gypsy medicine, and I fear that there are many ailments that I cannot cure."

"Let's hope we do not have to worry about that," Tasmin retorted, thinking that they had enough to fret over without thinking about sickness.

"Do you think we should make one more attempt to talk to Savana, and ask her if she wants to come with us?" A deep look of guilt furrowed her dark face as she turned toward her friend.

"No, I don't think we should," Tasmin replied, wishing that somehow she could convince her friend that Savana's attitude was selfish and unjust. Many times, she had tried to ease Persia's feelings of guilt, but to no avail. Persia was convinced that Savana was justified in hating her for her betrayal to the pact they had made, and Tasmin knew it would be useless to discuss the subject again. "I'm afraid she might interfere with our leaving, and I would rather that no one be aware of our plans because I don't want to see Romalio again. I don't think I could bear it." She cleared her throat and turned away, pretending that she was busy tying a bow in the long ends of the colorful scarf which was draped around her shoulders.

Persia did not try to induce her friend to speak about the pain she was feeling toward Romalio, but she hoped that soon Tasmin would be able to ease herself of the heartbreak she was suffering because of the king. It hurt Persia, too, to think of the agony that Romalio was in at this time, but she could not help him. Because she was *marime,* he would not be allowed to speak to her. A shooting pain burned through Persia every time she thought of how much they were all losing because of the ancient laws regarding purity and sin. Only a few days ago, everyone in this small *familia* had been so close to one another that there was nothing they would have not done to help each other. Now, because of circumstances that no one could have changed or controlled, their lives had been thrown into turmoil and despair. Tasmin had been right when she had said the old customs were silly and foolish, and Nanna had also been right when she had said that they could never be changed.

From the main fire, a violin and a dulcimer began to play a melody that was as ancient as the timeless Gypsy customs. Both girls turned their attention toward the music. *"Le Rakli Kai Barili Ando Lulojai,"* Tasmin said, her voice choked with emotion. Over five hundred years old, *The Girl Who Grew Up in a Flower* was Tasmin's favorite song. She had danced to this tune hundreds of times, but she knew she would never dance to its beautiful chords again.

Persia placed her hand on her friend's back, but because of the complex emotions she was experiencing, she did not feel adequate to the task of consoling Tasmin during her time of confusion and trouble. She knew that Tasmin's pain was a mixture of guilt because of Romalio, and the uncertainty of her feelings for the *gajo.* All through the years, when

234

they had been growing up, they had been told by Nanna and every other Gypsy woman that they should never be friendly with non-Gypsy men. *"Rom Romesa, Gajo Gajesa,"* the women would warn. "Gypsy with Gypsy, gentile with gentile." Stories of Roms who had defied this custom usually ended in tales of tragedy, and although Tasmin's fortune spoke of love and happiness with her green-eyed *gajo,* Persia could not help but to wonder how long it would be, and how much she would have to suffer before this would be within Tasmin's grasp. "Someday, you will dance again for the *gajo.* "

"Yes," Tasmin answered in a whispered tone. "But never again around Gypsy fires."

No retort came from Persia. How could she dispute the truth? After tonight, the Gypsy princess would forsake all that was associated with her past, and her royal heritage . . . After tonight, Gypsy fires would be extinguished forever.

"We should go now," Persia said when the music had ceased and the camp had grown silent outside the *vardo.* They planned to ride at night, hoping the darkness would be safer for two females traveling alone. During the day, they would seek shelter and rest. Their ultimate destination was unknown, but they were headed south. When Persia and Savana had encountered the *gajo* at the creek on their return to the Gypsy camp, he had been south of where Tasmin had parted company with him. Both girls knew of the huge *gajo* city San Francisco, and though the idea of entering this enemy-infested area was terrifying, they knew this was where their search for Blayde Chandler would begin.

Tasmin picked up her bags and clutched them to her breast as she took one last look around Nanna's *vardo.* How she missed the *Rawnie* already, and how she would miss this little wagon where she had lived for the past five years! She blinked but could not halt the single tear that escaped from her ebony eyes as she hurried from the *vardo.* She waited outside for Persia, knowing that it would be even harder for her friend to leave the *vardo* for the final time. Her eyes kept being drawn toward the direction of her brother's *vardo,* where she knew her tiny niece and nephew slept. If only she could see them one more time, just to hold them and tell them of how she would always love them. But this was not possible. Earlier today, she had tried to speak to them, but after the *diwanya,* Soobli had issued orders to everyone in the camp that his sister was to be kept away from his *chavvies.* When she had started to approach Danso and Cyri, they had been hustled away from her by Nura. Tasmin recalled Nanna's vision of how Nura and Giorgio would eventually raise the *chavvies,* and though it saddened her to think that they would not be raised by their own blood kin, she also knew that Vilo's parents would be good to her niece and nephew. There was nothing she could do for the youngsters now anyway, and it would have to be enough just to know that they would be taken care of after she was gone. Still, she would always wish that she had been able to say good-bye to them.

Her own torment was interrupted when Persia did finally emerge from the back of the wagon. Her sorrow was evident by the glassy sheet of tears that coated her gaze, which were visible even in the darkness of the night. Neither of the girls spoke as they quietly made their way through the sleeping encampment. Each of them was engrossed in poignant and painful thoughts of their life among the wandering Roms, and of the happy memories that they would treasure in their hearts for all time.

At the edge of the campsite where the Gypsies had bedded down their herd, Tasmin and Persia paused to mull over their next move. They each needed a horse, and it was imperative that the mounts they chose be able to keep up with a fast pace. At the last farm where they had picked grapes, the tribe had been cheated out of over a hundred dollars that the farmer had promised as payment for their labors. A sturdy Arabian mare had been acquired for their herd when the *gajo* had refused them their money. It was this horse that Tasmin chose for her own, while Persia unhobbled a pinto; both horses could endure long distances without water and would not tire easily.

The women's movements were cautious but hurried, for each of them felt a sense of urgency at beginning this strange journey on which they were destined to embark. But as they started to lead the horses away from the Gypsy camp, a low, barely audible voice rang out through the tense air.

"So ceres le grastesas?"

Tasmin and Persia gasped as they swung around toward the source of the voice. The night afforded them with only an outline of the man, but they both knew that it was Soobli who staggered toward them and whose slurred voice had asked them what they

237

were doing with the horses. Tasmin slid from her horse's back and approached her brother as quickly and quietly as she could manage. If he woke up the entire tribe, their departure would not go as planned. Her eyes immediately sought Romalio's *vardo,* which was dark and silent. Once she was close to her brother, though, the fury that shrouded his face made Tasmin cringe. *"San mato akano,"* she said, accusing him of being drunk. An obvious state, since he was barely able to stand up without wobbling from side to side.

"And y—you are a horse thief," he spat back at her through clenched teeth. His raven eyes flashed with light as he swayed forward. With his face only inches from his sister's, he could see the fear in her expression. A wicked smile curved his mouth with this realization, and it grew even more sinister when he noticed her panic increase as they stared at one another in the dim glow of the Gypsy moonlight.

"Please, Soobli, just let us go in peace." Tasmin attempted to reason with him, but she knew it was a wasted effort in his drunken state.

A crude snicker escaped from deep in his throat. Did she think that she could run away and start a new life, when she had just destroyed *his* entire life? His cold gaze raked over her trembling form, the chilling smile still intact as he reached out and roughly grabbed her chin between his forefingers. The pain and terror that flooded through her face made him elated. "Princess Lovell," he said, then spat at her, spraying her face with his spittle. "You are not worthy to wipe my feet. You are worse than a *gajo."* His last comment was the lowest of reproach for a Gypsy; being considered worse than a *gajo* meant that you were nothing.

Tasmin jerked away from his pinching hold on her chin and ran the sleeve of her blouse over her face to wipe away his spit. Persia was already at her side, and clutched at her arm in an attempt to pull her away from the crazed man. "He is dangerous," Persia cried, remembering the vision that had flashed through her mind of Soobli trying to prevent his sister from fulfilling her destiny.

The princess's attention remained focused on her brother, although she did not ignore Persia's warning. If Soobli had not been so drunk, she might have tried to reason with him, and for her mother's sake, she would have liked to make peace with him before their final parting. But now she wanted only to get away before he became even more vicious, and before Romalio and the others became aware of any disturbance. For an instant she allowed her eyes to ascend and lock with the brutal gaze of her brother. Like everything else in this camp, she knew she was looking at him for the last time. If only she could have seen a spark of humanity in his savage gaze, but only selfish contempt lurked within his flashing stare, and it was this cruel image she would carry with her for the rest of her life.

"*Del O Del baxt, Prala.*" In spite of the hatred that he held for her, Tasmin wished for her brother God's luck as her final words. She twirled around and pulled herself onto the back of her Arabian once again before Soobli's liquor-laden body could make another move toward her.

"*Aven!*" Persia called out. "They're coming!,"

239

she repeated, in a voice that rose with hysteria as she motioned toward the camp with a frantic wave of her arm. While the two girls swung onto the bare backs of their mounts, Persia was overcome with a sense of victory. She realized that they had outsmarted the fates that had threatened to block the *Drom* which they were meant to travel on this humid summer's eve.

Tasmin, however, made the mistake of looking back over her shoulder in the same instant that she spurred her horse and sent him flying out into the darkness beyond the Gypsy camp. Along with the image she would take with her of her brother's venomous wrath, she would also carry forever in her heart her last glimpse of the Gypsy king as he ran toward her in the pale moonlight. On his tortured face was a crucifying look of unrequited love, and for a fleeting instant Tasmin thought of reining her horse and running back into Romalio's outstretched arms. But in a flash he was gone from her view, and she had time only to concentrate on clinging to the back of her horse as the animal streaked through the black forest, and toward a future which had only been glimpsed in old cards and murky tea leaves . . . a future that could prove as dark as the night that loomed over this foreign land.

Chapter Twenty-Two

Blayde Chandler eased his stiff body down into the tepid water, sighed, and leaned back against the smooth, cool porcelain tub. He couldn't remember the last time he'd had a real bath; a quick dip in a murky pond or river didn't count. But a bathtub was an indescribable luxury for a man who spent most of his time in a saddle, and Blayde planned to enjoy this extravagance for as long as possible. His eyes closed as his mind wandered back over the past few days . . . beginning with the first moment when he had glimpsed the dancer spinning through the orange glow of the campfire. In his imprisoned mind, he could see her red dress twirling around her shapely legs, could envision her flashing ebony gaze as clearly as if she were here in this room now. He had vowed that he would not permit himself to dwell on the memory of the Gypsy after they had parted company in the forest. But his mind refused to be cooperative, and she constantly traipsed through his thoughts as if she had been invited.

The bounty hunter shook his auburn head with annoyance and sat up in the tub. Couldn't he have a moment's peace from that witch's spell? How far away did he have to run to escape her sorcery? In anger, he grabbed the towel which hung at the side of the tub and tossed it across the room. To be distracted by anything or anyone was dangerous to a man in his profession. And to allow himself to squander precious time remembering a woman he would never see again was even more foolish. He stared at the towel, now heaped in a pile at the far wall, while his mind began to paint a picture of the Gypsy's red dress falling to the ground around her satiny limbs.

"Witch!" he growled. Would she never leave him alone? He sought penance—and escape from the dark-eyed visage—by summoning Emma's memory. But to his horror, he found that the features of her lovely face grew more vague each time he sought her memory. How powerful must be the Gypsy's evil magic, that she could replace Emma's image with her own, for it was Tasmin's face which his mind unveiled without a moment's pause.

"Forgive me, Emma," he said, shaking his head in a vain attempt to clear the empassioned visions which danced before his eyes. "She could never take your place; no woman could." In annoyance he quickly washed his long reddish-brown hair and scrubbed his body with vigorous motions that did nothing to ease his frustrations. He then rose from the tub, his much-awaited bath now ruined because of that witch's interference. Water dripped from the tips of his long hair and rivulets ran down his taunt frame as he stepped over the high, curved sides of the tub and walked across the room to retrieve his towel. As he dried himself, he was careful not to touch the knife wounds that still marred his shoulder and gun hand. It was amazing to him how fast the injuries were healing, though, and this served to fuel his belief that the Gypsies used something unnatural in their medicines. In just a few days' time the wound in his shoulder no longer caused him pain, and he was already able to bend his hand and move all his fingers. However, he knew he was not ready to use the hand for a fast draw, and for the first time in three years he wished he had just a little more time before he faced Ben McCalister.

After draping the damp towel over the side of the tub, Blayde carefully bandaged his wounds with small dressings that would not inhibit his movements. When this tedious task was finished, he walked to the bureau, where, spread out on the top, was an assortment of shaving supplies and toiletries. A quick swipe of the razor at the river's edge was his usual routine for shaving, but today he planned to take time to tend to his grooming—that is, if the witch would leave him alone long enough so that he could lavish the extra attention on himself. Naked, he stood before the bureau and observed his image in the oval mirror which hung on the wall. He was thirty-one years old and only a few fine lines mapped the area around his eyes, but they were not visible unless he smiled, and he rarely smiled these days. Picking up the comb that lay on the bureau, he

243

began to comb his long, straight hair back away from his face. Wet, the dark auburn strands hung several inches past his shoulders. Although many gunfighters tended to grow their hair to longer lengths, Blayde did not wear his hair in this style to fit an image. He had not bothered with a haircut merely because his appearance was the least of his concerns lately. Today, however, was different.

Hair combed and face clean-shaven, Blayde eyed himself in the mirror again. Emma used to exaggerate about his good looks, but he was not blind to his appeal to women. He remembered how she would tease him about being so handsome that it took no more than a glance from his twinkling green gaze to make her grow weak-kneed and fevered. The memory brought a poignant smile to his lips. But the handsome face that encased the emerald green eyes which had once been lit with a mischievous sparkle and were the talk of all the women in El Paso lacked the devilish charm it once had. Women still took notice when the gunman sauntered into a room. But the cold, bitter aura which emitted from him now made women leery of the handsome stranger. This suited Blayde, because until recently he'd had no interest in women anyway. Only the Gypsy—Tasmin—had managed to put a crack in the hard shell that he had erected around his wounded heart.

"Tasmin," he said to his reflection in the mirror. Why did her name seem to taste like sweet honey on a hot day as it rolled over his tongue? His taunting mind answered him—Gypsy Witch!

His jaw squared; his thick auburn brows furrowed into straight lines over his narrowed eyes. Surely her spell would wear off soon, or so he hoped as he turned away from the mirror and strode to where his new clothes were spread out on the bed quilt. The sinewy muscles in his back rippled like a fine-tuned machine as he reached out and picked up the white shirt, gingerly slipping it over his freshly-bandaged hand and shoulder. With his other hand he fastened the pearlized buttons which ran down the front, then added pearl cuff links to the buttonholes in the material that encircled his wrists. He did not bother to don underwear before he slipped his long legs into the black jeans he had purchased when he had first arrived in town. Carefully he tucked the shirttails into the waistband. Then, when he was satisfied that the garment was not bunched up around his lean middle, he fastened the brass snaps. A narrow black belt was then drawn through the belt loops, even though his snug-fitting jeans did not need the belt to secure them. It was vital that his appearance be impeccable today.

He worked the bottoms of his pants over the tall tops of his shiny black boots, then picked up the black suede vest that still lay on the bed. With the garment slung over his arm, he went back to the bureau and hung the vest from a top knob of the dresser drawer. His attention was then focused on the black silk scarf that was spread out at one end of the bureau. Although he took special care to wrap the scarf around his neck and to tie it just right, when he finished, the knot hung to the side of his neck and the long ends draped over his shoulder in a careless manner, which was the exact effect he was striving to achieve. Next, he slipped into the vest, leaving the front unbuttoned and the white shirt peeking out starkly from in between the dark suede.

From the bedpost he retrieved his black gunbelt and holster. He positioned the belt so that his gun hung slightly to the front of his leg before he tied the thin leather strap around his muscled thigh to ensure that the holster would not move when he walked or drew his pistol in a sudden gesture. Over the entire outfit he donned a black jacket which hung past the gun on his thigh and hugged his broad shoulders and lean waist with precise measure, as if the garment had been specially designed for his muscular form. Only his wide-brimmed black hat remained to complete the ensemble. He moved to the bureau again and gazed into the mirror as he slicked back his hair with his fingers, then placed the hat on his head, tilting the brim at an angle that sat low on his forehead.

He stood back, scrutinizing his appearance. Once, he had represented all that was good and just; now he was the epitome of a killer. Perhaps after today, though, The Prosecutor would finally close the file on his last case.

A knock on the door snapped Blayde from his thoughts of vengeance and immediately drew his hand to the handle of his Colt .45. He felt a dull throb in his palm, but fortunately the ache was not severe enough to keep his hand immobile, even though he still lacked his previous speed. But now he could not worry about his limitations. "Who's there?" he called out as he moved to the side of the doorway, poised, his gun aimed face-level at the closed door.

"Sheriff Balhorn."

Blayde hesitated for a moment, taking the time to recall his last encounter with this man. He had traveled through San Francisco twice before, and each time he had sought a reward for the outlaws he had brought in, three men all together—two dead and one mortally wounded. Balhorn had been amicable, but his attitude toward bounty hunters was typical of the one most lawmen harbored toward men like Blayde Chandler. Bounty hunters walked a precarious line with the law. Many of them were outlaws themselves who had been pardoned from their crimes or had already served time. Since they knew the workings of the criminal mind, their choice of career was logical. But men who made their living tracking other men also had a free rein when it came to murder, and this was a freedom that most lawmen did not condone.

Without holstering his gun, Blayde turned the key in the lock and allowed the door to open. He waited to the side of the door until the other man was in plain sight and he could be certain the man was who he claimed to be. The sheriff showed no surprise to find a gun pointed in his direction, and he merely gave his head a slow nod. "You can put that away now."

Blayde imitated the lawman's gesture, nodding slowly, then slipping his weapon back into its holster

247

in one smooth movement. "Sheriff?" he said as he stepped back to permit the man to enter the room.

"I reckon you know why I'm here."

"I do."

The lawman nodded again, his gaze sizing up the other man in a slow observation. Dressed in black— dressed for death, the sheriff said to himself. He knew this man's reputation well, and knew about the past, too. He reckoned he might feel the same way if it happened to his family. Still, he had a job to do, too, and he would feel a whole lot better when Blayde Chandler was no longer around. "He's not here," the sheriff stated.

"I know he is."

Sheriff Balhorn shrugged in a nonchalant manner, but inwardly he was beginning to grow nervous. His previous encounters with Chandler had been occasions which had not concerned the McCalister gang. The sheriff had known even then how dangerous the bounty hunter was, but now that Chandler thought that he was about to close in on the man he had been chasing for three years, the lawman saw an even more deadly side of him. There was a chilling glint in the green eyes, one he had not noticed before. The sheriff felt as if he was staring at a wild animal who was crouched and ready for the kill.

"McCalister rode out sometime during the night." A weak feeling overcame the sheriff when he observed the fury that masked the other man's face. He only hoped Chandler would not make him the object of his rage. The lawman was fast on the draw, but he knew he was no match for the bounty hunter's gun hand.

For an instant Blayde's anger threatened to steal away his senses. He had known McCalister was in town last night; he had tracked him to the brothel down the street. Disgusted, Blayde had observed the outlaw through a window as he had staggered up the stairs with the help of his female companion. Blayde had seen him disappear into one of the upstairs rooms, but he would have been willing to bet that McCalister had been too drunk even to perform with the whore he was with, and because of this had decided that it would be a wasted effort to call him out for a showdown.

Blayde had not seen any of the other gang members, figuring they were either in other rooms somewhere in the whorehouse, or in any of the numerous saloons which lined the streets of San Francisco. They had to be lurking somewhere nearby, though, because McCalister never traveled without his pack of killers at his side. Still, Blayde thought that he had been careful not to be seen by anyone, and he had even registered under a false name when he had checked into this room in the early morning hours so that he could ready himself for the showdown he had been certain would come before this day was through. Obviously one of McCalister's men had spotted him, or someone had tipped them off that he was in town, and they had gotten themselves and their drunken boss out of town before the sun had risen this morning.

"Damn it!" Blayde growled. His uninjured hand

drew into a tight fist and raised up as if he was going to punch something—anything or anyone—but then he managed to corral his fury before he lost all self-control. So close . . . again! He should have marched into that whorehouse last night and put a bullet right between McCalister's beady eyes. But no, he had waited, wanting to show the scum just how good he had become with his gun; he had wanted to see the outlaw's smug expression melt into fear and defeat as he slumped to the ground to meet his death.

"Damn it!" he shouted again as he twirled around and stalked to the window. From his hotel room he could see the building where he had observed McCalister last night. It was the closest he had been to the man in three years—since the day he had broken out of the El Paso jail and murdered his family. But as he had glimpsed him through the window, Blayde had marveled at how little the outlaw had changed through the years. Even drunk, McCalister still managed to evince an aura of irreproachable virtue that had always made Blayde bristle ever since the first moment he had seen the man's smiling face on a Wanted poster. Blayde was aware of how drastically his own appearance had altered in the past few years. Where once he had been the image of a dignified, well-dressed man, and his handsome, well-groomed features conveyed the gentle life he lived, Blayde now had a face as rugged and worn as the rough backroads he traveled night and day. It had taken him an hour just to scrub off the trail dirt and shave the long, scraggly whiskers

250

that sprouted from his weathered face. Until he had stopped at a store on the other side of town yesterday to purchase the new outfit, his only clothes had been the dust-creased duds that he had worn for the past several months with only an occasional wash in the river.

McCalister, though, appeared to be no worse for wear. Last night he had been garbed in a fancy suit of brown linen, not new, but pressed and immaculate on his small, lean form. His dark blond hair was cut short and neatly combed behind his ears. A trimmed beard of the same shade of blond rimmed his chin from ear to ear and was joined at the corners of his mouth by a perfectly-shaped mustache. Twinkling blue eyes, though glazed from liquor, had crinkled with laughter as he had flirted with the whore who had caught his interest. Blayde had always thought the outlaw looked like a Mormon preacher, and perhaps this was one of the many traits that had initially outraged him so much about the killer. How could a man who could murder so many people with such little conscience appear so innocent and kindly? It was a deceitful facade that never faltered, for even as McCalister was about to snuff out a life, he always managed to put a sincere-looking smile on his shining face and a glint of humor in his blue gaze which made his victims feel as though at any moment he would embrace them rather than slaughter them.

Blayde wiped the image of the ruthless killer from his mind as his rage returned with renewed intensity, and all directed at himself. How could he have been so stupid as to let McCalister slip through his fingers again? The murderer had never engaged in a fair fight in his life. Why had Blayde felt an obligation to grant him this advantage now? Next time, he vowed, nothing would stop him from killing the scum, regardless of the circumstances.

Sheriff Balhorn made no attempt to converse with the man until his anger had subsided. He had never seen a man's face fill with such hatred, and he hoped that when Chandler did catch up to McCalister, they would be far away from San Francisco. He jumped when the gunfighter turned suddenly and focused his cold, emerald gaze in his direction.

"What way did they ride?"

"S—s—south, I figure."

"Why's that?"

Balhorn shrugged, while trying to regain his composure. "Red Eye got a late start. Reckon he was too busy in one of them rooms over there," he motioned toward the window, indicating the bawdy house down the street before adding, "He didn't head out till around dawn. One of my deputies followed him out of town."

"He was the only one anyone saw leave?"

The sheriff rubbed his jaw in a thoughtful manner, then gave his head a positive nod. The same deputy had also alerted him to the bounty hunter's arrival. How McCalister and his men had been warned, the sheriff did not know. His only certainty was that he would not breathe easily until he knew that this man was gone, too.

"I suppose my business here is finished, then,"

Blayde said, his bandaged gun hand unconsciously twitching at his side.

The sheriff's gaze was drawn to the unnatural movement of the man's hand as he once again nodded in agreement. The knot in his chest kept him from answering with any sense of coherence.

Blayde began to gather his gear, oblivious to the man who stood nearby. When he was ready to leave, he did not bother to speak to the lawman, never even glanced in the man's direction again. His thoughts were consumed with an urgency that could not tolerate the minor details of common courtesy. He would not allow McCalister to get away from him again. His time to collect on past debts was running out.

Chapter Twenty-Three

Blayde knew which trail to follow out of San Francisco; he had traveled this route before. The least traveled path was the one always chosen by McCalister and his men, and as Blayde studied the faint trace of hoofs in the dust, he could tell that several horses had passed through this area recently. They were still moving southward, but Blayde had a feeling their destination was Texas. McCalister had been away from his homeland for almost a year now, and he always migrated back to his familiar stomping grounds when he grew bored of terrorizing other areas of the country.

He knew his theory was correct when the trail he was following turned inland a few miles out of San Francisco and headed southeast, toward Nevada. As Blayde began to lead Eclipse away from the shoreline, he experienced the same odd sensations that he always felt when he knew he was headed home again. Although he had been in parts of Texas, the bounty hunter had not been back to El Paso for three years. It appeared McCalister purposely avoided that area, and for this Blayde Chandler was grateful. Every time he was anywhere in Texas again, it always brought back a flood of memories in the life he had once lived as a lawyer, father and husband. But now he felt an even stranger range of emotions as he thought of leaving California, alien feelings of regret and yearning that increased as each step of Eclipse's hooves took him farther away from the Gypsy . . . the witch whose spell seemed to grow stronger as time passed. Every mile that he traveled added to the finality of their parting, especially since he knew that her people had been headed to the north, while he continued to move in the opposite direction.

Blayde tried to push the hauntingly beautiful image of the dancer from his mind, but as usual, she managed to possess him completely. He still did not understand his own feelings toward the young sorceress, and he was certain he never would. She had bewitched him, but eventually he would forget her, or so he told himself over and over again . . . each time her dark, mysterious visage teased him with her memory. *Tasmin,* his inner voice called out again and again, and Blayde knew that he would never be able to escape from her spell completely. Her magic was too powerful and he was too weak from longings that he was forced to deny.

The sun was high over the Californian country-side when Blayde drew a tight rein on Eclipse and stopped to study the lone figure who rode through the gully below the crest of the hill where he was riding. Even with the glare of the midday sun upon the man's back, Blayde knew at once that the man was Red Eye. He was surprised to see that the outlaw had not caught up to the rest of his murderous cohorts, but because Red Eye was alone, Blayde's hopes of encountering McCalister before nightfall were dimmed. Obviously McCalister had ridden hard and fast when he had fled San Francisco, a mixed blessing for Blayde, since he was so obsessed with catching the outlaw. But he knew that the added time would aid in the healing of his gunhand. This turn of events, however, was a spate of bad luck for Red Eye. The bounty hunter smiled to himself as he watched the outlaw's horse meander through the draw. Next to McCalister himself, Red Eye was the most ruthless of the outlaw gang. Without his right-hand man to back him up, McCalister's defenses would be weakened considerably, and after tonight, Blayde had no doubt that Red Eye would no longer be a threat to anyone. In a moment of shocked revelation, Blayde became aware of his own behavior and quickly wiped the savage smile from his face. He had become too much like McCalister, he realized as the thought made a bitter taste rise up in his throat and settle in his mouth.

From the ridge, the gunman knew he could take aim and finish off the outlaw with one bullet. But as he had proved last night, when he could have shot McCalister through the whorehouse window, that was not Blayde's style. Though he hated to admit it to himself, he had begun to crave the danger of a showdown with his prey. He almost enjoyed the look of fear that contorted their faces when at the final second they realized that they had been outdrawn. Of course, he told himself that he was only being fair by inducing his opponents into a gunfight, and this is what he was telling himself now, as he swung down from Eclipse and positioned himself at the edge of the cliff.

"Red Eye," he called out in a victorious tone. A rush of excitement charged through his veins when the outlaw swung around. Even from a distance, Blayde caught a glimpse of the terror that flooded through the man's face. The bounty hunter was overwhelmed by his good fortune at finding this man alone. Together, Red Eye and McCalister might have been his downfall, but now, his confidence in fulfilling his final quest only expanded and fueled his courage. Blayde began to move down the slope of the hillside with long, pantherlike strides. His lean body was slouched, his arms held out to his sides, and his eyes fixed solidly on the outlaw's face.

Red Eye remained unmoving in his saddle, almost as if he was hypnotized by the unwavering stare of the approaching gunman. The look on Chandler's face did not seem human as he stalked down the hillside, and Red Eye felt as if he was glimpsing Hades as the man drew closer. He told himself he should kick his horse in the sides and make a run for his life, but he couldn't move. His eyes could not look away from the black-clad figure who now stood only several yards away. The band of outlaws had managed to elude the bounty hunter for so long now, that Red Eye had allowed himself to grow careless. He now realized he had made a deadly mistake by not leaving town with the rest of the gang, who had snuck out in the wee hours of the morning.

Since he had not been this close to The Prosecutor for three years, Red Eye was taken aback by the visible change in the lawyer. But it was more than just the man's toughened exterior which threw him off guard. Outwardly, and inwardly, the bounty hunter emitted a sense of doom, and it was this aura of death that surrounded the man, which made Red Eye too shaken to make a move to defend himself.

"Get down off that horse," Chandler said in his slow drawl. His brow cocked slightly above one emerald eye as a sinister grin unconsciously curled his lips. He felt his hand throb beneath the bandage, but not because it was hurting; it was the worry of knowing that at any second the hand would move into action.

Red Eye continued to stare at him, his eyes never wavering from the man's face. He, too, was a skilled gunman, and he knew that the eyes told more than the gunhand. This knowledge told him that Chandler would not draw until he had dismounted and presented him with a fair fight. But the outlaw was not concerned with fairness. He only wanted the Prosecutor out of his life for good. His boss, Ben McCalister, would be indebted to him forever if he finished off this troublesome man once and for all. For a second, however, Red Eye felt his fear return. What if he was wrong about the lawyer's sense of humanity? The outlaw decided this was a chance he had to take as his hand flew down to his gun. His only thought as he tumbled from the saddle was that he had been wrong.

Blayde did not even think about his actions; drawing his gun was more reflex than premeditated movement. His trained vision had seen the change in Red Eye's gaze, a barely noticeable glint that had filtered through his eyes at the same instant that he had gone for his gun. Still, the bounty hunter's hand had been swiftest, and his aim fatal. The bullet hit the outlaw in the throat, spraying blood out from the bullet hole like a ruptured dam. He hit the hard ground with a loud thud, twitched spastically, then remained unmoving, face down at his horse's hooves.

For several minutes, Blayde did not move either. His mind had traveled back through the years again, with tormenting visions of Emma falling to the ground beside her flowerbed. Years ago, the outlaws had bragged of how Red Eye had terrorized Emma, smacking her around and fondling her, before McCalister had done the actual slaying with a bullet to her head. A raging anger overcame him—Red Eye had died too easy, too fast. Ben McCalister would not have it so easy! he vowed as the smoke rose up from his gun, hitting his flaring nostrils and reminding him of the house where his young son had been burned alive.

With a cautious approach, he walked over to where the outlaw laid in the dirt. He never trusted an opponent's death until he was certain he was not being tricked. The amount of blood which soaked the ground around Red Eye's body eased Blayde's suspicions. Yet, he still took the extra precaution of keeping his gun aimed at the other man's head until he had rolled him over with a kick of his booted foot.

Red Eye gazed up at him with a sightless stare and a silent scream on his parted lips. Below his chin, a perfectly round hold drilled through his jugular vein, where a trickle of scarlet blood still oozed out and dribbled down the sides of his neck.

Blayde stared at him for several minutes as an odd sensation overcame him. The end truly was drawing near, of this he had no doubt. But once, he had wanted the end to come only so that he could join Emma and Timmy. The new and conflicting emotions which had been induced by the Gypsy dancer made him feel guilty and selfish. He longed more than ever to put his gnawing revenge behind him, but now he realized that there was another quest that he must fulfill before he was ready to leave this world . . . an obsession he must quench, or was it a spell he could not break?

After tying Red Eye's body on the back of his horse, Blayde debated over whether or not he should continue to travel in the same direction as he was going when he had encountered the outlaw, or if he should return the man's body to San Francisco. The bounty hunter pulled several tattered, yellow papers from his saddlebags and thumbed through the pages. Thoughtfully, he eyed what remained of an old Wanted poster. Red Eye was worth a thousand dollars—dead or alive—and this poster was almost three years old. Since the gang had never ceased their murderous tirades over the years, the reward on the killer's head might be even more by now.

A thoughtful expression brought a slight frown to Blayde's freshly-shaven face. He still wore his suit of black and only a light layering of dust on his new clothes disturbed the polished appearance he had strived to achieve this morning when he had been in the hotel room. Glancing down again at the torn and faded poster he held in his hand, then out toward the barren hillsides that loomed before him, Blayde made a decision. For miles ahead of him there lay only a scattering of little towns where he might spend days waiting for the reward money on Red Eye's corpse. But he knew he would be able to collect his money from Sheriff Balhorn right on the spot, and in the long run, he would save time. A few days ago, the money would not have mattered; catching up with the rest of the gang would have been the important thing to Blayde. But again he was aware of the sudden change that suddenly had taken rule of his actions and thoughts. For a reason he could not explain to himself once again, he felt that he had to return to San Francisco. Something—or someone— was drawing him back, and the call was too strong for him to ignore.

Chapter Twenty-Four

The two dark-skinned girls tried to appear nonchalant as they reined their horses at the hitching post outside the sheriff's office. However, it was impossible to ignore the stares and the snide comments which came from the curious gathering of onlookers. Roms always aroused attention whenever they entered a non-Gypsy settlement, and the pair of beautiful young women who had ridden into town alone drew more than a mild interest from the crowd, especially the rowdy cowpokes and drunken sailors who roamed the San Francisco streets. Although the sheriff's office was not close to the waterfront, where the roughest part of the city was rapidly acquiring an infamous reputation, there were still plenty of saloons and bawdy houses in this section, as well as an array of respectable businesses.

Tasmin tossed her head back defiantly, refusing to act ashamed or humble, in spite of the rude comments that were being tossed back and forth by the men who were huddled nearby. A group of haughty-acting women, dressed in the latest fashions, chartered a wide path around the two Gypsies as they made their way down the street. From behind lace handkerchiefs, as if they were afraid of contacting germs, they whispered to one another as they hurried past the girls. Tasmin returned their raking stares, letting her own gaze travel up and down their bodies in the same intimidating way they were scrutinizing her. She noticed the scarlet flushes that rose up in their pale cheeks, but she was determined not to be affected by their snooty attitude.

"I don't think coming here was a good idea," Persia whispered as she clasped Tasmin's arm. She was not as brave or strong as Tasmin, and the men's rude comments and the debasing behavior of the women had left her embarrassed and frightened.

Refusing to give in to her own feelings of uncertainty and fear, Tasmin shook her head in a defiant manner. But unconsciously she took the time to smooth down the long strands of her ebony hair that cascaded from the scarf she wore on her head and hung over her shoulders and down to her waist. She straightened the black satin *jodka* apron she wore over her tiered skirt before she realized how foolish she was behaving. Their appearance would not affect the outcome of her mission in this *gajo* village, so why was she wasting time primping when they needed to finish their business and be on their way as soon as possible?

"The sheriff is the only one who might be able to help us," Tasmin said in an annoyed tone of voice, although it was herself she was angry with. "Maybe

he will know if the green-eyed *gajo* has been here."
She pulled the other girl along with her as she made
her way to the doorway of the lawman's office.
Before she had a chance to turn the doorknob,
though, the door swung open. Tasmin's eyes met
with the shining badge that flashed from his breast,
then slowly rose until she was looking directly into
the frowning countenance of the lawman.

Sheriff Balhorn had just settled down for an
afternoon nap when the disturbance outside his
office woke him. His habit was to take a quick
snooze in the late afternoon so that he would be
ready for the toughest part of his job, the nighttime,
when danger lurked around every corner. Knowing
that the McCalister gang, as well as Blayde
Chandler, were gone from his town made the sheriff
rest much easier, and he was filled with annoyance
that he had been bothered again. When he pulled the
door open, he was surprised that all the hullabaloo
was caused by the arrival of two young female
Gypsies. He stared at them with a perplexed look for
an instant before he glared over their heads at the
leering men who crowded around his doorway.

"Get outa here," he growled, and waved his hand
through the air.

For a moment, Tasmin and Persia thought that he
meant for them to leave. They huddled together and
stepped backward. But before they made another
move, the sheriff returned his attention to the
Gypsies. He didn't have much use for Gypsies; it
seemed they always managed to get into some sort of
trouble whenever they passed through the area. He
had never set eyes on these young women, though,

and he suspected that for them to brave riding into town alone, they must have good reason.

"You two," he said as a deep scowl possessed his face. "Come on in here." He stepped back and motioned for the Gypsies to enter his office. His annoyance visibly increased when they cringed away from him again instead of coming forward. "Well, do you want to see me or not?" he demanded in a loud voice.

Tasmin's fear of the man began to be replaced by her own annoyance. She had just vowed that she would not allow herself to be intimidated by any of the *gajo* in this town, and already she had broken that pledge by letting the sheriff scare the wits out of her. She straightened her trembling form and tossed her head back again. "I wish to speak to you," she replied, gazing directly into the lawman's eyes.

The girl's bold stare unnerved Balhorn for an instant. Her rare beauty was obvious, but the mysterious aura that surrounded her was even more intriguing. With nothing more than her presence, the sheriff in his imagination began to paint pictures of flashing dark eyes and glistening dark skin on a moonlit beach. He gave his head a quick shake to disperse these unorthodox ravings. What on earth had made him think of such things when he was supposed to be on duty? he wondered as he forced himself to behave in a rational manner. "Then get on in here," he ordered again, and quickly turned away and stalked to his desk, while telling himself it must be time to pay another social call on that sweet little blonde who worked down the street in one of the local whorehouses.

Tasmin tugged on Persia as she stepped through the open door and followed her friend into the building, grateful for the opportunity to escape from the crowd on the boardwalk. The sheriff, however, did not appear to be much more cordial than the men who lurked outside. Once they were in his office, their uneasiness was still evident as their worried gazes flitted around the interior of the lawman's domain. The confinement of such a structure was suffocating to the Roms, and the two girls felt imprisoned just being inside one of the *gajo* establishments. Tasmin shuddered as she glanced down the long, narrow hallway that led to the cells where criminals were held. She could not image anything worse than being locked up in a place where her wild spirit could not be free to roam. When she tore her eyes away from the dark, ominous-looking hall, she met the piercing glare of the sheriff once again as he impatiently waited for her to speak.

"W—We are looking for someone," she announced in a shaky voice. She still clung to Persia, and in an effort to look more serious, she turned loose of the other girl and forced herself to take a step forward.

The sheriff was mildly impressed by her bravery. "Ain't seen none of your type around these parts for quite a spell." He wondered if her skin was as soft to the touch as it was to the eye. Her face, he noticed, appeared as smooth and unmarred as brown satin, and he had a feeling her whole body was just as luscious. An impatient sigh escaped his parched lips.

266

It was definitely time for a visit to his favorite whorehouse!

"A Gypsy is not who we seek," Tasmin said, her courage retreating as she noticed the hungry glint in the man's gaze. She could also see the battle he waged within himself as he fought against his lustful thoughts. Her appearance had provoked this sort of behavior from *gajo* before, but she had always had the protection of her tribe in the past. Now, there was only two of them to fight off anyone who might decide to make unwelcome advances toward them. Nervously she glanced at Persia and was dismayed to see the look of sheer terror on the other girl's face. The remembrance of her recent encounter with *gajo* was apparent in her terrorized expression, and Tasmin knew that Persia's fragile mind could not survive another frightening experience. The urge to protect her friend from any further pain fueled her own courage as the Gypsy princess once again faced the lawman.

"We are searching for a *gajo*—a non-Gypsy—a man who we believe was traveling this direction." She swallowed hard, and took a deep breath as she stepped forward again. The surprised look that filtered across the lawman's face gave her even more strength, but his expression began to harden as she drew nearer. Tasmin halted her steps, and attempted to calm the frantic beating of her heart as she desperately tried to conceal the fear that was running rampant through her being.

The sheriff shrugged, glancing away from her dark gaze. Her boldness no longer impressed him, it only increased the wanton thoughts that continued to pour into his mind; thoughts that he could do nothing to acknowledge while he was supposed to be upholding the law and order. "What business do you have with this man if he's not one of your own?"

Tasmin was rapidly coming to the conclusion that this man would be of little help to them if she did not think of something to say that would overcome his resistance, which was obviously prompted by the fact that he felt no obligation to aid a Gypsy. "The man is my—my husband," she blurted out in her accented voice. "Yes, my husband," she repeated when she heard Persia gasp with disbelief. "We were to meet here in San Francisco, but I am not familiar with non-Gypsy names, and I can not remember where he told me to meet him." Her foreign accent grew more predominant as her lie increased.

The sheriff rubbed at his chin in a thoughtful manner. He had a distinct notion that this Gypsy gal was lying to him, and the skittish way the other one was acting added to his suspicions. "Husband, uh? Well, what's his name?"

"Chandler . . . Blayde Chandler," she retorted without hesitation, and with barely a trace of an accent as she said his name loudly and clearly. His name evoked a rush of tingling sensations that inched through her body and at the same time brought a look of stunned shock to the sheriff's countenance.

With his mouth gaping open, Balhorn stared at the dark-eyed female who stood before him, his thoughts an entanglement of confusion. She was Chandler's wife? Not possible! The bounty hunter was still grieving over his dead wife . . . or was he? The sheriff's gaze roamed over the beautiful Gypsy once again, lingering on her layers of colorful clothes, which only accented the luscious curves of her ripe young body. Her waist-length hair was like spun silk—a man could lose himself in those black tresses. Lord, she was a sight! All fire and desire, he thought to himself. It was entirely possible that a woman like this could have eased the bounty hunter's grief. But still the sheriff found it hard to believe that Blayde Chandler had actually made a Gypsy woman his wife. He started to dispute her, but then wondered if he dared. The gunfighter was a peculiar one, and Balhorn knew for a fact that a man like Chandler carried a grudge forever if he was crossed. The last thing Balhorn wanted was to have the gunman seeking revenge against him because of some woman, especially some Gypsy wench.

"I saw him just this morning," he finally answered, deciding that he had nothing to gain if he tried to dispute her. Who was he to say that Chandler had not married her somewhere along one of the backroads where he was always traipsing back and forth? "He was headed out of town—south, I reckon."

A quivering breath echoed from deep in Tasmin's throat. They had taken a grave risk by coming here today, and had figured that learning anything that would be pertinent in their quest, was a long shot. Still, Tasmin had been compelled to take the chance. She was certain now that fate was leading them, because it was too coincidental that this man had seen her green-eyed *gajo* just this morning!

"South?" she repeated, twirling around to look at Persia. "Did you hear?" She started to say more as her enthusiasm bubbled over at the realization that they were on the right trail, but she stopped herself before she said too much in front of the lawman that might reveal her lie about being the *gajo's* wife. Persia only nodded, not trusting herself to say one word that would interfere with Tasmin's fabrication.

The Gypsy's excitement was obvious yet the sheriff's mind still whirled with questions. "I've known Chandler for some time now. He never mentioned that he'd gotten married again. How long have you two been hitched?"

A cold chill slivered down Tasmin's spine. It never occurred to her that the sheriff might personally know Blayde Chandler, nor had she ever thought about the possibility of the green-eyed *gajo* belonging to another woman. Her mind went blank for a moment as the sheriff's words spun through her like a knife slashing away at her defenses. But before she was forced to answer his question, he began to divulge more information about the man whom she claimed was her husband.

"Reckon three years is long enough to mourn the death of your woman, even for a man like him." He shrugged again and shook his head as he added, "Too bad he didn't give up his unnatural obsession with doggin' McCalister, too."

Tasmin nodded in agreement, but she didn't trust herself to speak. She only wanted to get out of here, and out of San Francisco, as fast as possible. So far, the sheriff had not challenged what she had told him but they might not be so lucky if they stayed any longer. "We must be on our way," she said in a hoarse voice as she looked up at the sheriff again. His words had shaken her to the core, but she knew she had to act as if she was already aware of everything that involved Blayde Chandler. At this moment, however, she would have given just about anything if she could have asked the sheriff to tell her all that he knew about the green-eyed *gajo*.

"It ain't likely that you'll catch up to him soon. He was hot on the heels of Ben McCalister and his gang. If he told you that he'd meet you here, then you'd be wise to wait until he comes back for you." Balhorn neglected to add that there was a good chance that the bounty hunter would never return.

A strong shake of her head was Tasmin's reply. She had no intention of hanging around this *gajo* settlement any longer than necessary. Her sole intention in coming here was to attempt to determine whether or not they were on the right trail in their search for the *gajo,* and already she had learned that and much more that she had not expected. "Come," she said to Persia, then glanced back at the lawman. "Thank you for your kindness, but we must go."

Sheriff Balhorn did not attempt to dissuade her again. He had no desire to see Chandler again, and with this foreign woman hanging around, there was the possibility that the bounty hunter would return . . . that is, if she was telling the truth about being Chandler's wife, which was something the sheriff was still inclined to doubt as he followed the Gypsies to the door. Outside, only a couple of curious sailors still lurked in front of his office. San

Francisco was a circus of activity, and the interest in the Gypsies had been diverted to the arrival of a wagonload of fresh fruit down the street. The sheriff anxiously waited for the women to be on their way so that he could head down the street himself. But it was not fruit that drew his attention; it was the thought of that sweet little blonde he planned to visit, the one he hoped would ease the ache in his loins aroused by the raven-haired Gypsy.

Tasmin swung up onto the back of her Arabian mare, then waited until Persia had mounted her pinto. They were in such a hurry to get out of the *gajo* town that neither of them noticed the man whose attention they had caught, the man who drove the fruit wagon . . . the same man who owned the horse Tasmin now rode.

Chapter Twenty-Five

"Horse thief!" the man cried out as he saw his stolen Arabian mare gallop off in the opposite direction. "Horse thief!" His fruit wagon forgotten, the man ran toward the startled sheriff, who had no idea what the man was screaming about until the fruit farmer was standing directly in front of him. "That's my horse, Sheriff! Those Gypsies stole my horse! You gotta go after them!"

"Are you sure?" The sheriff glanced at the ring of people who had already gathered. "Did anyone see the Gypsies ride in on those horses?" he asked no one in particular. Several heads nodded in reply.

"That don't make no difference," the fruit farmer insisted. "They stole that mare from my farm a few weeks ago when they were working on my place." He pushed himself up against the sheriff so that their faces were even and they were belly to belly. "Now, are you going to do your job or not?"

A murmuring echoed through the crowd as Sheriff Balhorn moaned to himself. He swung around, uttering a low rash of profanities to himself. Lord, if that Gypsy wench was Blayde Chandler's woman, and a horse thief as well, he would have himself a barrel of trouble. "Yeah, yeah, but I'm goin' alone," he shouted back over his shoulder. "I don't need no help to capture two helpless women."

"I comin', that's my horse!" the fruit farmer announced as he swung back around and asked, "Anybody got a horse I can borrow?" The reins of a nearby horse were immediately thrown into his outstretched hand, while the farmer wasted no time in swinging up onto the animal's back. He sprinted past the sheriff before the lawman had a chance to mount his own horse, which was tied to the hitching post in front of his office. He cursed out loud as several more riders flew past him, spraying him with dust and rocks in their haste to follow the fruit farmer. Obscenities still spewed from his mouth as he spurred his horse and sent him galloping down the street behind the rest of the crazed men who were hell-bent on capturing the accused horse thieves.

The two girls had just barely turned the corner at the end of the street when a loud thundering of hooves roared up behind them. Though they had no idea that they were being pursued, the horrible recollection of every bad encounter they had ever had with *gajo* in the past dominated their thoughts. Their first inclination was to flee, but the fruit farmer and his cohorts had come upon them so quickly that the Gypsies did not have a chance to attempt a getaway. Tasmin felt another horse slam against the side of her little mare, and before she

274

knew what was happening, she was crashing against the hard ground. For an instant she saw hooves flash before her face and thought that she was about to be crushed beneath the flailing legs of the panicked animals. Before this became a reality, though, a man's body smashed down on top of her, knocking the wind from her lungs and almost rendering her unconscious.

Tasmin was not aware of the sheriff yanking the man from her body, only of the pain that pinned her to the ground and filled her entire being; her mind was too numb with shock to think beyond anything else. Until the face of the lawman loomed above her, Tasmin could not even begin to focus on what had happened.

"You hurt?" the sheriff asked, leaning down close enough so that his lips were all she could see. She could not move, nor answer him, but she saw him rise up and turn on the man he had just pulled away from her. "You ass! This here is Blayde Chandler's woman. Do you know who Blayde Chandler is?"

The fruit farmer shrugged and gave his head a negative shake. He could not think of anything other than the victory of recovering his stolen horse. "I don't care," he answered defiantly. "I want those horse thieves to hang!" An immediate round of agreement echoed from the rest of the men. The charge of horse thief meant that a hanging, or in this case two hangings, were imminent.

The sheriff dropped his hands to his sides with a hard thud. This meant even more trouble, especially if this woman was telling the truth about her association with the gunfighter. He leaned down toward her again. "Are you hurt?" he repeated.

"Persia?" she choked out in a voice still weak from lack of air. Her first coherent thought was for the welfare of her friend, and as she struggled to sit up, the sheriff surprised her by bending down and clasping onto her arms as he pulled her up to a sitting position. As soon as her head stopped spinning, Tasmin glimpsed her companion, who was held in the tight grasp of one of the men who had ridden after them. The horror of this latest attack appeared to have left Persia in a shocked trance, but other than her fragile mental state, she did not seem to be injured. The knowledge that her dear friend was still alive though, made Tasmin's thoughts begin to focus on the reason behind this *gajo* madness. She took a raspy breath, then directed her narrowed gaze at the sheriff. "Why d—did you do th—this?" she managed to gasp in a heavily-accented voice.

A sheepish expression crossed the lawman's face as he glanced at the fruit farmer, then back at the Gypsy. "He says you stole his horse." He waited for her to answer, silencing the farmer with a look of warning that defied dispute.

A sinking feeling filled the pit of Tasmin's stomach. She could never convince these *gajo* that she had not stolen the horse, even though she knew that the men of her tribe had taken the animal as payment for monies they were owed by the farmer. When Tasmin attempted to explain this situation to the sheriff, the fruit farmer vehemently denied that he had not paid the Gypsies all they had earned.

Sheriff Balhorn stood between the Gypsy and the farmer while he digested the story each had told him. Ordinarily he would have been inclined to believe the farmer, but he could not forget about Blayde Chandler, and this woman's claim to be his wife. "I'm taking you into custody," he finally announced when he found that he could not make a clear decision while standing here in the middle of this dusty street, surrounded by a bloodthirsty lynch mob. Locked in a jail cell, the Gypsies would be safe until he could decide what to do.

"What about the hangin'?" the farmer demanded.

"There ain't goin' be no hangin' until I do an investigation." The sheriff ignored the arguments that circulated through the crowd, even though he could understand everyone's confusion about his submissive attitude toward an alleged horse thief. He grabbed the Gypsy's arm, then motioned toward the man who held Persia by his side. "Let's get these women to the jail, and," he turned toward the rest of the crowd and announced, "I don't want to hear another word about any hangings until I've examined all the evidence." He began to stalk back toward the jail, dragging the reluctant girl beside him. He motioned to one of his deputies, who stood among the crowd, to bring the other Gypsy.

"I didn't steal his horse," Tasmin said again as they entered the jailhouse, even though she knew her denial fell on deaf ears. But the realization that she and Persia were about to be locked in a cell was terrifying. Without warning, she yanked away from the lawman's tight grip and backed up against the nearest wall. "Please, don't put us in there," she begged. A glance at Persia told her that her friend was near the end of her sanity; imprisonment might push Persia over the edge.

The sheriff's irritation with this entire business concerning the two females was apparent on his scowling face. "Look," he said in an equally annoyed tone. "I'm putting you in here for your own protection. If you really *are* Chandler's wife, then I don't want any harm to come to you." He raised his hand up and shook his head when she started to dispute him again. "You've got no choice in the matter. After all, you have been accused of horse theft, and that is a serious charge. I could have left you to them," he added with a wave of his arm toward the men who stood outside the door of the jailhouse.

In defeat, Tasmin mulled over his words as she glanced at the unfriendly group that had followed them down the street. A noticeable shiver shook her slender form as she realized that he was right and that their only hope for survival now was protection from the mob who wanted to see them hang. She drew in a hurtful breath through her bruised lungs and gave her dark head a tired nod. "But please," she added, "Let us be in the same cell." She motioned toward her friend. "She is not well."

With little interest in the other girl, the sheriff nodded. What had happened to the quiet one did not matter; it was the fiery-eyed one who concerned him, since she was the one who insisted she was the wife of Blayde Chandler. The remembrance of the bounty hunter flexing his bandaged gunhand in the hotel room this morning flashed through the lawman's mind, reminding him of the importance of his impending investigation. He would hate to unjustly accuse this Gypsy of horse theft and have Blayde Chandler dogging him in the same way he had relentlessly followed Ben McCalister for three years. Of course, if she *was* found guilty, he would not let the gunman stand in the way of justice.

"Fetch the doctor to look them over," he said to his young deputy, who had followed the sheriff's orders so far, but who obviously objected to the handling of the situation.

"They're just a couple of heathens. Why—"

"Just *do it!*" he demanded when the other man started to object. With an angry glare at the two young women, the deputy stalked out of the jailhouse. A tired slump became visible on the sheriff's shoulders as he motioned for the women to start down the narrow corridor that led to the cellblocks.

Tasmin took Persia's arm and solemnly began their trek down the dimly-lit passage. They walked past several empty cells, but at the end of the corridor she could hear voices which she knew belonged to other prisoners. As they dragged their reluctant feet along the wooden plank floor, Tasmin felt as if she was walking toward Beng's lair. The thought of any type of confinement was almost worse than death to a Gypsy. As she led Persia into the tiny, dingy room the sheriff pointed at for them to enter, which housed only a narrow berth that

279

served as a bed and a washbasin in one corner, Tasmin was certain they had died and gone to hell. The sound of the heavy door gave a creaking moan when the sheriff began to pull it shut, and induced a fierce panic in Tasmin. She turned loose of Persia and swung around to clasp the narrow bars of the tiny window in the heavy iron door. But the sheriff only shook his head as he met her frantic dark gaze before he quickly turned and stomped back down the hallway as if he needed to retreat from her pleading eyes. His footsteps echoed along the wooden planks and when they died out completely, Tasmin realized the grave seriousness of the farmer's accusation.

She twirled around in a frenzy of terror and stared at Persia, who still had not shown any reaction to anything that was happening around her. "Persia?" Tasmin asked, her worry evident in her voice as she gently shook her friend for a response which she did not receive. Persia's eyes wore a look void of any emotion, and as she stared at her friend, not even a hint of recognition filtered into her dark, empty gaze. Tasmin was at a loss as to how she could help her friend, yet she knew there was little she could do as long as they were locked in this cell. Taking Persia by the hand, she led her to the narrow cot and gently pushed her down onto the thin mattress. The girl lay back without any resistance, but her eyes remained staring at whatever it was that only her barren gaze could see. A feeling of hopelessness overcame Tasmin as she tenderly smoothed Persia's thick black hair back away from her clammy brow. She wondered if Persia would ever come back to her. Maybe Persia had found the perfect escape from this hellhole, and all the rest of the pain she had been forced to endure in the past few days. At this moment Tasmin almost wished that she, too, could find a dark cavern in which her overburdened mind could retreat. Angrily, she reprimanded herself for wanting to give up. Her strength had to be powerful enough for both Persia and herself. At this moment, her fear seemed to be rapidly gaining control over her.

She sank down on the hard floor and leaned back against the cot where Persia lay, her mind vivid with images of their limp bodies dangling from swinging ropes. This was one fate that neither Persia or Nanna had read in the cards, and as Tasmin fought against the terror of this twisted turn of the *Drom,* she began to wonder if the fortunes they had always believed would rule their lives were as foolish as the ancient customs that now were nothing more to her than a bunch of irrational gibberish. Her eyes closed tightly while she tried to reaffirm her belief in the promising future that the fortunes had foretold for her and the green-eyed *gajo.* But as she crouched in this suffocating cell, this picture eluded her, while her mind produced only the image of dangling ropes. Her eyelids flew open again as she clutched at her throat, the feel of the rope tightening around her neck growing stronger with each passing second. The walls of the tiny room felt as though they were closing in around her, and she began to feel as helpless to save herself as she had felt when she had

281

attempted to draw Persia out of her trance.

She drew her knees up to her chest and hugged them tightly in her embrace. Persia's withdrawal from reality no longer seemed so distant, and as Tasmin let her mind slip slowly from the realm of consciousness, she began to envision the soft glow of Gypsy fires. The rhythm of pulsating music drew her further into her peaceful retreat, while the blackness closed in around her . . . into a darkness where her perfect world was once again intact.

Chapter Twenty-Six

As Blayde rode his horse down the darkened, fog-shrouded streets of the oceanside settlement, he realized how much he despised cities. The roaming life that he had grown accustomed to living for the past three years suited him just fine, and when he decided to settle in one place again, it would have to be far from civilization. Now why, he wondered in annoyance, would a thought like that enter his head? All day his mind had been hallucinating about things that would never happen . . . like making love to the Gypsy dancer, whom he would never see again. Now, the idea that he would someday settle down was the craziest notion of all. But maybe these thoughts were still induced by that witch's evil spell, he reminded himself as he turned his horse down the street that led to the sheriff's office.

There was little activity along the boardwalk, but the establishments which housed the saloons and whorehouses were bustling with excitement at this late hour. After he collected his reward money for Red Eye, Blayde planned to pay a visit to the nearest saloon, where he intended to purchase a bottle of bourbon before riding out of town once again. He did not want to spend the night here, but he would sleep once he had left civilization behind. The bourbon would help him sleep—without the haunting dreams of the raven-eyed witch, he hoped. Blayde tied Eclipse's reins at the hitching post, and beside him he tied Red Eye's horse. The outlaw's body was bound tightly in a burlap tarp, but the heat of the afternoon sun had already produced a pungent odor that emitted from the corpse. The smell caused a lump to rise up in Blayde's throat. He would never get used to the distinct odor of death.

He pinched his nose with the fingers of his unbandaged hand and turned away from the dead man in disgust. That bottle of bourbon was needed to help him forget a lot of things tonight. He stepped up on the wooden planks that ran in front of the sheriff's office and was overcome with another odd sensation, a feeling that his entire life had just come full circle. But that was impossible, because this would not happen until he killed McCalister. Still, a rush of adrenalin filled him with shards of nervous excitement, and as he turned the knob on the door that led into the building he experienced an avalanche of intimate emotions. He vaguely remembered feeling like this each time he waited for a verdict on a case that he had just tried, or when he had waited for Emma to say "I do" on their wedding day. This strange sense of anticipation had been present as he had waited outside the bedroom door for Timmy to be born. Only the dancer, Tasmin, had evoked a similar emotion. Earlier today, though, when he had glimpsed Red Eye riding in the gully below him, a hint of this same type of unknown anticipation had surged through him. Now, however, this feeling was as strong as he could ever remember. A knot formed in his stomach, his legs shook like a baby taking his first step; Beads of sweat formed on his upper lip and he felt his face grow flushed and feverish. Even his hand, which rested on the doorknob, suddenly felt too wet and clammy to turn the knob.

Blayde's steps were rooted to the spot as he fought to regain his lost composure. What was it, or who was it, that waited on the other side of that door? It had to be McCalister, Blayde told himself, because only McCalister could evoke such an intense, overpowering sensation, along with the feeling that his ultimate destiny was finally within his grasp. With this thought ruling his head, Blayde shoved the door open; it banged against the back of the interior wall with a loud explosion, causing the sheriff and the deputy who occupied the building to bolt from their seats as their hands automatically went for their guns. The gunfighter saw their actions, and before either the deputy or the sheriff could pull their six-shooters out of their holsters, Blayde's gun was aimed and ready to fire.

Sheriff Balhorn gasped; beside him his deputy imitated the same type of noise. They both remained frozen in the positions they had assumed when they realized they could not outdraw the bounty hunter. The sheriff could imagine only one reason for the man's outburst and he knew he'd better do some fast talking. "Your wife—she's safe. I locked her up for her own protection."

"What in the devil are you talkin' about?" Blayde asked, his voice nearly as tense as his crouching body. He glanced around, expecting to see Ben McCalister, and only half listening to the foolish chatter of the sheriff.

"Y—your wife. She's—" his words stuck in his throat as the bounty hunter's cold gaze locked with his frightened wide-eyed stare.

"Wife?" Chandler growled. The word sounded alien to his ears as he spoke. What sort of cruel jest was this man playing? Blayde wondered as his eyes leveled a lethal glare toward the man.

"G—Gypsy wife," he gasped, his gaze moving slowly down to the Colt .45, which had not wavered from its poised position and still held a precarious aim toward his heart.

The sheriff's words spun like a wild top through Blayde's mind. Gypsy! Gypsy wife? Gypsy witch! What madness had she brought upon him now? The tension in his body shifted to his mind, drawing his thoughts to a complete halt. It was not Ben McCalister who had waited on the other side of this door, it was her . . .

"Tasmin," he said without conscious thought. His gunhand grew slack as his mind sought for control of his pounding heart and wayward thoughts— thoughts of the raven-haired dancer and the reality that he would actually see her again.

"Yes, that's her," the sheriff readily agreed. He had not bothered to ask the Gypsy her name, but Chandler's reaction proved that he knew about whom the lawman spoke. Balhorn sighed a ragged, yet relieved, breath when the bounty hunter allowed his gun to return to its holster. Still, the fire that flashed from the gunman's emerald gaze did not suggest that the man's temperament had improved. "You want to see your wife?"

Once again, the mention of his wife sent icy fingers traipsing down Blayde's spine. Still, he remained silent, only giving his head a slight nod as a reply. He could tell the sheriff he was crazy to suggest that he had a wife, but he had learned long ago to keep his mouth shut until he had gathered all the evidence. He waited until the sheriff had stumbled over to where the cell keys hung from a hook on the wall, then started to follow him down the dark corridor, which led to the cellblocks. Each step that took him farther down the hallway felt as if he had walked a mile. The wild pounding of his heart threatened to explode in his chest as the strange feelings of affinity and anticipation clutched at his entire being. And they continued to grow stronger, even after he peered through the tiny window in the cell door and saw her huddled on the floor. The whites of her eyes shown starkly in the faded light of the cell as her face tilted upward. Blayde was reminded of the first time their eyes had met, when she had knelt before him in the hazy glow of the Gypsy fires.

This time when their gazes touched, she lacked the

287

passionate promises of unspoken enchantment, and now Blayde could see only terror screaming out from the raven depths. He had no idea why she was here or why the sheriff believed her to be his wife, but at this moment he did not care. His only thought was that he was with her again, he would worry about the consequences later. Right now, he wanted her out of this cell and into his arms, and with this his only goal at this time, his eyes never faltered from her face as he spoke to the sheriff: "Release her."

The demand brought her to her feet at once. She closed the distance gap in one bound, pressing her face up toward the iron bars of the tiny window, only inches below where his countenance waited. Was he really here? her shocked mind kept repeating. She had prayed over and over to Del that he would come back for her, but never had she believed that such a miracle was possible. She yearned to reach up and touch him, but she feared that her hand would only meet with an image created in her mind. O Del! Thank you! she cried inwardly when he spoke again, and she felt the warmth of his words whisper across the top of her head.

"I want her released," he demanded once again. Movement on the narrow cot drew his eyes away from her for an instant, but his gaze quickly returned to the girl who stood so close, yet still remained unreachable.

"Well, there is a bit more to it than that," Sheriff Balhorn said, his courage fleeing once again when the gunman gave him a deadly glance. "See, there is a man—just a dirt farmer—but he says she stole his horse."

Blayde cringed inwardly. A horse thief! His previous conceptions about Gypsies returned with renewed strength. But the lawyer he had once been rallied to the surface. "Do you have proof of this charge?"

"She was riding the horse when he accused her."

The pit of his stomach drew into a tight knot as he glanced toward the silent figure who still lay on the cot. In the dim light he could barely make out the features of the other girl, but he was certain she was the fortune-teller who had stolen his money and Emma's picture. Had these two been on a thievin' spree? he wondered. He was filled with indecision: by leaving them here in this jail cell until he had caught up to McCalister, he could pay them *both* back for all the aggravation and injury they had each inflicted on him in the past few days. This thought fled his mind as quickly as it entered, however. He wanted—*needed*—to be with Tasmin with a desperation that he did not understand, and if he had to put up with the other one too, then he would have to submit. First, though, he had to figure out a way to get them out of jail.

"Did you steal the horse?" he asked Tasmin point-blank. He saw a glimmer of anger flare up in her dark gaze as she tossed her head back in a defiant manner.

"No," she relied as her eyes shifted nervously toward the sheriff.

"Says the farmer owed her people some money, so the men in her tribe took the horse as payment," the lawman intervened. "Of course, the farmer denies this."

A thoughtful frown knitted Blayde's rugged features. "I want to talk to this farmer." Then, as if his interest in the Gypsy and her dilemma had completely disappeared, he turned to the sheriff and added, "I need to collect the reward money for Red Eye."

The sheriff was taken aback by the man's sudden shift in conversation. Although he knew the answer, he was still compelled to ask. "D—dead?" He exhaled sharply when the bounty hunter gave his head a slow nod. Knowing the significance of the outlaw's demise, Balhorn almost felt as if he should offer the man a word of congratulations for finally eliminating one of his family's murderers. Instead, he turned to his deputy and ordered him to fetch the fruit farmer. Chandler still made him more uneasy than any man he had ever known, and the sooner he could be rid of the bounty hunter and anyone who was associated with him, the better he would feel about this whole business. He gave the Gypsy another unsteady glance, then motioned for the gunman to follow him back to his office.

Blayde did not look back at Tasmin as he departed from the cell block. For the moment, he had managed to corral his wild array of emotions, and he intended to keep them under tight rein until he could separate his own feelings from those induced by Gypsy sorcery. But as he walked away, he could feel her raven gaze following him down the corridor as strongly as if she was clinging to his back. Shivers traced down his spine as his mind echoed its usual sentiment . . . Gypsy witch!

"The reward is up to two thousand," Sheriff Balhorn said as he singled out a tiny key that dangled from his keychain. He bent down and unlocked a side drawer at his desk, and removed a carefully-folded paper. Smoothing the white sheet out on the top of his desk, he proceeded to fill out the necessary papers concerning Red Eye's capture and death. He did not bother to observe the body first, because he had no doubt in Chandler's word. "I'll get the coroner's signature tomorrow," the sheriff added, handing the papers to the bounty hunter.

Blayde laid them back down on the desk, not bothering to read the documents, since they were the usual forms he signed whenever he delivered a wanted man to a lawman; they stated that he had collected all and any monies due him for his services. He pushed the papers toward the lawman, his signature absent until he had the two thousand dollars in his hand. His tone of voice was impatient as he stated, "I need the money tonight. I have to keep moving."

The sheriff's hand shook visibly as he folded the papers and placed them back in the desk drawer. "That's a lot of money, and the bank ain't open till tomorrow morning."

"Open it; you have the authority." His unyielding attitude did not allow for any further discussion on the subject.

His mouth opened, then clamped shut when the sheriff decided that it would be simpler to ask the bank president to open the bank tonight and withdraw two thousand dollars than to contend with

291

Chandler's presence until tomorrow. He sighed with annoyance, but shook his head in agreement. "What about your wife? Are you planning to leave her here?"

"No," the bounty hunter added. Without another word, he stripped off his long black coat and tossed it on the sheriff's desk. Then he sat down on the garment and began to undo the pearl cufflinks that he had meticulously donned early that morning. He rolled his shirtsleeves up to his elbows, crossed his arms over his broad chest, and stretched his long legs out in front of him as he leaned back in a casual manner. His shimmering emerald green gaze then focused on the door as he waited for the fruit farmer to appear.

The sheriff was overcome with his own sense of nervous anticipation as he watched the gunfighter's calm actions. He had just killed a man who had participated in the murder of his wife and son. His new wife was in jail for stealing a horse, yet he was acting as if he was waiting for nothing more important than Sunday dinner. The lawman swallowed hard and sat down in the chair behind his desk. It just ain't natural for him to be so composed, Balhorn thought to himself. Watching this man was kind of like watching a long fuse burn its way toward a keg of dynamite. Fascinated, a man would stare at the spark as it traveled along the fuse, while his heart would beat faster and faster, because he knew that when the fire reached the end there was going to be one hell of an explosion.

Balhorn was still eyeing the bounty hunter

cautiously when the door opened and his deputy entered with the fruit farmer. Chandler's gaze moved in an intimating manner up and down the length of the man before stopping on his face with a direct stare. "Are you the one whose horse was stolen?" His voice was flat and disinterested, as if he was already bored by this entire subject.

His ploy worked as planned, reducing the farmer to a speechless idiot who could barely mumble an answer. "Y—yes, sir." The man looked to the sheriff for reinforcement, but the lawman would not meet his gaze, leaving the farmer to fend for himself against the cold-eyed gunfighter. All day, ever since it had become common knowledge that the Gypsy claimed to be the wife of the notorious bounty hunter, the farmer had been told wild tales of how fast the ex-lawyer was with a gun, and of how revengeful he was when he felt he had been wronged. The farmer's confidence had already suffered gravely because of the talk; now, after meeting the man, he wished he had never even ridden into San Francisco today, let alone accused the Gypsy of stealing his horse.

Blayde Chandler rubbed his clean-shaven face. His dark auburn brows drew into a straight line over his narrowed gaze, which had not wavered from the farmer's sweating countenance. "My wife says she believes the horse was part of the payment that you owed her people."

"No, s-s-sir. I did not give them Gypsies the horse, they stole it."

His sudden bravery impressed Blayde, but he did

293

not let the man know this as he crunched up his face in a thoughtful frown. "So, we have your word against that of my wife, and I'm inclined to believe my wife." He paused, inducing a long silence that cloaked the room in noticeable tension. Several times tonight he had referred to the Gypsy as his wife; still, he was shocked at how easily he had pulled off this ruse. A few days ago, even pretending that he had another wife would have been unthinkable.

When none of the other men made any attempt to speak, Blayde knew he had them right where he wanted them. He had used this ploy many times in the courtroom. There were two sides to every story, regardless of who was right and who was wrong. He had already stated the Gypsy's case, and also whose side he had taken. Now he only needed to present his final argument. "My association with Gypsies, through my wife, of course, has brought to my attention that these foreigners are accused of many injustices which are not entirely their fault." To provide a more convincing pose, the ex-lawyer rose to his feet, standing several inches above the head of the farmer, whose eyes ascended with a bulging stare at the dangerous man who towered over him.

"I—I don't recall sayin' exactly w—who stole the horse," he stammered. "Could have been any of them Gypsies. I suppose your wife might not have realized the animal was stolen." He glanced at the sheriff, shrugged his shoulders, and gave his head an uncertain nod.

"Are you dropping the charge, then?" Blayde

leaned down so that his face was even with that of the farmer. His eyes drilled into the man's unsteady gaze with the most imposing expression he could introduce at such close range. He did not intend to wait for the man to have second thoughts about his last train of thought, and he especially wanted the issue solved before the sheriff had a chance to intervene.

Every inch of the farmer's body began to quiver in noticeable spasms. At this instant, he would do anything this silver-tongued man asked of him, although it took all his strength just to shake his head in agreement.

A thin grin curled the corners of the gunman's lips as he straightened back up and glanced at the sheriff. "You can release my wife now and fetch my reward money." He resumed his seat on the edge of the desk, but his body did not seem as relaxed as before, nor did his expression appear to be as nonchalant. Instead, his actions and appearance had an aura of impatience and his mood was spurred by a sense of annoyance over the whole situation.

The bounty hunter's tense attitude served as fuel to send the rest of the men into action as the sheriff quickly produced papers for the farmer to sign. Once the charge he had brought against the Gypsy was officially dropped, the farmer wasted no time in departing from the sheriff's office, while the deputy was sent to the house of the bank president so that the bank could be opened and the reward money collected. Sheriff Balhorn gave the deputy explicit orders not to take no for an answer and to bring the banker to the jail if he refused to cooperate. He wanted this whole mess cleared up before there was any more trouble, and it would not be finished until the whole lot of them—Chandler and the Gypsies—were out of this town.

The bounty hunter's jittery mood did not ease as they waited for the deputy to return. When the lawman returned, however, he did not have good news to report. The banker was skeptical about opening the bank late at night and demanded that the bounty hunter wait until morning to collect his reward money. As the sheriff went to discuss the situation with the uncooperative banker, Blayde was afforded with another opportunity to see the Gypsy. He walked back down the dimly-lit corridor, hesitating while the deputy proceeded him and unlocked the cell door. The girl emerged slowly, barely stepping out from the shadows of the cell. Her uncertainty about her release was obvious as she glanced at the deputy, then toward the green-eyed *gajo*.

"You and her are free to go now." The lawman motioned toward the other girl, who still lay on the cot.

Tasmin stared at the deputy with an expression of surprise while she digested his words. Then, as a look of relief lit her dark eyes, she turned back toward Blayde. "Thank you," she said to him. An embarrassed blush torched her face as she wondered if he knew that she had pretended to be his wife. She did not have long to wait.

"Couldn't let them accuse my wife unjustly, could I?"

His lips curled with a snide smirk, the closest thing to a smile that Tasmin had ever seen cross his face. She was reminded of the impassioned way those same lips had kissed her in the forest a few days ago, and another profuse rush of scarlet colored her cheeks. In the dim shadows of the lamps that lit the narrow hallway, however, her blush was not noticeable.

The gunfighter's impatience was growing more apparent with each passing second. He motioned toward the dark cell. "Wake her up," he commanded. "We need to be on our way."

Tasmin's entire being filled with happiness, despite his brisk mood. He had said, "We need to be on our way." This had to mean that he was taking her and Persia with him. She rushed back into the cell to collect her friend before he decided differently, and was overjoyed to see that Persia was sitting up, rubbing her eyes and looking as if she was beginning to regain her senses. The doctor who had visited their cell earlier today had said that her state of shock might last for days or weeks, maybe forever. Tasmin had asked the Gypsy God for his help, and it appeared that Del had answered all her prayers!

"Where are we?" Persia asked as her groggy eyes moved about the small cell.

"Come," Tasmin said in a quiet tone, helping her friend to her feet. "We were just resting here. But now it's time to return to the *Drom.*"

Her explanation brought a wan smile to Persia's lips. She did not remember why they were here, because her overburdened mind had blocked out their latest encounter with the evil *gajo*. Nor did she care what had happened during the blank time that filled the dark passages of her mind. She only knew that whatever was happening now was good, was part of the predestined *Drom* that Tasmin and her were meant to travel. She rose up on her unsteady legs, leaning heavily on her friend for support as they walked from the cell.

Blayde observed the two young women who moved toward him, wondering what in the world had possessed him to play along with this insane plot. He had a mission to complete; what had made him return to San Francisco? Then, as plain as the nose on his face, he realized the answer to all his questions . . . Gypsy witch!

Chapter Twenty-Seven

Blayde's moodiness increased as the long night wore on, but he did not make any effort to explain his brooding silence to the women who rode with him. Why should he try to explain what he could not fathom? He had been desperate to see the Gypsy when he had thought that he would never see her again. Now, here she was, and he was at a loss as to how he should feel, or what he should do with her and the other one. She'd told him that they had run away from their own people because they had been banished from their tribe. He could not assume responsibility for them though, and it was not even feasible to think that he could take them all the way back to Texas with him. They would never be able to keep up with the pace he planned to travel, and besides, he could not allow himself to be distracted from his three-year quest.

"Thank you for helping us to get out of jail."

The Gypsy's soft, lyrical voice startled him out of his deep concentration as she rode her Arabian mare up beside his silver roan. She had wanted to leave the horse with the fruit farmer, but Blayde felt that this would be an admission of guilt. Anyway, she needed a horse to ride, and she was used to this mare, regardless of how the animal had been acquired.

"You already thanked me." Just knowing she was so near made him a man without a mind. He would be a deaf-and-dumb mute if he stayed in her presence much longer. "Is she all right?" He tossed his head in a motion toward the other girl.

"She's better. It's just that she has suffered so much lately."

Blayde remained silent as he recalled how the young women had recently been at the mercy of McCalister and his men. She was lucky to be alive, he thought, also remembering what Emma had suffered at the hands of the same men. The memory of the past, which had entwined itself with the present course of events, gave Blayde an eerie sense of affinity.

"Nanna died," Tasmin added, even though the man did not appear to be interested in talking to her.

"Nanna?" Blayde could not recall to whom she referred. The only Gypsy name his mind had diligently retained was hers . . . Tasmin's name, and everything else about her that his memory could savor.

"The old one, Persia's grandmother. She was like my grandmother too." Tasmin's voice trailed off, making her sorrow apparent.

How could he have forgotten the old woman who had heckled him about her witchery? A shard of guilt stabbed at Blayde's chest; still, he reminded himself not to become too involved with this girl's life. To do so would only make leaving her again all the more painful. "I'm sorry," he replied in a brisk tone. He spurred Eclipse gently, making the horse speed up his steps so that they were no longer side by side with the Gypsy.

Tasmin made no attempt to converse with him throughout the rest of the night, since he had made it so obvious that he did not have any desire to talk to her. She was too relieved just to be here with him to be worried about his quiet, brooding nature. Both Nanna and Persia had told her what a difficult road she and the *gajo* would have to travel before they could find happiness together, and her journey with the man had only just began.

Though he did not offer any information to his traveling companions, the *gajo* seemed to know exactly where he was headed. Moonlight afforded them with minimal guidance along the route they were following, so they did not stop until the hour was approaching dawn and the early morning fog made traveling impossible. They had been on a road up until this point, but now Blayde steered them away from the roadway. They rode close together, so as not to lose one another in the dense fog. A short distance off the road, Blayde stopped and dismounted, then ordered the Gypsies to do the same.

"We'll sleep until the fog lifts." He took the reins from the two girls and tied their horses to Eclipse, whom he knew would not wander off. Then he untied his own saddlebags and tossed his bedroll on the ground. When the women made no attempt to move or help themselves, he grunted with aggrava-

301

tion and threw their bags at their feet. Still, the girls huddled together in a frightened clench.

"You'd best get some sleep. We're not stoppin' here for long. Unless—" he shrugged as he stretched his long frame out on his bedroll, "You two are planning on staying here." From his position on the ground, the fog prevented him from seeing their faces. The lower portions of their bodies from their waists down were all that was visible in the thick, murky air. Riding had left their many-tiered skirts and petticoats a mass of wrinkles, and Blayde was amazed that they could ride so expertly while wearing so many unnecessary garments. His suggestion that they remain here, though, brought an immediate response.

Tasmin pulled Persia down to the ground beside her and murmured something in Romanian. The girl stared at her friend as if she was terrified, but she began to roll out the quilt that served as her bed. When she had dived under the thin coverlet that was rolled in with the quilt, not even her head was visible.

"*Tsinivari,*" Tasmin whispered to the *gajo* when she turned her attention away from the other girl. Her voice was filled with dread, and though Blayde could barely see her face, he could sense her uneasiness.

"*Tss—*" he tried to repeat, but the Gypsy's hushed voice repeated the strange-sounding word for him.

"*Tsinivari;* the evil spirits that lurk in night fog." She scooted close to him, not stopping until she was pressed against his side. Among the Gypsies, this

302

close contact would be considered *marime,* but since they no longer lived under Rom rules, Tasmin dismissed the thought from her mind. "Persia believes in them," she added, attempting to calm the quivering in her voice.

A slight grin curled Blayde's lips. "And you don't believe in them?" He could feel her shiver against his thigh. Why did she think she had to be so darned close? His body tensed, an action that did not dismiss the odd ache which had originated in his chest when she had first touched him, but was now working its way down through his loins.

"I think there are things out there that will harm us, but they are not spirits."

A snide chortle emitted from Blayde. She was smarter than he had given her credit. He was reminded of the attacks her people had suffered, as he realized that she probably knew a great deal about living in fear. "It's not the ghosts and spirits we have to be afraid of," he said, trying to ignore the throbbing in his loins that had grown continually stronger. "It's the living ones that we can't trust."

Tasmin sensed that he understood this better than anyone, and she longed to talk to him about the things that had happened in his past that had made him so distrustful and cold. She did not know how to approach the subject though, so instead, she began with the most recent event in their lives. "Are you mad at me for saying that I was your wife?" She heard him take a deep breath before he answered.

"You said what you felt was necessary."

His reluctance to talk did not deter Tasmin. She

303

had to know more about this man who had changed the entire course of her life's *Drom*. "But you once had a wife." Still pressed up against him, Tasmin could feel his entire body grow taut as a strange, deep sound came from his throat. For a moment she thought he was angry at her, but when he spoke, his voice trembled with a different sort of emotion.

"My wife and son were killed by outlaws three years ago." Blayde was amazed that he had disclosed that information so easily. Rarely did he talk to anyone about his family. Was she using her Gypsy magic on him again?

His announcement also surprised Tasmin. This man had known much tragedy in his lifetime, too, but until now, she had not realized how much he had endured. For the first time, she had some insight into the makings of the man he was now. "I'm sorry," she whispered in earnest.

Blayde grunted a reply of thanks, then added, "You'd better get some sleep."

"Are your shoulder and hand better?"

Why did she insist on asking him one question after another? "I'd be a lot better if I could get some sleep." He purposely rolled over on his side, presenting her with his back. At least in this position their bodies were not touching. However, the ache in his loins was not put at ease, and it made sleeping impossible. Blayde was disgusted with himself for allowing his manly urges to overcome his reason. What was it about this witch that made him want to forget all his restraint, toss her into the deep grass, and make wild, abandoned love to her?

Tasmin did not move, nor did she make any effort

to sleep. Though no one spoke, none of them slept as they waited for the fog to clear so they could be on their way again. They were each engrossed in their own thoughts of what the future had in store for their disoriented lives. Tasmin knew she belonged with the *gajo;* Destiny had played too strong a hand in bringing them together in the first place, and then by bringing them back to one another. She told herself she had to be patient and not push him in any manner. When he was ready to confide more about his past, or ready to pursue their future, then she would be waiting. She sensed that there was something blocking their chance at happiness, and whatever it was, it must be eliminated before it destroyed the fragile hold on they had on their new and developing relationship. They had to overcome all the roadblocks, and just as the *gajo* had said . . . they had to do whatever was necessary.

The Gypsies were used to traveling, and they offered no complaint to Blayde's relentless pace. They constantly surprised him with their strength and endurance, and even more amazing was their lack of interference in his quest. He had been expecting Tasmin to bombard him with more questions about his family, but she did not approach the subject again. She did not ask him any personal questions and made a pointed effort to stay out of his way. He knew she worried that he would leave them behind if they interfered with his life, and he felt guilty that she had to work so hard at pleasing him when he returned none of her efforts.

The days rolled on, and though they became soulmates on the trail, Blayde still had not permitted

305

himself to think about the future. The two young women, he knew, had nowhere to go since they had been cast out from their tribe. He did not ask them what had prompted this action, though, and neither of them made any effort to tell him. With staunch determination, Blayde concentrated only on his own mission, and what would happen beyond that, he could not even begin to fathom. When he did speak to the young women, their subjects were limited to conversations about the weather, or discussions about the landscape. Blayde discovered that the Gypsies knew far more than he about horses, and their knowledge about tending to the animals impressed him.

As time passed, their days and nights became almost routine. They rode as far as possible during the nights when it was cool, and their days were spent resting, unless they were close to a *gajo* settlement. Then Blayde would leave them and go into the nearby town to inquire about whether or not the McCalister gang had passed through recently. They had crossed the tip of Southern Nevada and had already left Arizona behind them; still, Blayde had not encountered any traces of the outlaws he sought. But he hadn't expected them to stop until they reached Texas. They were moving along the back trails, fast and hard, obviously avoiding all civilization. Blayde attributed their actions partly to Red Eye's death, which had been splashed across all the newspapers in the Southwest. Articles about the bounty hunter's unyielding three-year-old quest brought about an uproar of sympathy toward the ex-lawyer's plight, and a renewed fury toward outlaws who escaped punishment.

Each time Blayde rode away, Tasmin wondered if he would return. She had no idea why he went into every town that they passed, nor did she have any desire to go into the *gajo* settlement with him. Their last episode with *gajo* was too recent, and when it had happened, Persia had still been suffering from the abuse of her captivity with the outlaws. Even now, her sanity teetered precariously on the brink of total retreat, and Tasmin did not want to do anything that might cause her more distress.

Persia's distrust of men was particularly obvious when she was around Blayde. Her mood during these times was always timid and nervous, and never would she look the man directly in the face. If Tasmin and the *gajo* engaged in conversation, she seemed to withdraw even further into her shell, retreating into long periods of silence. Once he was gone, however, the shadow of her old self would begin to show through. Then, it was as if her mind had vaulted back in time, for she would converse with Tasmin endlessly about their childhood, remembering events and details that the princess had long since forgotten. She spoke only of happy times from the past, for which Tasmin was grateful, since she felt that they had dwelled long enough on the sad memories. Though she talked of how she and Nanna used to predict the future through cards, reading palms, tea leaves, and fire gazing, she never once made any mention that she still possessed the ability to see the events that were destined to happen.

Tasmin had asked her to tell their fortunes one

evening as they had waited for the *gajo* to return from the town where he had gone earlier in the day. The girl had grown so distraught that Tasmin had worried that she was losing her grip on reality again. From Persia's reaction, Tasmin had grown leery of anything that lent a clue to impending events, and neither of them had mentioned the future again.

Chapter Twenty-Eight

For as hard as he concentrated on catching up to Ben McCalister, Blayde spent as much time dreaming of holding and kissing the Gypsy again. Their fevered kiss in the forest continued to taunt his lips, and knowing that she lay so near every time they stopped to rest was rapidly taking a toll on his mortal restraint. Though he constantly told himself that these undeniable cravings were the result of black magic, this explanation was becoming more foolish as each day passed. The Gypsies never did anything that suggested they were producing magic, nor did they attempt to engage in any unusual ceremonies or rituals. The absence of these traits made Blayde doubt his own beliefs; still, he sternly denied that his feelings for the beautiful dancer could be genuine. She had to be doing something—some form of sorcery—that kept him in such turmoil and wanton desire.

Contrary to their usual routine, Blayde decided to set up camp in a cottonwood draw, and remain here for a couple of days. He knew how weary he was becoming of their relentless pace, so he could imagine how tired the Gypsies must be from all their riding. Besides, he was certain he had to be closing in on McCalister soon. When he did finally encounter the outlaws, he did not want to be too exhausted to pull his gun from his holster, which was the point he was about to arrive at when he made the decision to take a much-needed rest from the trail. Throughout the first day, he had lounged peacefully in the shade of a spreading cottonwood that grew in a grove close to a riverbed. But now, as darkness fell heavy over the Texas ground, his slumber was disturbed by a movement nearby. Blayde opened his eyes, but did not make a move as his mind cleared enough so that he could focus on his surroundings. As his vision adjusted to the dark, he became aware of someone moving quietly through the campsite.

Alertness instantly claimed his mind and body as he tensed and slid his hand down to the gun which he had not taken from his hip, not even for sleeping. His head turned to the side with slow, barely noticeable movements until he was facing the directon of the activity. Through the obscure light of night, Blayde caught a glimpse of swirling skirts that disappeared from his view only an instant after he had spotted them. He rose to his feet cautiously, glancing nervously toward the empty bedroll which was spread out on the ground next to the sleeping form of Persia. A trembling sensation began to rumble through his body as he once again looked toward the area where the colorful kaleidoscope of skirts had disappeared from his sight. What was she doing out there all alone?

His vivid imagination began to draw a dozen different pictures of demonic rites and smoking caldrons of mind-stealing potions. Was she out there—somewhere in the darkness—chanting words in tongues that only the devil could decipher? He dreaded the idea of following her, yet he knew that he had to go—had to see for himself what evil powers she possessed. Perhaps then he would finally understand the unnatural fixation he had acquired for the enchantress ever since the first moment he had gazed at her dark, beautiful face. With steps that were etched in feelings of foreboding, Blayde began to make his way toward the river.

Tasmin had no qualms about going to the river alone, for she had finally overcome the fear of the dark that she had acquired when she and Persia had first set out on their fated journey. As she had felt before, she once again found intrigue and mystery in the nighttime. Her only regret was that there were no singing violins to serenade her by the light of Gypsy fires. In resignation, she dismissed the absence of the sweet music from her past and climbed onto a large, flat rock that jutted out over the river. She had scouted out this spot when they had stopped earlier today and had waited with anxious enthusiasm for Blayde and Persia to go to sleep tonight so that she could indulge in a long, leisurely swim.

A yearning to dance also invaded her on this moonlit night, and as she let the passion overcome her body, she began to sway rhythmically to a melody she hummed softly. As her gentle tune flitted through the night air, she paid no heed to her surroundings while she raised her arms up toward the starry sky and began to pull her blouse over her head in a gesture of total abandonment. She dropped the garment down on the flat surface of the rock and reveled in the freedom she felt as she continued to dispense her firm, young body of the rest of her encumbering clothes. Like a practiced seductress, her motions were slow and alluring, each movement coordinated with the dispensing of another garment . . . until, after a performance of sensual and hypnotizing motions, her dark, bronzed body stood atop the flat rock in a state as natural and free as the endless Texas countryside.

Moonlight, descending from the heavens like a spotlight over her body, made her shimmering skin appear incandescent and mystical. Every hollow, each curve of her enticing form was outlined by the bright beams of light as they, too, danced with exuberance over her silken skin. She raised her arms high up into the air, then swayed backward and around to the front as if she was in a trance. The long tresses of the most rich shade of black which draped down to her hips swirled around her lithe form like a fluttering raven fan and bellowed out boldly through the timid breezes that whispered out over the land. Her possession was the freedom produced by the darkness of night, and her obsession was to dance once again beneath the Gypsy skies. The moon—she thought—was the only witness to her impassioned performance. She allowed herself no limitations as she danced upon the rock with erotic movements that suggested a vastness so large that her spirit seemed to soar on swift wings of fancy over the tops of the highest mountains and across the widest ocean.

When at last she had quenched her desire to dance as she had only imagined in her wildest dreams, the Gypsy princess plunged into the clutching dark fingers of the river. She emerged from the water after only a few minutes, for even though the midsummer night was humid and smothering, the water in the river was much colder than she had expected. Still, the cold dip, along with the release of her pent-up frustrations, infused her with renewed vigor. She climbed on the rock again and stretched out her long, slender legs so that her body could dry while she meticulously combed the tangles from her long, wet hair. Butter or muttonfat was used by the Gypsies to keep their thick tresses shiny, but since Tasmin had neither of these commodities, she had to be satisfied with knowing that her hair would at least be freed of all the dust she had accumulated along the trail.

Until now, Tasmin had been completely oblivious to anything around her. But a sound like a branch being crushed beneath a footstep caused her to fear that she was not alone. She jumped up and grabbed her clothes, then quickly began to don only what was absolutely needed for her retreat back to the camp. Her loose-fitting white blouse and the outer skirt of colorful tiers were the only garments she tossed on over her damp skin. The abundance of petticoats, along with her *jodka* apron and tall riding boots, were clutched tightly in her hands and held against her breast in a defensive manner. She paused atop the rock for a moment after she had prepared

313

herself to flee and listened again for any more sounds. Hearing none, she carefully climbed down from the rock and stopped once again—this time so that she could slip into her boots. If she had to run, her bare feet would not aid in her escape from whatever—or whoever—she thought she had heard.

As she took several hesitant steps, though, the source of the noise became visible. A gasp of surprise emitted from Tasmin as she came face to face with the *gajo*. Once she realized who was causing the disturbance, she was no longer afraid, although she did feel a rush of embarrassed heat enflame her cheeks as she wondered how long he had been observing her. When she started to ask him this important question, however, the odd expression on his face caused her uneasiness to regenerate and her words to stick in her throat.

Blayde's mouth flapped open and hung in this awkward position while his mind fought to retain each and every second of the incredible ritual he had just witnessed. Though he wondered if she had been summoned to dance by the Prince of Darkness, at this moment he did not care. If he had not seen her with his own eyes, he never would have believed that something so breathtakingly beautiful could exist. Her essence atop that rock had been so spiritual, so filled with hope and desire, that he found it hard to believe that she could truly be a cohort in evil. Her enticing young body was like a temple of beauty, and Blayde Chandler knew that he would worship her for the rest of his life.

The couple stared at one another wordlessly for what seemed like an eternity. Neither of them knew how to put their overpowering feelings into words. If he had watched her dancing like a fool in the moonlight, Tasmin was not sure if she could ever face him again in the daylight. Yet the look upon his ruggedly handsome countenance did not suggest that he thought her insane. His expression provoked an intense ache to spring up through her loins and spread through her whole being like a wildfire that had lost all control. If he did not say—or do—something soon, the flames would surely consume her.

"For whom did you dance, Gypsy Witch?" Blayde finally managed to gasp in a hoarse whisper. His legs felt as frail as a new colt's as he held his breath and waited for her reply. Oh God, he prayed inwardly, please don't let her say that she danced for the devil.

Tasmin swallowed hard, then tilted her face back so that she could gaze directly into his eyes. The wet strands of her long tresses hung past her waist and clung to the damp material of her skirt, along the gentle swell of her buttocks. Her breathing quickened, making the tiny buds that stood alertly from the center of her full breasts strain against her moist blouse. Again the moonlight outlined each and every curve and crevice with shameless definition. And though the man was grossly aware of how the light played havoc with his waning control, the woman only sought an answer to his question. Someday, when he was ready to submit willingly to their love, she would dance only for him, but for tonight, she had to tell him the truth. "For myself, *Gajo*. I dance only for myself."

upon his bedroll. But like her, he did not find suf—
had either hisped Tasmin
wondered if it was her unabashed performance at

Chapter Twenty-Nine

"What are you cooking?" Tasmin asked in their native tongue. Whenever the *gajo* was gone, they reverted back to the language of the Roms. Her curiosity in the other girl's activities was only half-hearted since her thoughts had been usurped by Blayde Chandler, and what had happened last night down by the river. After the experience they had shared, though, Tasmin figured it was probably best that they were apart from one another today. Walking away from him at the riverbed had been sheer torture, but she had managed to find the strength to return to camp after his strange inquiry about whom she had danced for. Her answer had drawn him into a deep silence, and while he was momentarily entranced with his private thoughts, she had hurried back to the camp. While a part of her had fervently prayed to Del that Blayde would chase after her, pull her down into the wild grasses, and love her with the same unremitting obsession that drove him along the endless backroads that he traveled, another part of her had shouted that it was not yet time. But time for what? she was beginning to wonder. And what if time ran out before they had a chance to fulfill the prophecy of their future together?

He waited until long after she had returned to camp, and when he must have thought she was asleep, Tasmin heard him sneak back and lie down upon his bedroll. But like her, he did not find any rest either. As he tossed and turned, Tasmin wondered if it was her unabashed performance at the river that caused him such distress, but her own sense of embarrassment prevented her from making a sound. Still, she longed to call out to him, to ask him what it was that haunted him so, to plead with him to let it go . . . whatever it was that had steered his life's destiny so astray. She sensed that his dangerous quest had something to do with the murders of his family. But his pain was too personal, too deeply ingrained in his past, to allow him to share with anyone the crucifying torment that ruled his body and soul.

This morning, without any effort to tell her of his plans, he had quietly departed from the camp just as the sun was cresting over the distant horizon. How she had wanted to ask him where he was going again—and why. But instead, she had pretended to be asleep until after he was gone. She did not understand her own actions anymore, and she understood even less about this strange, green-eyed *gajo* who had captivated her heart. Somehow she had to find the strength to stand by him until he had accomplished whatever it was that drove him with

317

such a deadly obsession. But his unyielding determination to exclude her from his life made Tasmin wonder how much longer she could endure his cold silence.

"Would you toss in those herbs, please?" Persia asked as she motioned to a pile of mint leaves. She was engrossed in stirring a concoction that simmered in a pot over the open flames of the fire.

Tasmin complied, then took a whiff of the strong-smelling mixture, which emitted the rich fragrance derived from such spices as nutmeg, ginger, and cloves, as well as sage, mint, and an assortment of other herbs. Since she had been hoping that the pot contained something savory for consumption, Tasmin was disappointed to see that the other girl was obviously mixing a potion of some sort. She was reminded of how Nanna and Persia were always devising a potion for medicinal purposes, or inventing a magic drink that was supposed to aid in lascivious attentions or seduction. Tasmin's hopes flared as this thought passed through her mind. "Is that for the *gajo?*"

Persia gave her a curious glance as a timid grin touched her lips. "No, it is for me." She continued to stir the bubbly brew, but she kept looking over at Tasmin. "He does not need a love potion. He only needs to put the past behind him once and for all."

"Will that ever happen?" Tasmin stared down into the dark liquid that Persia stirred with such deliberation, becoming almost hypnotized by the rolling bubbles that boiled from the center of the mixture.

A shrug was Persia's reply. She was scared to

envision the future these days. Too much had happened that she had not foreseen, too much had happened that had changed the course of destiny. She returned her concentration to the potion once again as she tossed in a pinch more of seasoning. The mixture was not intended to please the tastebuds, but she had to drink all of it if she wanted it to work.

"You still have not told me what it is that you're mixing," Tasmin inquired once more as she wrinkled up her nose and shook her head in disgust. "Ugh! It smells like medicine." In panic, she glanced at the other girl. "Are you ill?"

"No," she replied with a negative shake of her head. "It is medicine for the soul," she added, afraid that if she told her friend the truth, Tasmin might try to stop her from drinking the potion.

Her brief explanation did not satisfy Tasmin entirely, but she was not knowledgeable in the medicines used by the fortune-tellers. Perhaps Persia was preparing a tonic that would help her to forget all the torment of her captivity and ease a bit of the sorrow she harbored over Nanna's death. Since it was apparent that Persia did not intend to divulge any more information about her unusual concoction, Tasmin could only assume that this was its purpose. She just hoped the bubbling brew would serve her friend well, and that soon Persia's old self would emerge from the shattered remains left by her broken dreams.

Blayde did not return by nightfall, as he usually did when he rode into a town, and Tasmin's worry increased with each passing minute as she paced back and forth at the edge of the cottonwood grove.

In this barren part of Texas, the cluster of shade trees was a delicious luxury, and the river that meandered nearby was pure heaven. She and Persia had idled away the hottest part of the day in the river, and for her friend's sake, Tasmin had pretended that she was enjoying herself throughout their lazy day. Although she did appreciate the fact that Blayde had afforded them with a chance to rest, her greatest concern at this time was that he had felt this would be a good spot to leave them behind as he continued on his ruthless journey. Tasmin tried to tell herself that she was worrying needlessly; so far, he had always come back. But what if he didn't this time? her spinning mind kept asking her frail heart.

She glanced back over her shoulder at the still form of Persia. The girl had downed her potion and retired to bed as soon as the sun began to fade from the Texas sky. Tasmin smiled to herself as she thought of how strongly Roms believed in the use of magic potions and mysterious incantations to cure ailments of the mind and body. If only it was so simple to find a solution to all the woes of the world, then surely their lives would not be filled with so much sorrow, Tasmin thought as she wandered out past the spreading branches of the huge cottonwoods and climbed the gentle swell that led to the sprawling plains beyond the river valley. The stars and the full moon lit the Texas prairie with an obscure glow that reflected the vastness of the countryside. In awe, Tasmin glanced up at the sky, where millions of tiny stars danced across the endless expanse of the velvet heavens.

This was her first trip into the heart of Texas, and

she had not cared for the flatlands of sage and mesquite, or the endless deserts of cactus and sand. The sweltering heat stripped her of her senses and left her yearning to return to the ocean, where the cool sea breezes blew the heat of the day away each night. The muggy heat of the Texas nights were as unbearable as the merciless days, and sleeping was sometimes made impossible as the suffocating air hung over the ground like a smoldering shroud. But this cottonwood retreat had been a lifesaver, and Tasmin felt as if both her own strength and Persia's had been revived. Her gaze ascended once more as she marveled at how big the sky seemed over the open prairie. The Texas sky, alive with so many twinkling stars, was by far the most beautiful sight she had seen since Blayde had told her that they had crossed the Texas border. Now she wondered if he was looking up at these same stars as he hurried back to her across the dark plains . . . or was his attention drawn in the opposite direction as he fled away from her in a desperate escape to outrun their destiny?

A sound coming from the campsite below snapped Tasmin's enslaved mind from the image of the *gajo's* desertion. She cocked her head to the side and turned toward the grove of cottonwoods. Another noise reached her ears, a distinct moaning, and Tasmin knew immediately that the sounds were coming from Persia. She did not take time to retrace her path down the incline as she charged back to the camp. The slick soles of her boots slid over the prairie grass that grew abundant on the small slope, but even as she lost her balance and tumbled down to the bottom, Tasmin did not allow herself to acknowledge the raw grass burns that had singed her arms and knees. The cries had grown louder, and all she cared about was reaching her friend. Visions of past *gajo* ambushes on her people clouded her thoughts, and painted grotesques pictures among the clutching branches of the trees. She had not wandered all that far from the cottonwoods that sheltered their camp, but it felt as though she had gone a hundred miles by the time she fell at Persia's side.

Darkness shrouded their camp since they did not dare to fall asleep and leave a fire burning underneath the brittle branches of the trees while they could not tend to the blaze. Besides, the heat of the Texas weather made a fire unnecessary for anything other than cooking. "What is wrong?" Tasmin asked as she reached out and clasped ahold of Persia's hand. The girl gripped onto her fingers with a deadly hold as she writhed in agony.

"It's the—the potion," she cried. "I waited too long to drink it."

Her words made no sense to Tasmin, but Persia's pain was evident as her nails dug into Tasmin's palm. She leaned close to her friend's face, squinting in the dark in an effort to see her more clearly, but in the blackness, she could barely make out the outline of her face. "What are you saying?" Her thoughts were aghast at the idea that Persia might have poisoned herself.

"I should have drunk it weeks ago," Persia said in a raspy voice. "Right after it happen—" her words were cut short when another spasm shook through her body. She clutched Tasmin's hand with both of her sweating palms as the unbearable pain ripped through her. A terrified scream tore from her throat, but she was not aware that the shrill sound had come from her. She struggled to sit up, but she felt as if a spear had just shredded through her abdomen and pinned her to the ground. When at last the searing pain subsided, Persia fell back against the hard ground, gasping for air and nearly incoherent from the lingering agony of the shock her body had just suffered.

"O Del!" Tasmin cried as she held fast to her friend's hand, though she couldn't have turned loose from Persia's deathlike grip if she had tried. She was convinced that the potion the girl had swallowed was laced with poison, and she could not think of any way to halt the rapid spread of the deadly serpent that had invaded Persia's body. *"Why?"* she screamed at her friend in anger. "Why did you drink the poison and do this to yourself?"

Persia moaned again when she heard the distant sound of Tasmin's voice. She wanted to explain to her dear childhood friend that she hadn't meant for this to happen. The potion she had drunk earlier was not a poisonous concoction. In her many teachings, Nanna had shown her how to mix a recipe which was used to induce abortion, but at the time that her grandmother had taught her this mixture, neither of them had ever dreamt that someday Persia would need to administer the potion to herself. Nanna, however, had stressed the fact that the medicine had to be taken immediately following impregnation. But because of all the turmoil in her life lately, Persia had not thought to take the precautionary measures until she had realized that she was pregnant as a result of the multiple rapes the outlaws had forced upon her. Though she knew how advanced her pregnancy was after all the weeks that had passed since her captivity, Persia determined that she would take the risk. Her reasoning was that she would rather die than allow her body to nurture the demon seeds of the *gajo* who had raped her. If only she could make Tasmin understand . . .

Tasmin's anger toward her beloved friend quickly subsided when the realization that she was dying made her crazy with fear. Wrapping her arms tightly around Persia's limp body, Tasmin held her close to her breast. "Please don't let her die," she pleaded to the Gypsy God. Almost everybody that she loved was dead; it was not fair that Persia would be taken from her, too. The ragged breaths that rumbled through her unmoving form as Tasmin held Persia told her that the other girl still clung weakly to life. How much longer Persia would hold on, Tasmin did not know, but she had to do something to try to save her. Since she was certain that Persia's condition was the cause of poison, she figured her first action would be an attempt to make the girl expel the poison by vomiting. As her panicked mind sought another antidote to the poison, however, Persia's weak voice broke the permeating quiet of the desert night.

"I'm here," Tasmin said when her friend called out to her. Once again she held the girl's clammy hand in her own perspiring palm. How many times over the years had they held hands for one reason or another while skipping through a meadow, giggling about

324

girl things, or when they had just needed a friend to hold on to?

Persia squinted in the darkness, but she could not see her friend's face. She did not need to, however, because she knew every contour of the other girl's face by heart. At this moment, she could clearly visualize the look of sorrow that masked the princess's face, and she wished she could do something to ease the guilt that she knew her friend was feeling. This was her only goal as she sought the energy to speak. "It wasn't poison," she whispered. "It was to kill the devil child that grew inside me— the one conceived from the outlaw *bengs*—" Her voice faded away, the last of her strength stolen by her effort to talk.

Though her words were no more than a hoarse whisper, her meaning was painfully clear. Tasmin knew at once what the other girl was talking about when the memory of Persia's abduction clouded her thoughts. "O Del," she sobbed, hoping he was aware of the insufferable pain he had caused for this poor Gypsy girl. "Why didn't you tell me?" she asked, leaning down close to Persia's ear. But the young fortune-teller was beyond hearing, for she had already crossed to the other side . . . to the land where Gypsy fires burned for all eternity.

Sunrise, and Blayde, found the two girls in the same spot, in the same position. He had not expected them to be awake, so when he first saw Tasmin sitting beneath the cottonwood he was mildly surprised that she was up this early. A pang of guilt flickered through his chest as he wondered if she had waited up all night for him to return. Since he had not bothered to tell her that he was leaving when he had ridden out of the camp yesterday morning, and since he always returned before dark, he knew she'd probably thought he had deserted them. But how could he ever hope to leave his Gypsy witch now? he thought as his mind and body vividly recalled the unforgettable image of her tempting form swaying shamelessly in the moonlight. She would only use her sorcery to bring him back.

As he drew nearer, Blayde began to sense that something was amiss. Tasmin was holding Persia in her arms, and there was a strange aura in the air. "Tasmin?" he called out as he approached them. When the girl turned to look at him, her tearstained face spoke of a hundred sorrows as their eyes met in the pale gray light of the Texas dawn. Blayde sensed that Persia was dead without Tasmin saying a word. Still, he knew he had to ask. "What happened?" Silent tears streamed from the Gypsy's ebony eyes, but she did not look away from the *gajo*. Her grief was no less for Persia, but knowing that he was here was the only thing that kept her from giving in to the torment that threatened to steal the last of her sanity. "I was afraid you weren't coming back."

He offered no excuse; his explanation for not coming back last night was not something she needed to know at this time. Yesterday, he had suffered a death of his own. His indescribable fury over this loss had not yet reached his obstinate mind. But he would explain all this to her later, when he had found a way to surrender to his defeat.

Without coming any closer, he motioned once

again to the dead girl. "What happened," he repeated.

Relieved to share the acute grief that she had endured alone, Tasmin did not hesitate to tell him the story that had spun through her traumatized mind all night long. "She drank a special potion to abort the child that she had conceived by the outlaws who kidnapped her from the Gy—"

The black rage that collected on Blayde's face was so terrifying that Tasmin's words froze in her throat. His mind conceived its own detailed account when her words faltered, and in the few seconds that passed until she spoke again, he lived a thousand deaths. His mind conjured up images of all the people who had been murdered by the McCalister gang. The distorted pictures mingled with his remembrance of the death and destruction of the Gypsy camp, and the day he had encountered the two Gypsy girls at the creekbed. Their haunted expressions, their bloody and torn clothes, had spoken of the abuse the McCalister men had inflicted on them. He'd thought then how lucky they were to have escaped with their lives, but after being with Persia for the past few weeks, he had come to wonder if she had really been all that lucky. The fiery-eyed young fortune-teller who had stolen money and his picture out of his shirt pocket on that mystical night when he had wandered into the Gypsy camp had been nothing more than an empty shell of herself since her encounter with the McCalister gang. All these thoughts whirled through his mind, a prism of deadly specters, but most of all he remembered how he had knelt beside Emma and held her dead body in his arms, just as the Gypsy was holding her friend now.

Blayde could not tell Tasmin that he knew or understood how she was feeling. He—better than most—knew that everyone felt grief at different depths. Still, as he carefully pried the young woman away from her dead friend, he wished he could somehow ease away all the misery that had been forced upon her in just the short time since he had known her. He pulled her unmoving form into his arms and held her tightly in his embrace, where he hoped she would cry and release some of the pent-up despair and anger that he was certain she was feeling. But she only leaned against him as if she did not have the strength or will even to stand on her own. He understood this feeling of false acceptance too. Eventually she would need his shoulder to cry on, and when she did, he knew that he would be there.

Chapter Thirty

Persia's death left a void in Tasmin that would never again be filled, and it reminded her of all the people she had lost in her young life. Her thoughts also dwelled on the Gypsies she had left behind, and especially on Danso and Cyri. If Nanna's predictions had been correct, Soobli would have deserted his children by now, and they would be living with Nura and Giorgio. Many of her thoughts centered around Romalio and the love they had once shared, and it made her painfully aware of the futile hope she had followed when she had come in search of the *gajo*. Many weeks had passed since they had left San Francisco together—so many that she had lost count. Yet he made no effort to talk to her about anything other than horses or the changing countryside through which they never ceased to travel. In the days which had followed Persia's death especially, he had pushed even harder to reach their unknown destination. But Tasmin was weary of his driven pace; she was tired of trying to decipher the haunted look that lurked in the depths of his green gaze.

In defense of her own shattered dreams, Tasmin had also corralled all of her feelings toward the bounty hunter behind a steel barricade as she fought with the conflicting emotions that raged through her heart since Persia had left her. After cremating the girl's body in Gypsy custom, along with her meager belongings, the couple had traveled almost nonstop for three long days. As always, Tasmin had no idea where they were headed, but she knew they continued to move deeper into Texas because they were still riding to the south. Unlike their previous plan, they did not travel solely by the cover of darkness, nor did they stick to the backroads and hidden trails. The easiest and most direct routes were where they now rode. Blayde's obsession to reach wherever it was that he was headed had taken on an invigorated sense of urgency.

When they stopped early one evening in a cottonwood draw that only vaguely reminded Tasmin of the spot where Persia had died, she was so exhausted that she could not show any reaction when the *gajo* said he was leaving again. She assumed they were close to a town and he was headed into the *gajo* establishment to do whatever it was that he did when he disappeared. Each time he left, however, he returned only to display a mood that had grown even more sullen and withdrawn. Since Persia's demise, he had not ventured out of Tasmin's sight until now. Almost as if he wanted to make it obvious that he planned to return, Blayde unburdened his horse of his saddlebags and bedroll.

Tasmin found this curious, since he had never bothered to leave behind any of his gear in the past. While he prepared to leave again, her tired gaze wandered out over the parched landscape as she fought a desperate battle within her breaking heart. Traces of a dry riverbed lined the scorching Texas ground close to where the thirsty-looking cottonwoods reached their parched branches up toward the sky as if they were pleading for release from the burning rays of the sun.

"I'll be back in the mornin'," Blayde said, breaking into the disoriented thoughts that wandered through Tasmin's weary mind. His drawling voice contained a note of regret as he thought of leaving her alone for the entire night. Still, he could not take her with him, for his mission was about to come to an end, and he knew that he must go alone . . . this one last time.

In slow reserve, the Gypsy's raven eyes ascended and settled on his face, a face that was very handsome in spite of the pain that was forever etched in its creases. The setting sun filtered through the brittle branches of the cottonwood they stood beneath, outlining him in a golden frame, and lending shadows to the rugged contours of his countenance. Her mind tried to memorize every line, every hollow of this man's essence in the brief time that he stood before her. She yearned to reach up to him, to pull him down into her arms and hold him there forever. Yet she knew that if she did this he would only reject her . . . would tell her that he had to go away again, and her heart could not stand this agony another time. So instead, she merely nodded her head in agreement, as if she understood his unspoken words and relentless motives . . . when in reality her mind—and her heart—were telling him good-bye.

For a moment, Blayde was made immobile by the strange look on the Gypsy's beautiful face. Her raven gaze bespoke an emotion he had not seen before—a sadness that went deeper than any she had suffered in the past. How he wished he could embrace her right now. But when he was finally able to profess his love to her, he wanted to know that he would never have to leave her again. Until he had settled the final score with the vow he had made three years ago, he was not prepared to make this declaration.

"I have to go. There is something I must do."

"I know," Tasmin retorted quietly. I have to go, too, her mind echoed. She stared up at him without further comment, wishing desperately that he would submit to the longings that she could sense were trying to divert his attention from leaving. But this was only a fantasy—she told her languished soul; he was deprived from her dreams and nothing more.

Blayde hung his head and took a deep breath, but the ache in his chest did not go away. Strands of his long auburn hair shadowed the sides of his mournful expression. Tomorrow, he would tell her everything . . . tomorrow he would show her how much he had grown to love her. Now, however, he had to go, because the longer he stood beside her, the harder it was for him to leave, and the time had come for him to terminate his haunting quest.

He did not allow himself to look back in her

direction again as he swung into his saddle and began to ride Eclipse toward the distant horizon. He had not ridden over that ridge for three years, ever since the day he had left his home for what he believed to be the last time. Back then, he had thought his route would be a simple ride of vengeance, which would be finished in a matter of days or weeks. How could he have known when he had ridden over the top of that ridge that years of ceaseless wandering and growing revenge would stretch out before him? And most of all, how could he have known that his embittered soul would discover love again?

"Love will once again smooth the jagged edges of this fractured heart." The words of the young fortune-teller echoed through the hollows of his mind, but at last, he knew that he could accept her prophecy without resistance.

The sun was almost gone as Blayde topped the tiny ridge and looked down into the lush valley, where a wide expanse of rolling buffalo grass spread out below him. Sand dunes rose up from in between a wide array of desert vegetation such as barrel cactus, cholla, prickly pear, and the tall, imposing shapes of the yuccas. A dozen or more blooming plants and cactus painted the evening desert with a pallet of colors ranging from the purest of white to the most vibrant of purples. Far off in the distance, Blayde could barely make out the blurred images of the town called El Paso, which from this vantage point was no more than a dark spot on the endless prairie. Even farther west, outlined in brilliant prisms of lavender produced by the rays of the setting sun, rose the majestic peaks of the Sierra Madres.

Blayde's gaze was drawn to the green valley that lay to the north of the town, where once had been the home he had shared with his wife and son. When he had left three years ago, he had never planned to return. A strange and eerie force accompanied him down the ridge as he rode toward his old homestead. Nothing had gone as planned, he realized, and now he had to make a final peace with himself for the promise he had made to his family three years ago. The sun was almost gone from the draw that had once housed his home, but the two tombstones that stood side by side beneath a large silver-barked cottonwood were still visible in the fading light.

A surge of unexpected sensations poured through Blayde and left him trembling with emotions he was not prepared to experience. Though he had faced many difficult trials in his life, he felt that coming back here had been his biggest challenge. Most shocking to him, though, was how he felt, now that he was here. He had tried to prepare himself for a cascade of pain and flashbacks that he had been certain he would have to endure once he set foot on this property again. Instead, a calmness like he had never known washed over him as he knelt down beside the two weathered graves where his son and wife rested. He slowly read the engraved names on the tombstones, yet as he did, his thoughts took an amazing twist. It was not the horror of their deaths that he began to recall as he had greatly feared; rather it was the beautiful times they had once shared that he so vividly retraced in the passages of his memories. Picnics, and laughter—oh, how he would like to hear the sound of laughter again!

A warm breeze began to blow softly through the branches of the towering silver cottonwood, showering the ground with balls of fluffy white fur that scattered the instant they touched the ground.

"Let us go . . ."

Blayde's head snapped up as his ears focused on the sound he thought he had heard whispering along with the wind. His mind was playing tricks on him, he said to himself.

"Let us go."

He heard the words again, as clearly and distinctly as if Emma was standing right before him. He even thought he felt the warmth of her breath upon his face until he realized it was only the gentle fingers of the wind. Still, he sensed her presence so strongly that he knew without a doubt that she was here.

"Emma, I have failed you and Timmy again," he said, speaking to the cold stone marker at the head of her grave. "For three years I have sought revenge for your murders, but I have failed." He paused as he pulled a jagged piece of newspaper from the shirt pocket where once her picture had been carried. His hands shook slightly as he unfolded the document and read again the detailed account of how Ben McCalister had been killed during a shootout in a small town in West Texas. This information had presented itself to him in the last town he had visited on the night that Persia had died. At first, he had been consumed with rage, feeling grossly cheated out of his revenge. Three years . . . wasted! Not once, in all that time, had it ever occurred to him that someone else might end McCalister's worthless life;

this had been his destined duty.

But lately, Destiny had led him down many uncharted roads that he had not planned to travel.

He thought of the beautiful young dancer who had suffered much more sorrow than most. Thinking of her now—here—made him feel guilty and ashamed. How could he think of another woman when he was kneeling at Emma's grave?

"Let it go . . . let us go . . ."

Blayde rose to his feet and gave a nervous glance around at the darkening landscape. He had heard Emma; this time he had no doubt. Was she trying to tell him something?

The breeze continued to echo through the branches, but its wispy gusts grew stronger and were hot and sweltering against his clammy skin. Profuse sweat broke out on Blayde's body, and an intense sense of the intangible threatened to steal away his senses. It was not Emma's gentle spirit he feared, though; it was his own failure that he so desperately wanted to deny. But as he glanced at the piece of newspaper that was now fluttering across the tops of the stirrup-high buffalo grass, Blayde began to realize that the past had already run its course. Once his mind finally began to grasp this knowledge, a peacefulness settled over the entire area. The air became void of the scalding wind, and the suffocating heat subsided as if it had been swiped away by some giant hand. Blayde ceased to sweat and felt as though he had just walked into the cool spray of the ocean tide. A revitalizing shower of new emotions washed over him as hopes of the future helped seal the broken images of the past.

It was over . . . finally over. A part of his heart would remain forever in this little valley, but at last he was able to separate life from death. He couldn't have done it without Emma's help, though, and as he looked down at her grave, he said a final word of thanks. In his heart, he knew she had heard.

Overhead, the sun had disappeared, and Blayde debated on the sense of trying to ride in complete darkness. Traveling through this valley at night was next to impossible unless there was a full moon to help illuminate the black hollows and desert swells, which was why he had told Tasmin that he would not return until morning. The previous evening, less than a quarter moon had hung in the Texas sky, and tonight just a sliver of the silvery sphere would be evident and would offer almost no light at all. Still, Blayde felt a need to return to the camp where he had left the Gypsy. There was so much he needed to tell her.

One brilliant star lit the dark heavens, and as Blayde swung up on Eclipse's back, he gazed up at the lone star. Surely he was imagining that the star had appeared solely to guide him back to the Gypsy girl who waited on the other side of the ridge. However, many unexplainable things had occurred recently. And he was a mere mortal man . . Who was he to dispute Gypsy magic?

Chapter Thirty-One

The past was firmly planted in the treasured crevices of Blayde's memory, and as he rode over the desert swells and up the ridge, the future was clearly etched in his anxious mind and body. He felt alive for the first time in three years, and with this new lease on life, he also became aware of his abiding love for the Gypsy. He felt as if he had dealt her a cruel hand in the past few weeks that they had been together, especially when her longtime friend had died such a brutal death. But, he would make up for all his inconsiderate actions as soon as he held her in his arms.

He realized how little he knew about her, and he yearned to ask her to tell him all her secrets, all her fantasies. He would tell her his, too, and once he was holding her, they could begin to realize every one of their dreams and desires. As Eclipse crested the ridge once more, Blayde remembered the last time he had ridden away from El Paso. This time, he knew without a doubt that he would not return.

Somewhere, though he did not know where, he sensed there was a place where he and the Gypsy could live in peace and freedom. He would worry about these trivial things later, though, after he had proved the extent of his love to the raven-haired witch.

Once he had descended to the open plains, his journey was almost finished, although the hour was past midnight—the witching hour—he mused, as he began to envision himself lying down next to the sleeping Gypsy. How many times over the past few weeks had he watched her sleep? . . . watched with waning restraint the way her long black lashes rested across the tops of her cheeks as she lay in silent repose, the manner in which her tempting lips curved gently at the corners and parted slightly as her soft breathing echoed in the silence of the night. How many wasted hours had he spent longing for what he had thought would never be within his grasp?

He followed the dry riverbed, but the trail was difficult in the darkness. Several times Eclipse stumbled over a protruding tree root or jutting rock. Blayde hated to put his faithful mount through this hardship, but he had to keep going. Since he had been certain in which cottonwood draw he had left the Gypsy, he became confused when he thought he had reached the spot, only to discover that the area was void of any life. As he started to ride on, however, a dark heap on the ground next to the trunk of a tree caught his eye and filled him with foreboding once more. He spurred Eclipse gently and directed the horse to where the unknown substance lay. Before his hesitant vision could determine what it was that had caused him such dread, though, his mind summoned the memory of himself tossing his bedroll and saddlebags at the base of the silver-barked cottonwood; it was these objects that he was glimpsing through the obscure light.

As he slid to the ground and stared at his gear in numb disbelief, he tried to convince himself that this was only a bad nightmare. Yet he knew that it was cold reality. She was gone, and he could not even begin to conceive of where she might have gone. There were only a limited number of possibilities, and none of them were ones he wanted to face. She could have wandered off before dark and not been able to find her way back to the campsite once the sun had disappeared from the draw. But it was obvious that all of her belongings were nowhere in the area. He did not want to think about the possible chance that she had been kidnapped, and when this grim thought passed through his spinning mind, he forced his attention to focus on other routes that might account for her disappearance. Then, a revelation hit him full force as he recalled the way she looked at him when he told her that he was leaving again. She had been hurt too many times, and his last parting had been more than her overburdened heart could assume.

In a frantic spin, he glanced around through the blackness that engulfed the entire area. He had no way of knowing what direction she had gone as long as it was nighttime. With a sinking resignation, he knew that he would have to wait until morning before he could begin to pick out her trail. As he sat down on the hard ground, a frustrated sigh emitted from the man. Why was it, that no matter what course his life seemed to take he was always one step behind whatever—or whoever—he sought?

The first rays of dawn had the bounty hunter once again dogging his prey. But this time, it was his plan to use his lips rather than his gun, to silence his victim. He determined that he should make her sweet, moist lips plead for sympathy, after the long night she had made him suffer. Since she had not been able to travel far the previous evening, and since Blayde had gotten an early start this morning, he did not have far to go before he glimpsed her Arabian mare tied to the low-hanging branches of a mesquite bush. With cautious movements, he dismounted from Eclipse and dropped his reins to the ground. Unmoving, the silver roan observed his master with mild interest as Blayde sprinted across the dry ground on the tips of his toes. If horses had the same thinking capacities as men, then no doubt Eclipse was wondering if the man had finally lost his mind. At this moment, he hardly looked like the dangerous gunfighter he had come to be during the past three years.

Blayde's emotions soared like an eagle when he spotted her sleeping form stretched out on her bedroll. To him she looked like a bronzed angel. She lay on her side, her hands resting beneath her cheek, as if in silent prayer. The colorful skirt and petticoats she wore lay entangled around her slender legs, and only her dainty brown feet peeked out from the edges of the layered garments. Her long hair was not encumbered by the scarf she usually wore, and the raven tresses cascaded over her bedroll and out upon the hard desert ground in wild abundance. Blayde's gunhand flexed in a nervous gesture as he yearned to entangle his fingers in the beckoning black mass of silken tendrils.

The man continued his wanton quest until he was standing directly above her. Yet even with him so near, a deep slumber still claimed her weary being. The fleeting thought that she might think him someone who was here to cause her harm passed through his mind. With all the pain she had suffered, though, she had not lost her faith and trust toward mankind. From this day forward, he vowed, he would be the protector of her gentle soul. He knelt down beside her, just as he had in his impassioned dreams. With hands that trembled, he reached out and gently stroked the tresses that beckoned for his touch. The gesture finally brought a response from the sleeping princess, a startled gasp as her heavy lids flew open and she became aware of another presence. Instantly her fear was transformed into a stunned silence as her gaze locked with that of the green-eyed *gajo*.

"Am I dreaming?"

A smile lit the rugged contours of his face, a genuine smile void of all sarcasm and hostility. "If you are, then we are both having the same dream." His Texas drawl was husky, and desire flashed from his emerald eyes.

Tasmin blinked in an attempt to clear any lingering effects of slumber, because she was certain she was only imagining the changes that she thought she was seeing before her eyes. But she *was* awake, and the man who knelt at her side was truly the green-eyed *gajo*. Yet there was something so different about him that she hardly recognized him. Then it occurred to her: the haunting expresson of intense pain, which had previously lurked in the emerald facets of his riveting gaze, no longer possessed him. And the vindictive look of cold revenge that had masked his features had also disintegrated from his countenance. Tasmin gasped again, but this time it was from the elated joy that yanked the barricade away from her yearning heart and set her love for this man free at last.

It did not matter what had happened that had finally set him released him from the heavy chains of his hurtful past. All that was important was that he had not let her get away, and now that Fate had once again corrected their wayward hearts, neither of them would ever go astray again. Tasmin's throbbing lips parted as she started to say the words that had plagued her through each passing moment, ever since the night when he had first wandered into the Gypsy camp. But they never had the chance to emerge. His hands dived into the tangled jungle of her thick ebony tresses, pulling her head back as her breath was stolen away by his crushing kiss, a kiss that held the fiery promises of what this moment had only began to induce.

A thousand times or more she had relived his first kiss and longed for another. She did not intend to let this second kiss fade away unless she was certain that his lips would return for more of this sweet ecstasy. To ensure this, she returned his kiss with every ounce of devotion that her lips and tongue could produce. His hunger was no less than hers, and as their mouths devoured one another and their tongues entwined like shameless serpents, Tasmin yielded to the weight of his long frame as he stretched out over her quaking body with impatient demands that were evident even through the barriers of their clothes. As his bold male intentions strained through his jeans and pressed against Tasmin's abdomen, she trembled with unknown anticipation.

He had only taught her how much a kiss could provoke, and now she realized that there was so much more that she had to learn. Fear of *marime* had prevented her from becoming educated in the intimate details of this ancient rite. But she had left behind those fears when she had come in search of this *gajo,* and now the excitement of this impending knowledge caused her to strain upward unexpectedly, as if her body was too anxious to hold itself back. Blayde's attention was drawn away from her lips when he felt the tremor that shot through her body and extended into his being. He reminded himself that this was their first time together, and he was certain it was her first time to make love with a man as well. Only for an instant did he wonder if she had ever been intimate with the Gypsy king, but then he realized that whatever had happened in the past did not effect their future. Still, as his shaking fingers moved down over the tempting mounds of her firm, young bosom, he fervently prayed that no man had ever touched this tender flesh which he now claimed as his own.

Shards of delirious pleasure shot through Tasmin

as Blayde pulled her blouse over her head and began to fondle her in places that had never before known the touch of a man's hands. While his fingers toyed with pert buds of her passion-swollen breasts, his legs brazenly entangled themselves between her thighs and mingled among the layers of her skirt and many petticoats. Tasmin clasped her arms around his back, the feel of his supple muscles rippling beneath her touch. Though she sensed that he was trying to be patient with her, she could not bear this wondrous torment much longer. She made her meaning clear by sliding her hands down to where the buckle of his gunbelt pressed unmercifully into her tender skin. Her fingers shook as she undid the buckle and carefully shoved the weapon and belt to the ground beside them. He would no longer need his constant companion, for he would have her instead, at his side for all eternity.

A strange sensation passed through Blayde as he felt his hip bereft of the weapon, but he did not have time to dwell on this feeling because it was over-powered by his intense need to be freed from all his clothes and to feel Tasmin's silken skin bare beneath his fevered body. As proficient as he was with a six-shooter, Blayde was even more skilled at dispensing with the Gypsy's seemingly endless layers of clothes, as well as his own. Although it had been three years since he had practiced this acquired talent, he reasoned that there were some things that a man never forgot, and he was an expert at overcoming the barriers that threatened to block his path in this ardent quest. With their bodies cloaked only in the shimmering rays of the morning sun, the lovers were finally freed from the last obstacle that had stood in the way of the love which they were about to consummate.

A flame of desire coursed through Tasmin when the *gajo's* mouth reclaimed her hungry lips in an enslaving kiss that demanded complete surrender. His tongue also drew a fiery trail along her succulent skin as it escaped from her mouth and began to move over her chin, down her neck, and to the rosy tips of her breasts, where it teased and lavished each kernel with hot enticement. Her fingers raked through the strands of his long auburn hair, imprisoning his head close to her bosom. Bolts of wild passion shot through Tasmin's veins as his tongue ravished her breasts, while at the same time his hand slid down between her thighs to tantalize and stroke the most private area of her womanly realm. Though she was shocked by this sudden invasion, her only response was a weak, involuntary cry that echoed the welcome pain of this delicious torture.

Submission radiated from every pore of her enflamed being, and Blayde could no longer contain the rampant blaze that raged through his long-deprived essence. The time had come for him to vent the emotions that he had tried to deny for far too long. His hips eased between her silken thighs as naturally as if they had always known that the trail would lead to this uncharted terrain. She reciprocated without resistance, her slender legs spreading to accommodate his muscled form. A sweltering heat induced by their intense passion molded their bodies together in an inseparable conjunction as his body pressed her down into the

346

thin mattress of her bedroll. The tip of his swollen shaft pulsated with fire as he plunged into her moist orb with a sudden penetration that tore away the thin membrane which had guarded her innocence. The surprise attack stole away her breath for an instant as she wondered why his tenderness had turned to such an act of cruelty.

The moments that followed his brutal assault, however, were once more shielded by the return of his gentle embrace, and soft kisses that bespoke his regret. Inwardly he rejoiced in the knowledge that he was the first who had tasted her tempting delights, and he vowed that he would also be the last. His hips began to move rhythmically in ritualistic motions as old as mankind. She clung to him, digging her fingers into the steel muscles of his back as her body began to submit to the natural urge to arch up to meet each of his powerful thrusts. Their sweating bodies moved together as one perfectly matched unit, pounding together with a savage thunder, until at last neither of them could halt the searing ecstasy that exploded within their bodies like a hot bath of molten lava.

"O Del!" Tasmin's raspy voice called out as she gave all of herself, unabashedly, to this man who was her ultimate destiny. Once, she had believed that only her dancing could unleash such a frenzy of excitement, but it had not even began to elevate her soul to the lofty summit from where she now descended.

Exuberant, and exhausted, the lovers clung to one another in spite of the sweat that poured from their skin like millions of miniature cloudbursts. They were each overwhelmed by the feelings which had been induced by this first and long-awaited union of their mortal bodies and soaring spirits. Blayde wrapped the woman tightly in his embrace, almost as if he was afraid that she would fly away from him if his hold grew lax. The length of his muscled body nestled against her side as his dazed eyes traveled over the gentle swells of her lovely young form. She had bewitched his mind with her beauty, and his body was impassioned with endless desire. If she was the sorceress that he had always believed her to be, then she had just produced the most powerful of all magic.

"I love you," she whispered in an unexpected announcement. She felt his body tense and a sharp breath exhale from deep in his chest. He had shown her that he loved her with his actions, and for now, she would not allow herself to be hurt by his obvious aversion to admitting to his love for her with words. Soon she hoped that he would learn how to say what his body had already divulged.

A long silence followed her tender admission as the summer sun beat down through the craggy branches of the mesquite bush where they had loved in wild abandonment for a time that had seemed to extend past eternity. Though he had first knelt beside her in the early hours of the morning, Blayde realized by the position of the sun that it must be past noon by now. Their lovemaking deserved a blue ribbon, he mused to himself as he attempted to say the words that he knew she longed to hear. But they remained hanging in his dry throat. Instead, he buried his face in the thick raven mass of her hair.

"By Gypsy law, are you now truly my wife?"

A chuckle escaped from Tasmin at his unusual question, even though she knew that he was purposely prolonging his response to her declaration of love. "Gypsy laws are foolish," she retorted. "By *gajo* law, are we now married?"

Blayde laughed . . . laughed for the first time in years. The sound of his own laughter sounded strange to his ears, but it felt so wonderful. For an instant Tasmin was unsure about whether or not he was making fun of her, but his jovial mood was infectious, and she could not help but to join in his bout of laughter, though she had no idea what it was that they both found so humorous. He still held her in his tight embrace, reveling in all that he had regained on this smoldering summer day as their laughter subsided. Even he was uncertain as to why her simple question had affected him in such a manner, but the reasoning was unimportant. In the time that their lives had magically entwined, they had known the deepest depths of sorrow, had loved to the highest summit, and now, had laughed just for the sheer joy of it. He had no doubt that there was nothing they could not accomplish as long as they were together, and they would be together for all eternity.

However, there was still one more quest that had yet to be fulfilled.

"Will you ever dance for me again?" he asked, his voice deep and tinged with the desperate longings her nearness continually induced.

Tasmin twisted her head back and gazed up at his handsome face. The other night she had told him that she had danced only for herself, but as the moonlight had bathed her in its shimmering beams, she had dreamt of the time when she could dance once more for him. A shy smile curved her lips as she disentangled herself from his enslaving hold and rose up from the ground like smoke rising up from a Gypsy fire. Before his enraptured gaze, she picked up her thin white blouse and tiered skirt. Her actions were slow, deliberated movements that were almost as enticing as if she were disrobing, rather than donning her garments. Blayde sat up abruptly and drew his knees up to his chest in an effort to conceal the obvious effect her calculated motions were arousing in his shameless body.

Raising her arms high over her head, the dancer began to click her fingers together, her eyes closed as her body began to sway from side to side. In her head, violins and guitars created passionate chords of Gypsy music which floated through the humid air like the wispy tendrils of gentle night breezes. The glare of the sun was blocked from her mind, while an image of the moon danced over her shoulders. The man, the green-eyed *gajo* whom she loved more than life, was the flame that ignited her Gypsy fires.

Her bare feet tapped in rhythm with her clicking fingers as her body began to pulsate faster and faster. Draped in the curtain of her thick hair, she twirled and sashayed like a frail branch in a windstorm. Her skirt twisted around her bare hips, exposing copper limbs and glimpses of the soft, raven curls that concealed her womanly retreat. The breath caught in Blayde's throat as he witnessed the erotic performance. An ache in his loins grew with increasing urgency as he longed to delve into the moist, velvety crevice that he knew lurked beneath the swirling skirt. Her dance taunted him without mercy as her loose-fitting blouse slipped down from one bronze shoulder to allow a single flushed nipple to peek out over the top of the gaping garment.

Blayde moaned in sweet agony while he tried to concentrate on the beauty of her movements. He was taken in by the sense of affinity that her movements evoked. All the sorrows and joys they had suffered shone from her sultry dance, which was enhanced by the most graceful steps that Blayde had ever observed. She danced as he had never seen her dance before . . . as a woman dances only for a man.

When she stopped on bended knee before him, Blayde was too entranced to speak. Her lips were parted as quick, short breaths escaped from her kiss-swollen mouth and made her ripe bosom rise and fall rapidly. She reached out and picked up one of his limp hands, turning the palm upward, then gently kissing the lifeline, where the road of her own destiny was also charted. The raven eyes that flashed like burning coals were half-open and gazed into the green spheres of his unwavering stare. A breathless whisper flitted across his sweating brow as she clasped his hand to her breast. "I danced for you, and now I ask something of you in return."

Her soft kiss had already left him trembling with renewed desire, but he shivered with dread at her request. Why did women feel the need to hear those words? They were only words. He had told Emma constantly how much he loved her, yet his words were meaningless when she needed proof of his love.

With Tasmin, he was determined not to make the same mistake. He would not fail her, and he would show her how much he loved her by his actions rather than with mere words.

"You know how I feel," he began in an emotion-filled voice. "Isn't that enough?"

Her head dropped down as her long hair fell over her shoulders and across the hollows of her pained expression. Would he never let go of the past? she wondered. His hand, which she still clutched against the silken skin of her breast, could feel the wild beating of her ebullient heart.

"Only a witch could make me say those words again," he said quietly as the fingers of his other hand cupped her chin and drew her face up to meet his. "A Gypsy witch," he added, though a smile curved his lips with tenderness.

"I love you."

Tasmin's eyes locked in a silent embrace with the *gajo's* emerald gaze, and as the heat of his barely articulated words touched upon her face, she knew that Gypsy fires would never be doused again.